Praise for the Downward Dog Mystery series

A Fatal Twist

"If you're a fan of yoga, dogs, childbirth and murder cases, then Tracy Weber's *A Fatal Twist* is just what the fertility doctor ordered."

—*The Seattle Times*

Karma's a Killer

"Weber's clever assemblage of suspects is eliminated one by one in her entertaining novel."

—*RT Book Reviews*

"*Karma's a Killer* continues Tracy Weber's charming series."

—*The Seattle Times*

"[Weber's] characters are likeable and amusing, the background is interesting, and the story is ultimately satisfying."

—*Ellery Queen Mystery Magazine*

"Weber keeps readers guessing and populates the action with plenty of kooky characters."

—*Mystery Scene*

"Crazy, quirky critters and their odd yet utterly relatable human counterparts make *Karma's a Killer* an appealing story. But when you add the keep-you-guessing mystery with both laugh-out-loud one-liners and touching moments of pure poignancy, the result is a truly great book!"

—Laura Morrigan, national bestselling author
of the Call of the Wilde mystery series

"Tracy Weber's *Karma's a Killer* delivers on all fronts—a likably feisty protagonist, a great supporting cast, a puzzler of a mystery and, best of all, lots of heart. This book has more snap than a brand-new pair of yoga capris. Pure joy for yoga aficionados, animal lovers ... heck, for anyone who loves a top-notch mystery."

—Laura DiSilverio, national bestselling author of
The Readaholics book club mysteries, two-time Lefty finalist
for best humorous mystery, and Colorado Book Award finalist

"Yogatta love this latest in the series when Kate exercises her brain cells trying to figure out who deactivated an animal rights activist."

—Mary Daheim, author of the Bed-and-Breakfast
and Emma Lord Alpine mysteries

A Killer Retreat

"Cozy readers will enjoy the twist-filled plot."

—*Publishers Weekly*

"[Kate's] path to enlightenment is a fresh element in cozy mysteries ... [A]n entertaining read."

—*Library Journal*

"Weber's vegan yoga teacher is a bright, curious sleuth with a passion for dogs. A well-crafted whodunit with an intriguing mystery and a zinger of a twist at the end!"

—Krista Davis, *New York Times* bestselling author
of the Domestic Diva and Paws and Claws Mysteries

"An engaging mystery full of fun and fascinating characters and unexpected twists. An intriguing read that includes yoga lessons and feisty dogs."

—Linda O. Johnston, author of
the Pet Rescue Mystery series

"Weber's second yoga mystery, *A Killer Retreat*, is as delightful as her first. Readers will love the setting, the complex mystery, and the romance of Kate's second adventure. Especially noteworthy in this popular series is the appealing combination of strength and vulnerability that Kate and Bella share. Enjoy!"

—Susan Conant, author of
the Dog Lover's Mystery series

"Whether yoga instructor Kate Davidson is wrestling her hundred pound dog, her new love life, or trying to solve a murder, *A Killer Retreat* is simply a killer read! Witty, fun, and unpredictable, this is one cozy mystery worth barking about!"

—Shannon Esposito, author of
the Pet Psychic Mystery series

"Fun characters, a gorgeous German Shepherd dog, and a murder with more suspects than you can shake a stick at. *A Killer Retreat* is a must-read for cozy fans!"

—Sparkle Abbey, author of
the Pampered Pet Mystery series

Murder Strikes a Pose
An Agatha Award Nominee for Best First Novel

"Cozy fans will eagerly await the next installment."

—*Publishers Weekly*

"*Murder Strikes a Pose*, by Tracy Weber, is a delightful debut novel featuring Kate Davidson, a caring but feisty yoga teacher … Namaste to Weber and her fresh new heroine!"

—Penny Warner, author of
How to Dine on Killer Wine

"[T]his charming debut mystery ... pieces together a skillful collage of mystery, yoga, and plenty of dog stories against the unique backdrop of Seattle characters and neighborhoods. The delightful start of a promising new series. I couldn't put it down!"

—Waverly Fitzgerald, author of *Dial C for Chihuahua*

"Three woofs for Tracy Weber's first Downward Dog Mystery, *Murder Strikes a Pose*. Great characters, keep-you-guessing plot, plenty of laughs, and dogs—what more could we want? Ah, yes—the next book!"

—Sheila Webster Boneham, award-winning author of *Drop Dead on Recall*

PRE-MEDITATED MURDER

A DOWNWARD DOG MYSTERY

TRACY WEBER

MIDNIGHT INK
WOODBURY, MINNESOTA

FIRST EDITION
First Printing, 2018

Book format by Cassie Willett
Cover design by Kevin R. Brown
Cover art © Kim Johnson/Lindgren & Smith, Inc.

Midnight Ink, an imprint of Llewellyn Worldwide Ltd.

Library of Congress Cataloging-in-Publication Data
Names: Weber, Tracy, author.
Title: Pre-meditated murder / Tracy Weber.
Description: First Edition. | Woodbury, Minnesota : Midnight Ink, [2018] |
   Series: A downward dog mystery ; #5
Identifiers: LCCN 2017034859 (print) | LCCN 2017049375 (ebook) | ISBN
   9780738753904 | ISBN 9780738750682
Subjects: LCSH: Yoga teachers—Washington (State)—Seattle—Fiction. |
   Murder—Investigation—Fiction. | GSAFD: Mystery fiction.
Classification: LCC PS3623.E3953 (ebook) | LCC PS3623.E3953 P74 2018 (print)
   | DDC 813/.6—dc23
LC record available at https://lccn.loc.gov/2017034859

Midnight Ink
Llewellyn Worldwide Ltd.
2143 Wooddale Drive
Woodbury, MN 55125-2989
www.midnightinkbooks.com

Printed in the United States of America

To my precocious German shepherd pup, Ana.
Thank you for filling my days with laughter
and my nights with warmth.

ACKNOWLEDGMENTS

The longer I write, the more I realize that writing is a team sport.

Thanks go to my agent, Margaret Bail, and editor Terri Bischoff at Midnight Ink. I'm grateful that you were willing to take a chance on this newbie author five years ago. Without you, my series would still be gathering dust at the bottom of my closet. Thanks as always to editor Sandy Sullivan at Midnight Ink and freelance editor Marta Tanrikulu. Your insights and feedback both amaze and humble me.

Special thanks to Jane Gorman, Brandy Reinke, and Renee Turner, who helped me understand the complex process of immigration and the particular challenges faced by immigrants coming to the United States from Mexico. Any errors are solely my own.

I'd be remiss if I didn't mention the town of Cannon Beach, Oregon, which is one of my favorite places in the world. I took some liberties with the sandcastle contest, including moving it to autumn instead of early summer, but the loveliness of the town is unchanged. I hope to retire there someday.

My husband, Marc, gets extra kudos for designing and maintaining my author website, as well as for listening to all of my grumbles and supporting me through all of my challenges. Ana Pup, the new canine love of my life, gets my eternal gratitude for keeping life interesting.

Finally, thank you to all of my readers, who keep me glued to the keyboard even when I feel like giving up. I write for you.

ONE

I slipped through the restroom door, leaned my back against the counter, and tried—unsuccessfully—to slow the pounding in my chest.

Dad's voice echoed inside my head. *Take it easy now, Kate-girl. Remember what Rene told you. You have to act like everything's normal. You don't want to ruin tonight for Michael.*

Almost three years after his death, Dad was still right. Tonight wasn't about me. At least not just about me. It was Michael's night, too. Or it would be, provided I didn't die of heart failure.

Public restroom or not, I could think of worse places to die. The floor's shiny black marble was spotless. A trio of lavender-scented candles cast dancing light beams across the matching countertop. The purple blooms of a phalaenopsis orchid cascaded from a dark green plant in the corner. The place even sounded inviting, thanks to soothing classical music floating through hidden speakers. Normally, I would have been enchanted by the room's painstaking ornamentation. Not today. Today, I was too busy trying not to hyperventilate to revel.

My adrenaline-laced anticipation surprised me, especially since I'd spent almost a year avoiding the very conversation Michael and I were about to have. Then again, maybe I was worked up because I'd been avoiding it for so long. Until recently, I'd had no idea how important our future was to me.

Maybe a relaxing breath practice would help me calm down. I closed my eyes and inhaled, mentally coaching myself as I would one of my yoga students. *Inhale and slowly count to four. One, two, three, four. Exhale, one, two…*

A few cycles later, my heartbeat slowed. The chattering of my monkey mind subsided. My hands were still trembling too hard to touch up my makeup, so I picked stray dog hairs off the black cocktail dress I'd borrowed for the evening and ran a comb through my shoulder-length hair. I smiled to make sure lipstick hadn't coated my teeth, pinched my cheeks to give them some color, and headed back to join Michael at our table.

Every part of SkyCity, the Seattle Space Needle's upscale restaurant, had been designed to seduce multiple senses. The heels of my three-inch stilettos sank into the lobby's lush oriental carpet. Notes from a baby grand piano caressed my eardrums. Swirls of color burst from a Chihuly painting, exploding the piano's overture on canvas. A kaleidoscope of scents arranged and rearranged themselves in my nostrils, creating a fluid collage: garlicky pasta Alfredo, musky perfume, the sweet floral bouquet of deep red roses.

For most Seattleites, dinner at SkyCity was reserved for special occasions. For practically broke small business owners like Michael and me, the experience might be once in a lifetime. But man, was it worth it. SkyCity served more than delicious food. It provided unparalleled atmosphere and a rotating, panoramic view of the entire city.

Any other evening, I would have been glued to my seat for every one of the forty-seven minutes it took for the restaurant to complete a full rotation. Any other evening, I would have been transfixed by the view: toy-like rooftops, tiny ferries, the stark lines of the Olympic

Mountains. Any other evening, I would have been drunk on the surroundings before I took my first sip of champagne.

This evening, however, I'd barely noticed any of it. I hadn't even tasted the pasta I'd picked at for dinner. I was too preoccupied. Waiting. Waiting for Michael to stop pretending that we were here to celebrate my thirty-fourth birthday. Waiting for him to pull out the jewelry bag that Rene had spotted him carrying two days ago. Waiting for him to ask me to marry him.

Michael stood and pulled out my chair, grinning. "You were gone for an awfully long time. I was about to send in a search party."

"Sorry about that."

I glanced at him over my wine glass as he nodded discreetly to our waiter. On a bad day, Michael was pretty darned handsome, and today was far from a bad day. His sexy, blue-green eyes sparkled. The tailored suit he wore accented his broad shoulders and six-foot-tall frame. Curly brown hair brushed delightfully above his ear lobes, as if daring me to nibble them.

Unmentionable body parts tingled. If Michael didn't hurry up and give me that ring soon, I might consummate our engagement before the proposal.

I grinned. *Now wouldn't that give new meaning to SkyCity's 360-degree view.*

"Care to let me in on the joke?" Michael asked.

"Sorry. Nothing. I was just thinking about how happy I am."

As if on cue, a line of wait staff approached our table. One carried a huge ice cream concoction enveloped in a thick dry-ice fog. Another brandished a bottle of my favorite bubbly and two crystal champagne flutes. The rest surrounded our table in a black-and-white semicircle. Conversations around us grew muted as people stopped eating to watch the theatrics. I felt my face redden. Leave it to Michael to embarrass me with a grand gesture.

Michael grinned like a madman; a cork popped through the air; the entire restaurant burst into song.

"Happy birthday to you..."

Huh?

Ten seconds later, I blew out the candle and watched as the wait staff disappeared. The other diners resumed their conversations.

I surreptitiously picked through the ice cream, hoping to find buried treasure. Nothing but frozen dairy products and chunks of rich dark chocolate. No diamond lurked in the bottom of my champagne glass, either. My unmentionables stopped tingling, replaced by an awkward unease deep in my belly. Could Rene have been wrong?

Michael leaned across the table and clinked his glass against mine. "Happy birthday, Kate. I hope you've enjoyed it."

The smile I flashed back felt so stiff, it could have been molded from plastic. "Tonight has been wonderful, Michael, truly. The flowers, the dinner, the champagne..." My voice trembled. "Everything."

Michael frowned, confused. "What is it? Don't like the dessert? The reviews said it wasn't too rich, so I asked for extra dark chocolate."

"It's delicious, Michael." I lifted the spoon to my mouth, but pasta with garlic sauce threatened to leap for my throat. I laid the spoon back on the table.

"It was that damned birthday song, wasn't it?" Michael grumbled. "I should have known better. I know how you hate it when people make a fuss over you. I just thought... well, I thought it would be fun."

"It *was* fun," I assured him. "And the dessert is awesome. It looks like an erupting volcano." Tears burned the back of my eyes. If I didn't get out of this restaurant soon, I might erupt right alongside it. I looked pointedly at my watch and waved to get the waiter's attention. "It's almost eight. We should leave soon to pick up Bella."

"Already?" Michael didn't hide his disappointment.

"The twins have been fussy lately. I promised Rene we wouldn't be out late."

I lied. My German shepherd, Bella, suffered from significant separation anxiety, so I never left her alone for more than an hour or two. Michael already knew that Rene was dog-sitting tonight. What he didn't know was that Bella's visit was supposed to be a sleepover. Rene had insisted, claiming that my engagement night would be significantly more romantic without a furry, hundred-pound bed hog.

Make that *supposed* engagement night.

Michael didn't look convinced, but he didn't argue. "Before we go, I have something for you." He reached into his jacket and pulled out a small, foil-wrapped box stamped *Trinity Jewelers*.

In that moment, the entire world seemed to freeze. I would have sworn that the Space Needle stopped spinning. I was so excited—so relieved—that I didn't grasp the significance of the box's flat, three-inch square shape.

Michael slid it across the table. "Go on, open it."

My hands trembled again, but I managed to unwrap the paper, ease the top off the box, and gaze down at—

A necklace?

A simple gold heart suspended on a delicate chain. A locket.

Michael reached across the table and opened it. Two tiny pictures were nestled inside. On the left, a grinning Michael. On the right, Bella.

"I know you don't wear much jewelry," he said, "but I wanted to give you something special. This way Bella and I will always be close to your heart."

The necklace was gorgeous. Breathtaking, really. Michael had obviously put a lot of thought into the gift. Normally, I would have been stunned—in a good way.

But tonight wasn't supposed to be normal.

The tears threatening my eyes spilled down my cheeks. "It's exquisite."

Michael dropped the necklace back into the box and took my hand. "Kate, honey, what's wrong? You've been acting weird all night. I'm starting to get worried."

"Nothing. It's just that …" I swallowed. "I thought you were giving me a ring."

At first Michael looked confused. "A ring? In a necklace box?" Then his face turned ashen. "Oh."

Disappointment flashed to embarrassment, which I covered up by pretending to be angry. "*Oh?* That's all you have to say? *Oh?*"

Michael opened his mouth, then closed it again without speaking. The silence between us echoed like a shot to the gut, but it felt significantly more painful. The waiter eased next to Michael, slid the bill onto the table, and scurried away.

"I'm sorry, Kate," Michael said. "Really, I am. I didn't mean to disappoint you. But what made you think I was proposing tonight?"

I stared at the tablecloth, wishing I could disappear underneath it. "Rene went shopping for the twins at Westlake Center on Thursday."

Michael groaned and rubbed the crease between his eyebrows.

I pointed at the box. "She saw you walk out of Trinity's carrying this. We both assumed—" My voice cracked.

The restaurant's energy—or at least my experience of it—shifted. The room grew quiet. Sympathetic eyes burned the back of my neck. The dry-ice fog surrounding my uneaten dessert threatened to suffocate me. I gripped the seat of my chair with both hands, willing myself not to bolt.

"Kate, I *will* propose to you someday, I promise. But not tonight. I can't."

"Can't?"

Michael refused to look at me.

Deep inside my gut, I knew that I shouldn't keep pressing. If I kept pressing, Michael's explanation might change our relationship forever.

I pressed anyway.

"Michael, what aren't you telling me?"

His jaw trembled. "You know I love you, right?"

I did.

I loved Michael, too. More than I'd ever loved anyone, except maybe Bella. Still, I couldn't bring myself to say the words back. "Out with it, already."

Michael stared at the floor for what felt like an eternity. When he looked up again, his eyes were wet.

"I'm sorry, Kate. I'm already married."

TWO

"AND THEN HE SAID that it never occurred to him to marry me!"

My voice carried well beyond Mocha Mia's long line of patrons. The pedestrians on the sidewalk outside the coffee shop probably heard me, too. Then again, I wasn't trying to be discreet. I was still too upset. I wasn't even soothed by my all-time favorite aromatherapy—the bitter-sweet smell of Mocha Mia's Dark Chocolate Decadence Cake.

Michael and I had gone home from SkyCity and argued for hours. Or at least I argued. Michael apologized and begged me to listen to his side of the story.

I couldn't, at least not completely. Not yet. I was too stunned, hurt, and mortified. At a few minutes after midnight, Michael packed an overnight bag and left. It was too late for me to pick up Bella, so I spent the rest of the night alone, tossing, turning, and staring at the clock. At five o'clock, I got up and did a short yoga practice, proving to myself once and forever that for all of its benefits, not even the best yoga practice could mend a wounded heart. At the end of Savasana,

yoga's ending pose of quiet rest, my mental state still teetered dangerously between heartbreak, depression, and fiery indignation.

I waited until eight, then called and left a semicoherent message
with Rene's husband, Sam, asking her to meet me at Mocha Mia after
my All Levels yoga class ended at eleven. I started my harangue
about Michael the moment I saw Rene standing in line.

The barista avoided eye contact as she steamed soy milk for my
latte, poured the steaming brew into a red Tazmanian Devil coffee
mug, and slid it across the counter.

"This one's on the house. It's decaf."

Rene balanced a caramel hazelnut brownie in one hand and
handed me her double-whipped-cream, extra-chocolate mocha with
the other. She tucked a twenty into the tip jar and winked at the
barista. "Consider it hazard pay."

Rene chided me as we maneuvered our way through the crowded
café. "I know you're upset, but take a chill pill. Meditate on world
peace or something. At the very least, keep your voice down." She
pointed at the double-wide stroller she pushed in front of her. "This
is the twins' naptime. If they don't get their beauty sleep, they'll fuss
all night. Again. I swear, if they don't get on a sleep schedule soon, I'll
leave them at Pete's Pets and let you raise them."

I ignored her joking reference to the abandoned puppies she'd
recently adopted and examined her more closely. Rene *did* look exhausted. Don't get me wrong, my model-perfect friend was still, in
many ways, perfect. The twins were barely three months old, and
Rene already fit into her size-four jeans. Her shoulder-length brunette hair was styled to perfection. But her expertly applied makeup
didn't completely cover the dark circles under her eyes, and the skin
surrounding them somehow managed to look puffy and wrinkled at
the same time. For the first time since I'd known her, Rene looked
her full age of thirty-four.

"I'm sorry, Rene," I replied. "I was so self-absorbed this morning that I didn't think about how inconvenient it was for you to come here with the twins. I should have picked up Bella at your place."

Rene let go of the stroller and waved her hand through the air. "Don't be ridiculous. It's nice to be out in the real world. If I spend any more time cooped up at home with the girls, my voice will get stuck in singsong." She glanced out the window. "Are you sure the SUV is safe in the garage, though? I don't have one of those permit thingies to put in the window."

I knew Rene would bring Bella along, so I'd left instructions for her to park in my studio's cool, underground parking spot. "You'll be fine," I assured her. "They don't tow unless someone complains. Besides, everyone knows Bella."

"How could they not?" Rene quipped. "Bella's a legend." She pointed to an empty table near the window. "Give me a chance to get settled in and we'll talk." She held up a finger. "But no yelling."

While Rene maneuvered the stroller into an almost-space between tables, I sipped my latte and mused about how Mocha Mia's mismatched décor symbolized my muddled life. Scarred wooden tables adorned with Tiffany-style lamps. Gourmet coffee served in mismatched mugs. Oil paintings intermixed with crude crayon drawings. All reminded me of my newly renovated Ballard home, built on the foundation of a troubled relationship.

Rene tucked a green baby blanket around the brunette twin, Amelia, and a blue one around the blonde beauty, Alice. She took a long, slow drink from her mocha and nibbled at the edge of her cake. When she finally looked up, her eyes were uncharacteristically serious.

"Okay, Kate. Start from the beginning, but go slow. Between sleep deprivation and postpartum hormones, I can barely remember my own name. What happened last night?"

"You mean Sam didn't tell you?"

"Tell me what? He said you were obviously upset, but the babies were crying so loud that he couldn't hear you well enough to make out why. For a minute, he thought you said Michael was married."

At the sound of the M-word, my throat tightened. "He is."

Rene sighed. "I don't have the energy for sarcasm, Kate. I—" She stopped, midsentence. Her eyes grew wide. She jumped to her feet and shouted, "Michael is *married*?"

Amelia jolted awake and began screaming. The barista ducked behind the espresso machine. An elderly woman at the table next to us gave Rene a foul look.

Rene mouthed the word *sorry*, whisked Amelia out of the stroller, and rocked her hips back and forth, still standing. "Are you sure you didn't misunderstand? Between running Pete's Pets, dealing with your house remodel, and living with you, I don't see how Michael had time for a one night stand, much less a whole second family."

"Oh, believe me, I didn't misunderstand anything." I ripped my napkin into teeny, tiny pieces, imagining with each tear that I was separating Michael's head from his body. "They're separated. Michael claims that he hasn't seen her since he lived in Cannon Beach."

"Oregon? When did he live there?"

"Almost three years ago, right before he moved to Seattle and opened Pete's Pets. Get this: he said that he didn't think it would be an issue." I swept the napkin confetti into a pile and smashed it. "We've been living together for nine months, and he claims that it never occurred to him to marry me."

Rene stopped swaying and peered at me skeptically. "Kate, you said that earlier, but I don't believe it. In fact, I don't believe any of this. Michael loves you. Anyone not completely blind can see that. What *exactly* did Michael say?"

To be honest, I wasn't sure. I'd been so shocked and upset that I hadn't wanted—hadn't been able—to listen to him, at least not completely. As I closed my eyes and tried to remember, formerly unacknowledged details came into focus: Michael's pained expression; the guilt in his voice; the tears in his eyes as I slammed the door behind him. "Maybe I misspoke. He said that when we first started dating, he didn't think we'd ever get married."

Rene sat in her chair again. "That, at least, makes sense. You weren't exactly hungry for commitment back then. Michael had to trick you into going out on your first date, and you broke up with him midway through the second."

Amelia started fussing again. Rene unzipped a zipper on the left side of her shirt and nestled the baby up to her breast. The sound of the infant's suckling calmed me, like an ancient, primordial lullaby. My breath slowed. My throat softened.

Rene continued. "So, Michael says he and his wife have been separated the entire time you've been dating?"

I nodded yes.

"And you believe him?"

I considered her question. How could I know what to believe anymore? "I think so."

"What's his excuse for not telling you?"

"He doesn't have one, at least not a good one. He was too chicken, I guess. He claims that by the time he realized the marriage would matter, it was too late to tell me. He was trying to get divorced before I found out." I frowned. "He didn't count on the great birthday fiasco."

Rene's eyes softened. "I'm pissed at Michael, Kate, and I certainly don't agree with his actions. But they make sense, in a clueless man sort of way." She buried her nose in Amelia's hair and inhaled. "You've kept secrets from Michael, too. Don't forget about your not-so-dead mother."

Prickly defensiveness tingled my spine. "That wasn't the same. Not even close. My relationship with Dharma didn't have anything to do with Michael. Besides, do you remember how mad he got when he found out she was alive? Michael wasn't just clueless, he was a hypocrite," I huffed. "Not to mention a criminal."

"Criminal?" Rene's eyes widened. "Don't tell me he's a polygamist..."

"No, there's only one Mrs. Michael Massey, thank goodness." I paused, oddly wary about sharing the rest of the story. "It's a sham marriage. Michael married this Gabriella woman so she wouldn't be deported. That's why he didn't think twice about casual dating."

Rene leaned back in her chair and slowly shook her head back and forth. "Oh, Michael. You're an idiot."

"No kidding. If the feds find out, he could do prison time." I hugged my arms to my chest, subconsciously protecting my heart from further injury.

"Why did he do it? For money?"

"Heck if I know," I scoffed. "All he would tell me was that it was 'complicated.'"

Rene absently stroked Amelia's cheek. "You know, if the marriage was fake, Michael wasn't cheating by dating you. Not really. You two can get past this. He'll get a divorce, and you'll move on with your life." Tears welled in my eyes. "It's not ideal, but..." Rene's voice trailed off. "Kate? Are you crying?"

I quickly wiped under my eyes. "Michael promised her that they'd stay married until she gets citizenship. She applied a couple of months ago, but the process can take a long time. Years, sometimes."

Rene frowned. "That's a long time to wait."

"Longer than you think. I know it's old fashioned, but I don't want to get pregnant until we're married. At this rate, I could easily be in my late thirties before we start trying to have kids. Michael contacted his—" I choked on the word. "He contacted his *wife* a couple of months ago and asked for an early divorce, but Mrs. Michael said no. She said if they don't stay married, her citizenship application will be delayed. She's not willing to wait." I felt my teeth clench. "At least not unless Michael pays her for it."

Rene started. "Pays her?"

I nodded.

"How much does she want?"

"More than Michael can come up with, at least on his own. Pete's Pets is like Serenity Yoga—built primarily on sweat equity and bank loans."

"Has he consulted an attorney?"

"Yes. Evidently she's legally entitled, scam marriage or not. He signed an Affidavit of Support as part of her green card application."

"Why did he do that?"

I shrugged. "It's a requirement. She promised him that she'd never ask to collect on it, and he believed her. They were supposedly going to walk away from the marriage without ties, emotional or financial."

Rene didn't reply, but her face clearly conveyed her opinion: Michael was an even bigger idiot than she'd thought.

I shrugged in reply. "You know Michael. He believes in people. But now he's stuck. He can pay her what she wants now, or risk losing more in court." My jaw started to tremble. "Rene, he spent every penny of his savings on the house remodel. We could move, but ..."

I couldn't bring myself to finish the sentence. My childhood home was all I had left from my father. Selling it seemed impossible.

For several long seconds, Rene's and my silence was broken only by murmured conversations at the tables around us and the contented cooing of the infant at Rene's breast. When Alice began stirring, Rene detached Amelia, closed the left zipper, and lifted her toward me. I cradled the tiny angel while Rene unzipped the oppo-

14

site side and began feeding her twin. The yearning for a child of my own was so strong, I was surprised *my* breasts didn't start lactating.

"So what's next?" Rene asked.

"I don't know." I smiled ruefully. "I considered killing Michael in his sleep last night, but I couldn't. I'd already kicked him out of the house."

"Where's he staying?"

"I'm not sure. Probably with Tiffany." At one time, the idea of Michael bedding down anywhere near his blonde bombshell employee would have made my head explode, but I now knew that Tiffany was like a little sister to him. His foray into her apartment would be strictly of the on-the-couch variety.

Rene continued cradling Alice in one hand while sipping chocolate-laced caffeine from the *This Is Probably Vodka* mug she held in the other. "All of this sucks, Kate. But I don't think you should give up on Michael. Not yet. He's been good to you—good for you, for that matter. Since Michael moved in with you, you've become more mature. More balanced."

"Why are you taking his side?"

"I'm not."

I scowled.

"Seriously," she continued, "I'm not. I will always be on your side. Michael made a mistake. A bad one. If I'd found out that Sam was married while we were dating, I'd have strung him up by his man parts. But honey, Michael is still a good guy, and you know it. Besides, I feel partially responsible."

"Responsible? For what? For Michael being married, or for him not telling me?"

"For the way you found out. If I hadn't blabbed to you about seeing him at Trinity Jewelers, you wouldn't have expected an engagement ring last night. Michael might have come up with a solution."

I was about to assure her that the only acceptable solution would have been for Michael to admit that he was married in the first place, but my phone interrupted. I glanced at the screen, then tossed it back in my purse. Rene cocked her head quizzically. "Michael," I said. "He's left a dozen messages already this morning."

"What does he say?"

I shrugged. "I don't know. I deleted them without listening."

"Don't you think you should at least hear him out?"

"I can't." My upper lip trembled. "Not right now. I'm too mad. If I talk to him now, I'll ..." My voice trailed off.

"You'll leave him." Rene finished. She placed her hand on my arm. "Sweetie, are you sure that's what you want?"

"No. That's why I can't talk to him. I need space."

The opening refrain of "Strangers in the Night" sang from Rene's purse—the ringtone she used for unprogrammed callers. She dug around in her shoulder bag, pulled out the phone, and frowned at the screen. "Pete's Pets. It's probably Michael."

"Don't answer."

She pressed the screen and started talking. "Hi Michael. Yes, she's here." I held up both hands and forcefully shook my head. "She doesn't want to talk to you." I imagined Michael's charming, blue-green eyes begging for mercy.

Rene listened for several long moments, slowly rocking Alice back and forth. "I see," she finally replied. "When?"

I grabbed Rene's napkin and jotted, *When what?*

Rene waved me aside.

"What do you think that will accomplish?" More silence. "Yes, I'll tell her. I hope this works, for both of you." She ended the call and tossed the phone back into her purse.

"What did he say?" I asked.

"He loves you. And he's sorry."

"He called you for that? He told me that himself last night."

"He also wants you to know that he's leaving town."

A beach-ball-sized lump formed in my throat. "Leaving? To where?" As upset as I was with Michael, part of me (probably the delusional part) thought that we'd get through this. Not today. Probably not next week. But someday. That would never happen if he left Seattle.

"To Cannon Beach."

The beach ball turned into a lead weight, which dropped on my stomach. "He's going back to his wife?"

"No. He wants to fix things with you. In fact, he wants you to go to Oregon with him. He thinks the three of you might be able to work out an agreement in person."

"An agreement? What, now he wants us to be sister wives?" I didn't try to disguise my sarcasm.

Rene placed Alice in the stroller, then gestured for me to give her Amelia. "Michael wants to make this right, Kate. Is it that impossible for you to let him try?"

I stared fixedly at the table. "I can't do it, Rene. Not now. I'll strangle Michael if we spend time alone." I was lying, of course. Anger was my escape valve. The tool I used to cover up the pain of being abandoned. It always had been. But Rene already knew that.

She gazed at my scalp for several long seconds, then reached into her purse. "Who said anything about you and Michael being alone?" She pulled out her cell phone again and hit redial. "Hi, Michael, it's me. I talked to Kate. We're going with you."

THREE

WHICH IS HOW, ON the following Tuesday, I found myself coaxing my ancient Honda Civic down Highway 101 en route to Cannon Beach. Rene acted as copilot while munching on barbecue potato chips smothered in pineapple jalapeño salsa. The sweet, spicy scent filled the car and made my stomach rumble. Bella, who'd finally given up begging for handouts after two hundred unsuccessful miles, sprawled across the back seat, snoring. Michael, Sam, the twins, and Rene's two five-month-old labradoodle puppies, Lucy and Ricky, followed in Rene's new mommy car, a Passion Red Volvo SUV.

Michael and I hadn't worked out our relationship dilemma, but we'd reached two tentative agreements. The first was that we wouldn't break up—yet. The second was that we'd continue living apart, at least for now, to give me some much-needed space. I couldn't talk about Michael's betrayal without my head and heart simultaneously combusting, so we agreed to put discussions of his marriage on hold until after we returned from Cannon Beach—where he'd hopefully talk Gabriella into granting him a divorce. It made sense, in a convoluted, keep-all-of-your-options-open way.

Rene didn't agree with my strategy. She wanted Michael and me to work things out quickly, before I had time to officially bolt. Rene usually knew me better than a Seattleite knows Gore-Tex, but in this case, she was mistaken. I might someday forgive Michael, though I wasn't sure I could ever forget. But that day wasn't today. In this instance, time was on Michael's side.

I had plenty of substitute teachers to cover my yoga classes, and Tiffany volunteered to keep an eye on the studio. She and Chad, her underemployed hot-yoga-teacher boyfriend, would take turns staffing Pete's Pets. Michael wasn't completely comfortable having Chad work at the pet store, but Chad needed the money and Michael didn't have any better options.

I was surprisingly blasé about abandoning Serenity Yoga for an unexpected trip of unknown duration. Then again, what did I have to lose? With my home life in shambles, I couldn't have concentrated on the business anyway. Besides, if Serenity Yoga had remained standing during my Orcas Island fiasco a year ago, it could withstand anything.

And now I had Tiffany. She'd been helping out at the studio a few hours a week, and I'd grown to trust her. If she ran into a problem she couldn't solve on her own, she would either consult the building's manager, Alicia, or call me. As for Chad, well, he was Michael's problem.

Rene crumpled the empty potato chip bag and licked spicy red salsa off her fingertips. She pointed at a sign for the Tolovana Beach state park. "Take this exit."

Nervousness tickled the lining of my stomach. Arriving at our destination made the trip seem more real. I still wasn't sure how I'd survive meeting Michael's wife with my sanity intact, but without Rene along, I'd have ended up in the loony bin for sure. I owed her. Big time.

"I know I already told you this," I said, "but thanks."

"For what?"

"For coming with me. Having you and Sam along means the world."

"Nonsense," Rene replied. "It's nothing. I'm the one who should thank you. The timing is perfect." She pointed toward a side road that led to the beach. "Turn here. Sam's on paternity leave for another week and a half, and I'm between catalogues for Infant Gratification. This might be our last chance to take a family vacation."

Infant Gratification was Rene's new infant accessory business. She'd dreamt up the idea during her hospitalization for preterm labor. Two months of bed rest later, she'd launched the company on Facebook. Her pacifier purses and quilted infant stilettos had become overnight sensations. Sam, who owned a successful software company, had played no small part in the business's success. Between Sam's computer savvy and Rene's creativity, they were well on their way to amassing their second personal fortune.

As for taking a much-needed family vacation? We both knew she was lying. Rene and Sam were small business owners and the parents of twin infants. They needed sleep much more than a road trip. They had come solely to provide me emotional support. Reason number 537 why I loved my two best friends so much.

A huge smile lit up Rene's face. "Pull into the driveway. We're here."

My jaw dropped open. "Here?" She couldn't be serious. Rene wasn't known for understated frugality, but this level of opulence was over the top, even for her.

The modern, two-story home could have been the love child of an architect and an environmentalist—if one of them was a multimillionaire. Rectangular lines, oceanfront windows, deep brown siding. All offset by huge solar panels, rainwater collection barrels, and an emerald green, plant-covered eco roof.

I turned off the ignition and gaped. "Wow."

Rene's eyes sparkled. "I thought you'd be surprised."

"Surprised" didn't come close to my true reaction. I was horrified. Not at the house, which was beyond gorgeous. Not at the three-car garage, which was bigger than the ground floor of my tiny Ballard bungalow. Certainly not at the grounds, which were covered in deep green ivy, fragrant evergreen trees, and fall-blooming rhododendrons.

What horrified me was the small fortune Rene must be paying to rent it. When she'd offered to find a rental in which we could stay with the dogs, I'd assumed we'd end up in a cheap rundown cabin or a non-view room in a failing hotel. Who else in their right mind would rent to a party with two infants, two puppies, and a one-hundred-pound monster-dog? As usual, I'd underestimated my friend's resourcefulness.

Rene opened her car door and gestured for me to follow her. "The boys can deal with the twins. I'm starving. Let's go inside and check out the kitchen!"

I knew better than to get between Rene and her afternoon snack, so I clipped Bella's leash to her collar and tried to hold on. Bella dove out of the back seat and pulled toward the house like Rene charging the double glass doors at the Nordstrom Half Yearly Sale. She paused long enough to anoint the ground next to Sam's foot, clearly reminding him that she was still alpha. Sam's blond mustache twitched, but he didn't comment.

"Sam … this place … it's too …"

He waved off the end of my sentence. "Don't talk to me. This whole thing is Rene's doing." His head disappeared inside the Volvo, where he wrestled with Amelia's car seat.

Michael looked as shocked as I felt, but like Sam, he didn't say much. He was too busy trying to leash a squirming black labradoodle puppy while its golden littermate chewed on his arm. "Ouch!

Ricky, settle down! Lucy! Keep your teeth in your mouth! My arm is *not* food!"

Rene yelled from the front door, "Kate, get in here!"

She didn't have to ask Bella twice. Bella lunged towards Rene's voice, practically dislocating my shoulder. I slipped and slid and tried to hold on as she dragged me through the front door and down the long bamboo hallway.

Rene laughed and reached toward Bella's collar. "For goodness sake, Kate. Let her loose."

"I don't think that's a good id—"

The metallic clank of the leash's clasp hitting bamboo interrupted my sentence. One hundred pounds of pure German shepherd bliss galloped down the hallway, leaving me in a horrified silence punctuated only by the scrape of German shepherd toenails against flooring. Not a single room escaped Bella's inspection. A long drink from the guest bathroom toilet, a dig in the family room's rug, and a joy-filled roll on a bedroom's queen-sized mattress later, Bella flopped on the deep red couch across from the living room's stone fireplace. A storm of silky black undercoat snowed down on the fabric around her.

Shedding season. Fabulous.

Bella tracked my movements, ears pricked forward at full attention. A German shepherd master, supervising her slave. I reached out my arms and swiveled in a complete circle, fully taking in the gorgeous space.

Floor-to-ceiling windows showcased a huge deck that looked out over the ocean and provided a stunning view of Cannon Beach's iconic Haystack Rock. Shiny bamboo floors were covered by vibrantly patterned Oriental rugs, and an eight-person dining table bisected the open area between the living room and the kitchen. Black granite countertops nestled between a Viking oven and the stainless steel Sub-Zero refrigerator that Rene was currently scouring for snacks. A curved staircase with a driftwood railing led upstairs to what I assumed were additional bedrooms and bathrooms. I felt an odd combination of awe and sadness.

The home's opulent furnishings inspired the awe. The sadness was that I wouldn't be sharing them with Michael. Until our relationship was on firmer ground, Michael planned to stay with his sister, Shannon, who lived in Manzanita, a tiny town fourteen miles south.

Rene plopped a container of hummus on the counter and dragged a burnt orange tortilla chip through it.

"You're eating other people's food now?" I asked.

"Nope. This is all ours. I had the rental agent stock the fridge with some bare essentials. I even had them stock tofu and fake meats for you." She tossed me a can of Diet Coke. "Catch."

I paused before opening it. "Rene, I'm beyond grateful, but I can't let you and Sam pay for all of this. It's too much."

"Pfft." She waved her hand through the air. "It's nothing."

I glanced up the stairway, mentally counting rooms. "How many people does this place sleep? Twenty?"

"Not that many. It only has five bedrooms and six bathrooms."

"Only?"

"It's a little bigger than we needed, but believe me, when Alice and Amelia start fussing at three in the morning, you'll be grateful for a bedroom or two of sound buffer. Besides, we'll need at least one of the bedrooms to corral the pups."

"But it must have cost a fortune!"

Rene shrugged. "You paid for the cabin on Orcas Island."

"A one-bedroom cabin with a saggy pullout couch hardly compares. Besides, I didn't pay for that cabin. Housing was included in my teaching contract."

"You still provided the lodgings. It's my turn this time. Besides, I can afford it."

Rene wasn't lying. Sam's uber-successful software company had expanded so rapidly that it would likely go public. I had no idea how much money he made, and honestly, I didn't want to. But I had a feeling he could buy this house and a dozen or so like it. I felt guilty for not paying at least a token amount, but when I'd initially offered, Rene wouldn't accept it. She'd insisted that any extra money Michael and I had should go toward his divorce settlement. I gave up arguing, for now. I'd find some way to pay them back later. Like babysitting the twins until they graduated from college.

"Please tell Sam thank you for me."

Rene gaped at me in pretend indignation. "Sam? Honey, this trip's on me. I'm not simply the world's best wife anymore. I'm a successful businesswoman. I'm paying for this little trip out of my quarterly profits."

"Infant Gratification is profitable already?"

Rene beamed. "First quarter sales have been through the roof. When I started the business, Sam claimed we'd be lucky if we broke even the first year. Well, I showed him. We made a huge profit—and in the first quarter."

I bit back some unattractive (and ill-placed) envy. No doubt about it, Rene and Sam deserved every ounce of success that their businesses enjoyed. They both worked their butts off.

Then again, so did Michael and I.

Rene's profits purchased new cars and rented vacation houses. On a good month, mine purchased a single bag of kibble and a dozen or so unscented candles. If I hadn't loved Rene and Sam so much, I would have been forced to hate them.

Rene kept talking. "You'd be shocked at what people will pay for baby baubles. Wait until you see my jewelry line this fall. Infant Grati-

24

fication is going to be the Tiffany's of the toddler crowd. Eighteen-karat baby ankle bracelets, teeny tiny toe rings. I've even been working on edible faux diamond earrings that will be safe if the baby swallows them."

I rolled my eyes.

"Mock me all you want," Rene said. "Baby accessories are a heck of a lot more profitable than yoga classes."

I couldn't argue with that.

"I know this place is a little over the top," Rene continued, "but it wasn't easy to find a place that would take three dogs this close to the Sandcastle Festival. We had two choices: this house or a one-star roach motel in Seaside that was about to be shut down by the health department. Wait until you see the fenced yard. Ricky and Lucy will be in heaven."

The Cannon Beach Sandcastle Festival was the region's largest annual event, and the associated sandcastle-building contest drew artists from all over the nation. The sleepy coastal town of seventeen hundred residents would host almost ten thousand tourists the coming weekend, many of whom had driven hundreds of miles for the festivities. Rene was right: finding any available rental, much less one this amazing, was nothing short of a coup.

I glanced over at my German shedder, who had rolled on her back, burrowed her head into the couch, and was now waving her feet in the air. "I can't believe a place this nice allows pets."

Rene glanced down at her fingers. "Well, I may have had to beg a little and put down a few thousand as a damage deposit, but I'll get that back. Bella's well behaved." She glanced at the couch, which was now permanently impregnated with dog hair. "You brought a lint roller, right?" She ignored my silence. "And how much damage can little Ricky and Lucy do?"

I remembered the two weeks the tiny labradoodles had terrorized my house. Uprooted plants, a million potty accidents, and a sofa's worth of destroyed cushions. I gave Rene a droll look.

She chewed on her bottom lip. "On second thought, maybe we should keep Ricky and Lucy in their playpen."

Rene and I wandered upstairs. In addition to the guest bedroom on the main floor, there were two master bedrooms and two smaller ones, either of which would be perfect for the twins. Rene paused for a moment outside the second master bedroom, as if carefully choosing her words. She didn't make eye contact. "I was thinking..."

Always a bad sign.

"We have so much space here. It's a shame that Michael has to stay with his sister. I get that you don't want to live together right now, but if he stayed here, he could have his own room." She gestured at the stairwell. "You could each have your own floor, for that matter." She smiled. "If Michael tries to get frisky, we can put him in charge of the twins' diaper changes."

"Don't push it, Rene." I smiled to take the sting out of my reprimand. "If Michael stayed here, we'd end up in the same room, then sleeping in the same bed." Rene didn't argue. "Before the first night was over, we'd either fight or have sex. Probably both. Neither would be helpful right now."

Sam's grumpy voice yelled from the entryway. "Do you two plan to help, or are you going to stand there and watch while Michael and I do all the work?"

"The latter," Rene quipped.

Sam cradled Amelia over his chest in a front baby carrier. Alice squirmed in a similar contraption on his back. He held a heavy-looking suitcase in his right hand and two carry-on bags in his left. Michael staggered through the doorway behind him, trying to control two play-attacking puppies who were determined to murder his shoe-laces. He pulled an extra-large wheeled suitcase beside him.

"Geez, Sam," I said. "You two didn't have to bring everything inside at once."

"Everything?" Sam grumped. "I wish. Most of our stuff is still in the SUV. This is all Rene's." He dropped the bags heavily on the floor and tried to help Michael pry two mouths' worth of puppy teeth off his tennis shoes. I grabbed the suitcase from Michael. My fingertips accidentally brushed the back of his hand, creating a not unpleasant tingle deep in my belly. The sensation was so familiar, so comforting, that I almost relented and asked Michael to stay with us.

Almost.

Another trip netted the rest of the bags, along with three extra-large diaper bags full of baby supplies. I was unpacking Bella's pre-ground, premedicated food when the bleep of a car horn startled me.

FOUR

MICHAEL'S FACE BRIGHTENED. "THAT'S Shannon."

Bella gave me a look that clearly said, *Don't worry, I'm on it*. She charged the door, performing her most ferocious guard dog impression. The puppies scampered behind her, but Sam snatched them off the ground and awkwardly carried Ricky, Lucy, and the twins upstairs, causing all four to yelp in indignation.

I grabbed Bella's collar and dragged her to a bathroom while Michael went outside to greet his sister. By the time Rene and I reached the doorway, Michael was admiring a bright orange Mini Cooper. He hugged the five-foot blonde pixie standing next to it, took a step back, and appraised her at arm's length. "You look fantastic!"

He wasn't exaggerating. Even at the age of thirty-six, Shannon was perpetually cute, with bright blue eyes and a lopsided grin that telegraphed the phrase *Here comes trouble*. Her stylish new haircut bumped her appearance to a whole new level, however. The multilayer pixie cut was streaked with warm caramel lowlights. Flirtatious, professional, and playful all in the same package.

She ran her fingers across her scalp. "Thanks. I got a new cut and color for the occasion. It's not every day that my baby brother comes to visit." She winked. "Even if he only came to see me so I could get him out of trouble. I hate to say it, but..."

"I know, I know." Michael made finger quotes: "You told me so." He glanced my direction, then turned back to his sister. "You still like me though, right?"

"I don't just like you, Baby Brother. I love you." She flashed me an impish grin. "Don't worry, I'll charm Kate for you, too."

My smile back to her was forced. I'd met Shannon a few months earlier when she'd visited Michael in Seattle. I liked her—a lot—and I knew her intentions were good. But friendly sister or not, Michael would have to work *himself* back into my good graces.

He now pointed at the shiny orange vehicle. "The hairstyle isn't the only thing new."

Shannon grinned. "I'm supposedly a successful real estate professional. I figured it was time I looked the part. I haven't sold the Chevy yet. You're not in the market for a beater car by any chance, are you?"

Rene pointed at my Honda and yelled, "They've already got one of those. Quit standing around out there and come inside."

Shannon broke away from Michael, jogged up the stairs, and wrapped Rene in a huge hug. "You must be Rene! It's nice to finally meet you in person!" The two women swayed back and forth like old friends reuniting after a long separation. They seemed unusually chummy for two strangers, but I didn't think much about it. I'd told my best friend all about Michael's sister. Michael, undoubtedly, had told Shannon about Rene. I was delighted that the two women seemed to like each other.

While Shannon and Rene finished introducing themselves, I released Bella from the bathroom. "Bella, say hello," I commanded. As trained, Bella went into a perfect sit in front of Shannon and offered her paw.

Shannon gave it a firm shake and kneeled down for a kiss. "Good to see you again, Bella Baby," she cooed.

After Sam brought the twins back downstairs and Shannon made the requisite oohs and aahs, Michael glanced at his watch. "If we're going to make it to dinner before all the meatballs are taken, we'd better get going now."

The spaghetti dinner held the Tuesday before the Sandcastle Festival was a Cannon Beach tradition. According to Michael, it was a huge, crowded party at which the locals kicked back, drank significantly too much alcohol, and celebrated their survival of another summer before the tourists invaded for the weekend. He was confident that Gabriella would make an appearance. I didn't think confronting her in a crowded location was the wisest plan, but Michael insisted, claiming that if she saw him in public, she'd be forced to talk to him.

I wasn't in the mood for an evening of socializing with strangers, but I wanted to spend time with Shannon, and a crowded venue might prevent her from asking me questions that I wasn't prepared to answer. Besides, an embarrassingly jealous part of me didn't want Michael to see his hopefully soon-to-be-ex wife without me.

Rene and Sam opted to stay behind with the twins to relax, unpack, and unwind. The Cannon Beach Activity Center (or C-BAC, as the locals called it) was on the way to Shannon's house, so Michael and his suitcase rode in the Mini Cooper with Shannon while Bella and I followed behind in my Honda. I'd considered leaving Bella at the rental house, but she needed a break from the puppies. My adult dog could only tolerate short bursts of Lucy and Ricky's frenetic energy before her normal crankiness turned into a full-blown flare of her chronic digestive disease, Exocrine Pancreatic Insufficiency. Her mental and physical health would both benefit from a few hours of alone time.

Michael and Shannon pulled into C-BAC's main parking lot. I kept driving to a shady side street a block away. In spite of the cool September weather, Bella would appreciate both the shade and the street's relative seclusion. I parked under a huge evergreen, unrolled the windows a couple of inches, filled Bella's water bowl, and pushed the driver's seat forward.

"Want to go for a quick walk, sweetie?" My dog let out a sigh and rested her head between her paws, clearly declining my offer. I ruffled her ears, promised her that I'd be back soon, and headed for the center.

C-BAC was housed in a large cement building fronted by a huge parking lot and sandwiched between sprawling green lawns. The grassy area to my right was filled with an assortment of brightly colored playground equipment; the one to my left had enough open space for a makeshift soccer field. Three cement stairs led from the parking lot to the building's blue double doors. Each time they opened, live bluegrass music belted outside. Banjo, guitar, fiddle, and the telltale wail of a harmonica. I felt myself grin. It was impossible to be cranky while listening to bluegrass.

Michael and Shannon weren't waiting for me on the sidewalk, so I followed a group of boisterous teens into the building. I froze as the door banged shut behind me.

Good lord, Michael wasn't exaggerating.

Every citizen in the greater Cannon Beach area—and at least three towns outside its perimeter—seemed to be crowded into the large, cavernous space. People of all ages—retirees, young adults, teenagers, grade schoolers, and toddlers—milled around the room, animatedly chatting and carrying plates heaped with pasta and red sauce.

The live bluegrass band I'd heard earlier played "The Devil Went Down to Georgia" near a small dance floor, which was filled with children jumping up and down and flailing to the music. I closed my eyes and took a deep, calming breath. The delicious scents of simmering tomato sauce, oily garlic bread, and recently poured beer wafted into my nostrils, and the smile I'd felt earlier returned, times two. I'd been in town less than an hour, but I'd already reached one firm conclusion: Cannon Beachers knew how to party.

An ancient woman sat in a folding chair next to a seascape-themed quilt stitched in teals, blues, grays, and greens. A sign next to it read, *Raffle Tickets $5 each or 3 for $10. Proceeds benefit the Cannon Beach Animal Shelter.*

"Care to buy a ticket?" she yelled over the din.

I imagined Bella gleefully rolling on top of the gorgeous art piece, pulled out my billfold, and handed her a twenty. "Sure, why not?" It was for a good cause, after all. If I won the quilt, I would gift it to Sam and Rene.

I was writing my phone number on the tickets when a boisterous, dark-haired toddler wearing overalls, a bright red shirt, and the world's tiniest cowboy boots screamed toward me, followed by an exhausted-looking twenty-something I assumed was his mother. Loose tendrils of hair escaped her brunette ponytail, framing her frantic face. The boy zipped toward the door behind me—and the busy parking lot on the other side.

"Jimmy, slow down!" his mother yelled. "Wait!"

He pushed the door open, but I grabbed him a millisecond before his feet crossed the threshold. "Whoa there, partner," I said.

Evidently, being captured ruined Jimmy's fun. The now-howling beast-child kicked, screamed, and pummeled my chest with tiny, angry fists. Exactly how Dad used to describe my own three-year-old temper tantrums.

His mother gave me a wan smile and took the flailing child from my arms. "Sorry about that."

"Not a problem."

She gently chastised him as she led him back through the crowd. "I told you, Jimmy, you have to stay close to Mommy."

Disaster averted, I thrust my raffle tickets into a gallon Mason jar, stood on my tiptoes in a tennis-shoed Tadasana, and tried to locate Michael and Shannon. They weren't on the dance floor and I didn't spot them in the food line, so I carefully wove my way through long rows of tables, each of which was painted with a multicolored mosaic of kid-sized handprints. An early fall project, I assumed, for stir-crazy schoolchildren.

Shannon waved to me from a table opposite the dance floor.

"We were starting to get worried," Michael said.

"Speak for yourself, Baby Brother." Shannon poked him in the arm. "Mr. Worrywart here is convinced that you're going to dump him and run back to Seattle the first chance you get." She narrowed her eyes and frowned at me. "You're not, right?"

I grinned. "Not tonight."

Her frown lifted and she poked Michael again. "See. Told you, silly." She gestured toward the food line with her thumb. "Now go buy your girls some meal tickets."

Michael glanced at me, seeming uncertain. "Maybe we should all go together."

"Don't be silly. Why make Kate put up with all of that small talk?"

"What small talk?" he asked.

"You haven't visited in almost three years. You'll bump into tons of people who want to catch up." Shannon pointed to a sultry-eyed, dark-haired man about Michael's age who was staffing a table near the buffet line. "Von, for example. He and his new boyfriend, Andreas, are selling the meal tickets."

I glanced at the man she referred to, then quickly looked away again and tried to quash the unease gurgling in my belly.

Tried, without success.

Von was gorgeous. Gorgeous enough that Rene would have gone gaga. I might have, too, if it weren't for the thick, dark facial hair that smothered his chin. I'd been working hard to overcome my pogonophobia—the irrational fear of beards—since I'd discovered its origins a few months ago.

Intellectually, I knew that Von's beard, by itself, wasn't the problem. Facial hair was simply a symbol—a reminder—of a long ago, much darker day. Physically, however, I still felt the same reaction: cold sweat dotting the back of my neck; gripping nausea in my belly; jarring, staccato beats in my chest. I'd been learning to suppress these reactions, with some success. But Von's thick, bristly beard was particularly... well, particularly beard-like.

I mentally chanted *OM Bhuh*, the mantra used to overcome obstacles, and stared at the man seated next to him. Andreas, I assumed. He was clean-shaven, balding, and equally handsome. Each time he finished putting money in the cash drawer, he lathered his hands in hand sanitizer.

Neither man looked in our direction. Neither of them looked at each other, for that matter. The energy between them was tense. Their bodies angled away from each other. If they were lovers, I doubted there'd be any romance tonight.

Shannon nudged Michael's arm. "Go on. Talk to Von. It'll give Kate and me a chance for some girl talk. Just don't sneeze on Andreas. He's a huge germaphobe."

Michael didn't move.

"Seriously," Shannon chided. "Go. If Kate makes a break for the door, I'll tackle her."

Michael didn't look happy, but he acquiesced. He slowly made his way across the room, stopping every few steps for shoulder claps, hugs, and more than a few squeals of delight. Michael may have been gone from Cannon Beach for a while, but he was obviously still popular.

Shannon watched him work the room for a few seconds, then pulled a piece of paper out of her pocket and slid it across the table toward me.

"I forgot to give this to your friend Rene today."

I glanced down at it curiously. A check. For almost as much as my monthly salary as a yoga teacher. "What's this?"

"Isn't it obvious?" Shannon spoke slowly and enunciated clearly, like a teacher speaking to a not-very-bright student. "It's a check."

I gave her a droll look. "I get that. But what's it for? Blackmail? A bribe?" I smirked. "For the record, if you have extra cash burning a hole in your pocket, your brother needs it more than Rene does."

"It's for my next order from Infant Gratification."

"You're buying Rene's baby baubles? Are you expecting?"

"No, but some of my real estate clients are, and I'm always looking for creative housewarming gifts. After Michael told me about her business, I looked it up online. It's fabulous! When she heard I was Michael's sister, she offered me a friends and family discount. If I pay cash, I get twenty percent off. This check is for my third order."

No wonder Shannon and Rene seemed to be so familiar.

"Your real estate clients want pacifier purses?" I asked incredulously.

"Have you checked out her catalogue? It's super diverse, and it has products I haven't seen anywhere else, including products for new moms." Shannon rummaged around in her purse and pulled out a plasticized package. "Like this, for instance. Rene gave me this sample while you were letting Bella out of the bathroom."

The clear plastic package contained a spray bottle enclosed in a bejeweled leather case. I gaped at the label. *Mommy Mace. Designer Pepper Spray for Mommies Who Want to be Safe AND Stylish.*

"Are you sure about this, Shannon?" I asked. "Personal defense weapons don't exactly scream 'welcome to your new neighborhood.'"

Shannon opened the package and pulled out its contents. "I haven't given anyone the mace yet. Like I said, this is a sample." She placed her index finger on the trigger, held it up to the light, and tilted it back and forth, causing light to reflect off the royal blue rhinestones. For an insane, terrified moment, I thought she was going to spray me. Instead, she passed the canister across the table. "You're probably right. Consider this my gift to you. Mace is better for people who live in the big city, anyway."

Seattle wasn't exactly New York, and the one time I'd carried mace I'd almost been doused with it. But it wasn't worth bickering about. I tucked the canister inside my purse, vowing to dispose of it later.

Shannon continued. "You'd be surprised by how many baby gifts are appropriate for homebuyers, though. Lots of people buy new homes when they start a family, and everybody with a child under two loves baby baubles. The eighteen-karat infant ID bracelets have been a huge hit." She paused and tilted her eyes to the ceiling. "I wonder if I could talk her into making platinum dog tags for my dog-crazy clients…"

Who was I to argue with Rene's success? I folded the check in two, slipped it inside my billfold, and watched Michael disappear into the crowd.

Shannon followed my gaze. "He really *did* freak out when you drove past the parking lot. I told him you were probably looking for shade, but he still wanted me to follow you. He's convinced that you're going to leave him."

I didn't reply, hoping that she'd take the hint and change subjects. No such luck.

"Well? Are you?"

I sighed. "I don't know. I hope not."

She frowned at me for several infinitely long, uncomfortable seconds. I thought I was going to be chastised, but she surprised me.

"I'm sorry."

"Sorry?" I asked. "For what?"

"For my part in this whole fiasco. I should have told you about Gabby." She looked down at her hands. "I almost did. Dozens of times."

Shannon's contrition should have made me feel better, but in fact, it did exactly the opposite. Irritation prickled my throat. "Then why didn't you? Why didn't Michael, for that matter."

Shannon frowned. "It's complicated. I shouldn't say anything else."

Yogi Kate understood that Shannon wasn't to blame for Michael's actions, but Yogi Kate wasn't seated at that table. Betrayed Girlfriend Kate was. I felt exactly like Jimmy must have felt when I scooped him away from the doorway. *Happiness interruptus.*

Three days of frustration spewed out of my mouth. "Complicated? That's the same thing your brother told me. For God's sake, Shannon! How complicated can it be? Michael was dating me while he was married to someone else. It seems pretty simple. Calling it 'complicated' is just the lame justification of a cowardly, scumbag cheater."

Shannon's face turned so red, I thought her hair might ignite. She hissed at me through clenched teeth, "Hold up there, Kate. Let's get one thing straight. That's my baby brother you're talking about. I will *not* tolerate anyone—especially you, the supposed love of his life—berating him. Michael made a mistake, but he's no scumbag. Not even close. He's certainly no cheater. Until you give him a chance to tell you his side of the story, back off on the judgment. About both of us."

One look at her fierce expression and I understood why she was angry. Michael was her brother. She would always have his back, the same way Rene would always have mine. I buried my face in my palms, embarrassed by my outburst. "I'm sorry, Shannon. He's your brother. You have to be on his side."

Shannon's voice softened. "Keeping my mouth shut wasn't about taking sides, Kate; it was about loyalty. It wasn't my place to tell you about Gabby." She tapped her sternum with her index finger. "Make no mistake. I'm Michael's sister—his blood. I will always love him. That comes with the territory. Therefore, I'm allowed to say this. You aren't." Her jaw firmed. "Michael was an ass for not telling you about Gabby."

Michael spoke from behind her. "Don't mince words, do you, Shan?"

Shannon's shoulders tensed, so briefly that I almost missed it. A not-quite-real smile graced her lips. She winked at me, then turned toward Michael. "When have you ever known me to mince words? Don't worry, Baby Brother. You may be an ass, but you're family. That makes you my ass. I'll stick up for you. Always. Even though Kate deserves better."

Michael didn't smile at her joke. "You're right, she does." He avoided looking into my eyes. "Think she'll settle for a doofus like me?"

"She will if she's smart."

I crossed my arms and leaned back in my chair. Why were they talking about me as if I weren't there? I considered asking them exactly that, but I decided that I might not want to know the answer. I pointed to the long strip of red tickets Michael held in his hand. "What are those?"

"Drink tickets. I bought a dozen. I figured we could all use some liquid courage."

Shannon pushed her chair away from the table. "I know I certainly could. But first let's get some food. I'm starving." She grabbed Michael's wrist with one hand, mine with the other. "Let's go."

We made our way through the buffet line, plates piled high with a tantalizing assortment of pastas, breads, salads, and sauces. Michael skipped the meat sauce in favor of a vegetable marinara, a sure sign that my meat-loving boyfriend was working hard to get back into my good graces.

Back at the table, we ignored our prior conflict and settled into a comfortable camaraderie. We shared jokes; we sipped wine. We noisily slurped spaghetti noodles through pursed, O-shaped lips. Red sauce dripped from my lips and spattered the front of my shirt.

Michael dunked a napkin into his water glass and wiped oily red sauce off my chin. "You're getting as bad as Rene."

I couldn't explain why, but those cherished moments of normalcy—of hanging out with Michael and Shannon eating sloppy spaghetti—made me feel close to him again. I almost forgot why we were there. All worries of Michael, his marriage, and his yet-to-be-confronted wife disappeared from my mind.

I should have known it was too good to last.

Forty-five minutes later, we'd cleaned our plates and used up three-quarters of Michael's drink tickets. Shannon wadded up her napkin and dropped it on the table. "This has been fun, but I have to get up for a 7:00 a.m. meeting tomorrow."

"You're showing houses at seven in the morning?" Michael asked.

"I wish," Shannon replied. "That would be a lot more productive. No one gets any real work done this close to the Sandcastle Festival. It's a planning committee meeting. I'm in charge of the fun run this year." She looped her purse around her shoulder. "Do you want to hang out here with Kate and see if Gabby comes by?"

Michael stared at me, eyes hopeful.

I involuntarily flinched. Fun family dinner notwithstanding, I still wasn't ready for us to spend the evening alone.

Michael must have noticed, because he sighed and pushed back his chair. "We may as well go. It looks like Gabby isn't coming. Maybe that's a good thing. I'll call her again tonight. If she still doesn't answer, I'll leave a message saying I'm in town and that I plan to drop off divorce papers tomorrow."

"Do you think that's a good idea?" Shannon asked. "To drop off papers in person, I mean. Wouldn't it be better to use a process server?"

"A server would cost money."

Shannon frowned. "Money's that tight?"

When Michael didn't answer, she turned to me. I shrugged. "The house remodel was more expensive than we thought it would be."

Shannon paused for a moment, thinking. "The Mini Cooper put a dent in my savings, but I can loan you a couple of thousand if you need it."

"Thanks, Shan. If Gabby keeps insisting on a payoff in exchange for an uncontested divorce, I may have to take you up on that."

"You never told me how much she wants."

Michael swallowed. "Fifty thousand dollars."

My stomach constricted, just like it had the first time I'd heard the number.

"A-Are you kidding me?" Shannon's energy changed. Hardened. Her expression grew sour. "I warned you not to marry that manipulative parasite."

"Come on, Shannon. I asked you not to call her that."

"Why not? It fits. After everything you did for her, I can't believe she has the gall to demand that much money."

Michael massaged his temples, the way he did when he was trying to hold back his temper. I glanced back and forth between the two siblings, conflicted. Should I interrupt Mount Michael before he erupted or let the sibling quarrel play out?

In the end, Michael made the decision for me. He took a deep breath and held up his hands. "Look, I don't want to argue. I'll admit, Gabby's being selfish. Uncharacteristically so. But she's always been reasonable in the past. I have to believe that if she and I get in the same room, we can work this out."

"Skip the negotiations," Shannon insisted. "Call her bluff and take her to court. She'll back down."

"My lawyer says that's not a good idea. Between paying spousal support and giving her a good chunk of my assets, I'd end up out way more than fifty grand. I can't exactly admit to the judge that we only combined assets to fool the feds."

Shannon scowled but remained silent.

"Even if I sold the business…" He shook his head. "Sinking all of my savings into the remodel seems foolish now, but I had no idea Gabby would do something like this. The only way I can get the money is if Kate or I take out a mortgage."

"Which neither of us can qualify for," I added.

"Forget court then," Shannon said. "Let me handle Gabriella. I'll squash her like a cockroach." She smashed her palm against the table with a decided *thwok*.

Michael gave her a scalding look.

"Fine. No more insect metaphors. So basically, you're stuck paying off Gabriella, but all of your money's tied up in the house, and you can't get a loan."

I had a feeling I knew where Shannon was going. From the tension in Michael's jaw muscles, he knew it too.

"The market in Seattle is really hot right now. Why don't you sell the house?"

Michael crossed his arms stubbornly. "Absolutely not. That's Kate's childhood home. I'd rather split my time between prison and bankruptcy court."

This was the crux of Michael's dilemma, and the source of much of my inner conflict. Selling the house *should* have been a non-issue. A house was only an object. An object that held a lifetime of precious memories, but an object nonetheless.

Michael, on the other hand, was a person. My soul mate. My love. Losing Michael might break me. So why was I choosing the house over him, especially when I had another alternative? Another alternative Michael knew nothing about.

Rene.

Rene had offered to lend me the money on the drive that morning, claiming that she didn't want Michael's drama to ruin her vacation. I adored her for the generous subterfuge, but I'd turned her down without hesitation. I had no idea how Michael's and my story was destined to end, but we needed to write it together. Without taking handouts from our loved ones.

Michael's expression invited no argument. "The house is off limits. We'll figure out another way."

A few minutes later, Shannon, Michael, and I silently headed toward the parking lot, prior jovial mood completely forgotten. We were halfway to the door when a female voice yelled over the crowd:

"Shannon, wait!"

FIVE

"Susan, oh no!" Shannon exclaimed. "What happened?"

A tiny Asian woman seated near the dance floor waved Shannon toward her. She wore a light cotton dress, a brunette ponytail, and an ankle-to-upper-thigh knee brace. A pair of metal crutches leaned against the wall beside her.

Shannon turned to Michael. "Sorry, Baby Brother, but I need to talk to her. She's supposed to teach at the fun run on Saturday. I'll meet you at the car in a few minutes." She scurried halfway across the room before Michael could reply.

He shrugged. "We may as well take Bella for a walk. I have a feeling she'll be a while."

The sky was dusky when Michael and I exited the community center, but the parking lot still seemed bright, lit by an almost full moon and the voices of happy neighbors. Michael pointed to the gold heart adorning my throat. "You're wearing the locket."

I reached up and fingered it. "I like it." I grinned at him ruefully. "Don't read too much into it, though. I replaced your picture with

Rene's." I hadn't, of course. I wore Michael's gift because I wanted him near me, even if the closeness was merely symbolic.

He gazed into my eyes. "Kate, I'm so sorry about—"

I held up my hand, stopping him. "I know. And we'll talk it all out someday, I promise."

"When?"

"When I'm ready. For tonight, can we just hang out and pretend that everything's normal?"

He nodded, but his expression remained clouded.

A silence-filled block later, I unlocked my car and liberated Bella from her backseat prison. She leaped to the ground and did a quick happy dance around Michael's feet before pulling me down the street, seeking out spaghetti with meat sauce, no doubt. Michael and I made small talk as we headed back toward the parking lot, carefully avoiding all discussion of divorce attorneys, money, and soon-to-be-ex wives.

The distant sound of upbeat bluegrass serenaded us, but I still felt uneasy, and not solely about the conversation Michael and I were avoiding. As a yoga teacher, I had become attuned to subtle changes in energy, and the energy around me felt predatory. As if someone was watching us—watching me.

I surreptitiously glanced behind me. Nothing. But I still felt…

Someone.

Maybe it was Dad, giving me the evil eye from heaven. Maybe it was Patanjali, reminding me that I should treat everyone—Michael included—with unattached compassion. Maybe it was my conscience, telling me that refusing to talk with Michael about our future was cruel.

Then again, maybe it was simply my overactive imagination.

I lightened the atmosphere with a lame attempt at humor. "You know, it's probably good that we didn't see Gabriella tonight."

"Why's that?" Michael asked.

"You know me. I'd have sicced Bella on her or shattered her knee-cap." I grinned. "Nobody steals my man." I wiggled my eyebrows. "Not even if she had him first."

For the first time since my birthday dinner, Michael's smile didn't seem forced. "Gabby never had me, Kate. Not the way you do. I wish—"

Michael stopped speaking and peered forward intently. His relieved smile evaporated. I could have sworn that I saw the hair on the back of his neck stand up, the way Bella's did when she spotted the UPS truck.

"Michael, what is it?"

Bella sensed his tension. A low, deep growl rumbled from her throat.

I touched his arm. "Michael?"

He gestured with his chin toward the parking lot, voice somewhere between a growl and a whisper. "Gabriella. Two o'clock."

I followed his eyes to two women. The first was a thirty-something blonde with a short, asymmetrical haircut highlighted with pastel pink. The combination of harsh LED streetlights and thickly applied makeup made her skin seem plastic, like a knock-off Barbie doll covered in spray paint.

The Hispanic woman standing next to her had to be Gabriella. She was drop-dead gorgeous.

As in so gorgeous, I wanted to drop dead.

Like most women I knew, I'd struggled with body image issues since my first preteen bra fitting. I'd been more chunky than obese, but to my teenage psyche, that didn't matter. When I'd looked in the mirror, I'd seen the Pillsbury Dough Girl. Practicing yoga had helped. Dropping twenty-five pounds had helped more. Still, one look at the raven-haired Latina and I felt myself being transported back to every humiliating high school dance I'd attended with Rene. Dances during which I'd huddled next to the wall, hoping someone would talk to me.

Dances during which the only boys who approached me asked me for Rene's phone number. Dances during which I fervently prayed for lightning to strike me dead.

I hadn't been unattractive, simply average. Rene was anything but. She was the sun; I was Pluto. It wasn't her fault, and she certainly didn't eclipse me on purpose. She couldn't help that I disappeared in her shadow.

Just like I would have in Gabriella's.

According to Michael, Gabriella was almost thirty, but she looked at least five years younger. The dark, lush hair of shampoo commercials flowed between her shoulder blades. Her caramel skin was flawless; her body at most a size four. She wore a red, form-fitting T-shirt, faded capri-length jeans, and strappy high-heeled sandals. I couldn't bear to make eye contact, so I stared at her feet. A chain of red starfish encircled her ankle.

Symbols of the love goddess, Venus.

Fabulous.

Long-buried feelings of inadequacy flooded every cell of my body. I absently rubbed at the red pasta sauce staining my right breast, locked my eyes on the competition, and made up my mind.

I hated her.

So I looked for her faults. I found only one. Disingenuousness.

Gabriella was hiding something. Pretending to be something she wasn't. Her hands fluttered animatedly through the air, but her bright smile seemed forced, her energy guarded. Her espresso brown eyes flitted in every direction, as if she was looking for someone. Someone she hoped she wouldn't see.

I frowned at Michael. "You didn't tell me she was beautiful."

"She modeled in Mexico."

"A model," I repeated, deadpan. "Naturally."

Michael grunted. "It's nothing to be envious about. She was always hungry, often broke. Lunatics stalked her and made her life hell. Her manager got her addicted to cocaine. When I met her, she was working as a waitress, and she was a lot happier."

"Should we go talk to her?" I asked.

"Maybe. Give me a minute."

In my Kate-centered universe, I assumed that Michael hesitated either because he didn't want me to meet Gabriella, or because he didn't want Gabriella to meet me. It never occurred to me that there might be a third option. It never occurred to me that Michael might be gathering courage.

He took a deep breath. "Stay here." He strode toward the two women without looking back.

Like hell.

I pulled Bella's leash tight and marched behind him. Gabriella glanced at me curiously. When her gaze flicked to Michael, she jolted, then froze, hands suspended mid-gesture. She didn't speak, so I tried to read her facial expression: wide eyes, tense jaw, open mouth.

Was she surprised?

She had to be, of course, but I read something else. She certainly didn't seem happy. If pressed, I'd have said her expression looked an awful lot like fear.

Of Michael?

Gabriella said something to the blonde, then pointed at Michael.

The blonde turned toward Michael, flashed him a huge, bright smile, and wiggled her fingers. Michael looked through her as if she were invisible. Her smile fell.

I know how you feel, sweetheart. The invisible handmaiden to the beautiful princess.

Michael's voice, when he spoke, didn't sound friendly. "Hi Gabby," he said. "I've been looking for you. But then again, you already knew that." He then spoke to the blonde, but his eyes never left Gabriella. "Crystal, would you give Gabby and me a minute?"

The blonde (who was obviously named Crystal) narrowed her eyes. "Gabby?"

Gabriella nodded a curt yes.

"Okay, but I'll be right inside. Yell if you need me." She retreated to the building, glancing over her shoulder at Michael and Gabriella every few steps.

I stood there watching, my muscles frozen. This was it. The moment I'd been waiting for. The moment I hoped would knock Michael's and my relationship back on kilter. I stood completely still, but the world swirled around me like a surreal merry-go-round, as if I were an audience to my life versus a participant.

No one else seemed to notice the impending drama. Families wandered in and out of the center, focused on their own conversations. Children played on swings and ran through fragrant green grass. A teenaged couple made out on the hood of an ancient blue Chevy Malibu.

Bella's growl knocked me out of my stupor. Her upper lip wrinkled, exposing sharp canine teeth; the guard hairs between her shoulders prickled at high alert. I followed her glare to an olive-skinned man skulking near the children's play area. He wore a camouflage baseball cap pulled low over his eyes. His energy felt hungry. A jackal waiting to scavenge.

Normally, when Bella growled at a stranger, I said the phrase, "This is our friend," which was my signal for her to stand down.

Not this time.

Bella didn't trust the man, and I was inclined to agree with her.

I kept the stranger in the periphery of my awareness but moved next to Michael so I could listen to his conversation with Gabriella. Gabriella ignored me, much as Michael had ignored Crystal. She spoke in heavily accented English. "Why are you here?" It sounded more like an accusation than a question.

"You haven't returned my phone calls," Michael said. "We need to talk."

Rapid-fire Spanish tumbled from Gabriella's lips, faster than any nonfluent speaker—such as yours truly—could hope to understand. Her tone, however, was universal. The woman was pissed.

Michael didn't sound happy himself. "What do you mean, we have nothing to talk about?"

More Spanish.

"That wasn't our agreement, and you know it," Michael spat. "Even if it were, I don't have that kind of money."

Gabriella's voice grew louder. Even her hands seemed to yell. The plain gold wedding band on her left ring finger swiped through the air with each emphatic gesture.

People around us stopped talking to stare at the spectacle. Michael lowered his voice and switched to Spanish. I cursed Dad for convincing me to take German in high school. Unless one of them ordered a Margarita or asked where the bathroom was, I wouldn't understand a word.

Several crescendoing accusations later, Michael crossed his arms and stepped his feet wide. "Forget it. That is never going to happen."

I recognized his expression. Pure. Stubborn. Male. I placed my hand on his arm, hoping the gesture would calm him.

Gabriella frowned at me. *"Quien es?"*

"Gabriella, this is my—" Michael hesitated. "My friend, Kate."

Friend? Now I was his friend?

Gabriella pointed at me, shook her head, and sputtered an unintelligible reply. Then she leveled a hard stare at me. "You must leave." She stomped a high-heeled sandal for emphasis. "Now."

I had news for Ms. Venus, Goddess of Love. I wasn't going anywhere. Neither, apparently, was Bella. She growled at the rude, stomping stranger.

"Bella, down," Michael commanded.

Astonishingly, Bella obeyed. She flopped to the ground, but she kept her back legs tucked under, ready to spring to my defense if needed.

Michael stared into Gabriella's eyes for several long seconds. Then his facial expression softened. He stepped toward her and reached for her hand. His voice was barely above a whisper. "Gabby, what's going on with you?"

Gabriella glanced behind her. Her eyes grew wet. *"Dejame. Por favor."* Her voice didn't sound angry anymore. It sounded frightened. She turned to me, face pleading. "Leave. Please."

"Not until you tell me what's wrong," Michael countered.

Gabriella shook off her tears. Her face hardened to concrete. She took three quick steps toward Michael and slammed her palms roughly into his chest. "I said go!"

The shove must have caught Michael off guard, because he stumbled. I saw a flash of light, then he hit the pavement with a sharp clank, a muffled thud, and a volley of swear words.

That's when Mount Rainier erupted.

Or at least that's what it felt like.

Bella sprang from the ground and hurled herself at her human's attacker. She barked. She snarled. She snapped at the air on either side of Gabriella's head. Gabriella screamed and stumbled away, yelling what I assumed were obscenities in Spanish. I yanked on Bella's leash. Michael scrambled to his feet and grabbed for her collar.

"Bella, knock it off!" I yelled. "This is our friend!"

Shannon charged down the community center's front stairs and screamed, "Leave my baby brother alone, you ungrateful tapeworm!"

Crystal ran behind her, yelling, "Rabid dog! A rabid dog is attacking Gabby! Somebody shoot it!"

The cowboy-booted toddler zoomed behind them both. He spied Bella, pasted on a huge grin, and ran toward her, waving his arms and chirping with glee. "Doggie!"

Everything next happened in an impossible fast-forward slow motion. Shannon threw herself at Gabby, clubbing her over the head with her purse. Michael dropped Bella's collar and grabbed for his sister. Crystal dove after them both.

Bella stopped lunging and whipped toward the child. The ecstatic toddler bee-lined it toward Bella, across the busy parking lot. The blue Chevy Malibu (driven by the male teenager that had been making out earlier) sped toward him, seemingly unaware that a child was careening toward his front bumper.

"Stop!" I yelled.

In a freeze-framed moment of gut-wrenching clarity, the teenager's face twisted in horror. He slammed on the brakes and the car flew into a skid. I dropped Bella's leash and dove for the child, praying that Bella wouldn't go after Gabriella again. Tires screeched on pavement. Burning rubber stung my nostrils. My knee scraped painfully against the sidewalk, but I grasped hold of the child and yanked him toward me.

Gotcha!

I'm not sure who cried louder—the toddler, in noisy frustration, or me, in grateful abandon. Bella loped next to me, nuzzled the child, and covered his face in sloppy, wet, German shepherd kisses. Jimmy's mother—who appeared seemingly out of nowhere—pulled him into her arms. "I told you, you have to wait for Mommy!"

Meanwhile, back in the parking lot, Michael held Shannon's arms behind her back while Crystal brushed dirt off of Gabriella's jeans.

"What in the hell is going on here!"

51

The voice came from a uniformed police officer. He wore a navy blue—almost black—uniform with short sleeves, a large silver star, and a name tag that read B. Boyle. He was a good two inches shorter than Michael, but his rigid posture made him seem taller. His dark beard quivered with authoritarian indignation.

I averted my eyes to avoid looking at his facial hair and they landed on his hands, which hovered frighteningly near the gun on his belt. Michael released Shannon's arms. Crystal scooped Shannon's purse off the ground, handed it to her, and disappeared to the sidelines.

The officer pointed at Bella, who was drowning the child in German shepherd saliva. "I heard someone yelling about a vicious dog. Was it attacking this child?"

"Bella would never harm a child," I assured him. "She loves kids."

Boyle narrowed his eyes at me and frowned. "You the boy's mother?"

The ponytailed woman balanced the snuffling toddler on her hip and stood. "No, I am." She smiled, trying to break the tension. "I'm Zoey Brown. This is my son, Jimmy." Officer Boyle replied with a curt nod. "The dog didn't do anything. Jimmy is fine. Incorrigible as ever, but fine." She kept talking. "He's been out of control since we moved here. I know I should discipline him more, but his father was so tough on him …" Her voice trailed off. "Anyway, this time, the little stinker ran out in front of a car. This lady saved him."

An onlooker pointed at Gabriella. "The dog wasn't going after the kid. It was attacking that woman."

Boyle turned toward Gabriella. His eyes widened, then softened. "I didn't see you there. Are you hurt?"

Gabriella stared at the ground and remained silent.

Bella, who was less fond of beards than I was, leaned toward the officer and growled. "Quiet!" I whispered. "We're in enough trouble already."

"Everybody's fine," Michael replied. "It was just a little misunderstanding."

Officer Boyle gave Michael a look that would have melted lava. "Stand over there on the sidewalk, sir." He turned to me. "Maybe I should call Animal Control. Let them deal with this."

"Bella's not dangerous," I assured him. "She just makes a scene. She barked, but she never intended to bite anyone." My words were true. Bella had never harmed anyone, human or animal. Like all dogs, Bella's reflexes were much faster than any human's. If Bella had intended to bite Gabriella, Gabriella would be bleeding. Period.

Officer Boyle examined Gabriella with dark, unreadable eyes. "Is she telling the truth? Did this dog hurt you?"

Michael stepped forward. "Everything's fine, Officer, we—"

"I told you to stay on the sidewalk," Boyle snapped. "I'm not talking to you."

An onlooker interjected, pointing at Michael. "Well, you should be. That man was harassing her. He's the reason the dog attacked."

"Harassing her?" Boyle clenched his fists. "Gabriella, do you know this joker?"

Gabriella held up her palms and blocked him from Michael. "Brock, *por favor. No hay problema.* No problem."

With Gabriella's thick accent, the name sounded like "Broke," as in having no money, but I had a feeling his real name rhymed with "rock." As in *the angry police officer bludgeoned the innocent German shepherd with a rock.*

She flashed a fake smile Michael's direction. "*Es mi esposo.* My husband." Her eyes begged Michael not to argue.

Officer Brock Boyle tilted his head and examined Michael more closely. "Your husband? I thought your husband lived out of town." He narrowed his eyes at the onlooker. "Are you telling me that you witnessed a domestic violence incident?"

"Believe me," Shannon snapped, "there's no domestic *anything* going on here." Michael gave her a warning look.

"She means there was no violence," I interjected. "Shannon and I both witnessed everything. It was just an argument. Some yelling. A shove or two." I pointed at Gabriella. "Most of which came from her."

Officer Boyle ignored me and stared enigmatically at Gabriella. "Are you sure that you're safe? We take domestic violence pretty seriously around here. All you have to do is file a complaint, and I'll make sure this joker spends the rest of the evening in a jail cell."

"No." She placed her palm on the officer's forearm. "Please. Everything is okay."

Officer Boyle didn't look convinced. He reluctantly turned away from Gabriella and pressed his index finger against Michael's chest. "I'd better not hear about any more problems from you." He marched three steps away, then turned back to me. "Keep that dog under control or I'll shoot it myself."

I held my breath until he disappeared inside C-BAC. He wouldn't really shoot Bella, would he?

The crowd dispersed. Crystal, Gabriella's blonde friend, reappeared. "Come on, Gabby. Let's get out of here."

"Not now," Michael said. "Gabby and I still need to talk."

"You can talk later," Crystal growled. "You've done enough damage for one night."

Michael's upper lip quivered, but Crystal's tone left no room for argument. Gabriella followed her across the parking lot, and the two women climbed into a dark gray SUV.

Michael stared after them, clearly upset. But he wasn't angry, at least not anymore. His expression was much more nuanced than that. He was confused. Worried. Perhaps even wounded. Something was brewing in his smoldering blue-green eyes. Something I might not want to know about. Something that a simple divorce decree might not fix.

The two women had driven a full block away before I realized that the man wearing the camouflage cap had vanished.

SIX

"We certainly know how to liven up a party, don't we, Baby Brother."

Shannon might as well have been talking to a Michael-shaped statue. He ignored her quip and stared stonily down the street as if pining for Gabriella's return. Like the third point on a bizarre, twisted love triangle, I stared at Michael, pining for him.

Zoey thanked me for corralling her son. I pretended to listen, but my mind and my heart were elsewhere: back in Seattle, three days ago, when Michael's and my future held so much promise. Promise that might be nothing more than a fairy tale with a yet-unknown, tragic ending.

A few minutes of small talk later, Zoey disappeared with the rest of the onlookers, who had wandered back inside the center.

Shannon approached me, wearing an expression that was half consternation, half worry. "When Mr. Tall, Dark, and Brooding is ready to go, tell him I'm waiting in the car."

I gave Michael a few more minutes of alone time, then edged next to him.

"You okay?" I asked.

His eyes flitted toward me, then settled back on the road. "No, I'm not." He frowned. "Something's going on with her, Kate, and it isn't good."

"You've got to admit," I replied, "Gabriella didn't have a good day." I grinned, trying to lighten the mood. "First she was introduced to her husband's mistress, then she got clobbered by her sister-in-law. I'd be a bit peeved, too."

Michael's mood snapped from pensive to prickly in a heartbeat. "This isn't funny, Kate. I'm not here to traumatize Gabby. She had enough of that back in Mexico. If you and Shannon plan to use her as a human punching bag, then maybe you should both stay away."

His response stung like a slap to the face, which was exactly how he'd intended it. I pretended annoyance to cover my hurt. "Hey, buddy. Back the truck up there. I didn't do anything to harm Wifey Dearest. That little scene was all Shannon. And Bella," I conceded. "But Bella was protecting you. If anybody's the victim in this circus, it's me. Why are you taking Gabriella's side all of a sudden? Isn't she the one essentially holding you hostage?"

Michael lifted his hand. For a brief, delusional moment, I thought he might slap me. His arm lifted a foot, then fell back to his side. He shook his head and groaned. "I'm sorry, Kate. I don't know what's gotten into me. I hate what this whole situation is doing to you. To us." When he looked back up, his eyes were shrouded. "I don't expect you to understand this, but..." His voice trailed off.

I wasn't sure I wanted to hear the rest of the sentence, but I asked anyway. "But what?"

"I'm not in love with Gabby. But I *do* care about her, and something's wrong. She's a good person. Refusing to talk to me isn't like her."

"And extorting fifty thousand dollars is?"

Michael stared at his sneakers as if the answer were neatly tied in his laces. "No. I mean..." He ran his hands through his curly brown hair, the way he did when he was upset. "Oh crap. I don't know anymore. Lord, what a mess."

As I witnessed Michael's struggle, my own chest tightened. No matter what happened, I loved this man. Which meant that when Michael hurt, I hurt. I reached out and touched his hand. "Hey, it's okay. We're not going to fix any of this tonight. Let's go home and get some sleep. I'll come over tomorrow morning and we'll come up with a new plan." I made a final, lame attempt at humor. "If Gabriella keeps giving us trouble, I'll sic Rene on her. Unlike Bella, Rene actually bites."

Michael shook his head. "Sorry, Kate. You're out. I never should have involved you in this fiasco in the first place. I thought meeting you would guilt-trip Gabby into agreeing to the divorce, but it only seemed to scare her. I need to talk to her alone."

"Are you sure that's a good idea?"

"No, but I'm not sure any of this is a good idea anymore. I came here to get Gabby out of my life, but maybe that's not realistic. Maybe we'll have to stay married until she gets citizenship."

My heart dropped to my knees. My face fell by that same amount.

"You don't get it, Kate. You can't. You don't know Gabby's and my whole story. She's frightened, like she was before I agreed to marry her."

"Frightened? Of what?"

"I don't know, at least not for sure. But I intend to find out." He swallowed. "I don't expect you to understand. Shannon never did."

I placed my hand on his forearm. "Then you don't expect enough of me. I *do* understand." I parroted back my own revelation. "When someone you love hurts, you hurt. If Gabriella's in trouble, we'll help her. Together." As much as my heart ached, I meant it.

Michael nodded, but he didn't make eye contact. "I'll call you tomorrow." He shuffled toward Shannon's Mini Cooper without kissing me goodbye.

It shouldn't have surprised me. I'd rejected all forms of affection from Michael since the great birthday dinner debacle. Still, that missing kiss felt like a kick to the gut. Of course Michael would help Gabriella. He had a kind heart and an incredible capacity for forgiveness. Otherwise he'd have kicked me to the curb eons ago. Michael's kindness and loyalty were two of the many reasons I loved him.

The question was, did Michael still love me?

For the first time in our relationship, I felt alone. It was ironic, really. I'd spent the past three days obsessing about whether or not I should leave Michael. It never crossed my mind that he might leave me.

Until now.

Bella nudged my hand. I kneeled next to her and rubbed the soft spot behind her ears. "We'll always have each other, sweetie." The steady look in her eyes agreed. Bella would be by my side for the rest of her life.

I watched the Mini Cooper disappear into the distance, then loaded Bella into my Honda and returned to the rental house. After giving a quick and purposefully obtuse recap of the evening to Sam and Rene, I collapsed into bed, where I stroked Bella's fur and stared at the ceiling. I lay there for hours, long after Bella's smooth, whispering breaths turned into deep, long snores. I finally drifted to sleep around three in the morning, wondering how my life had gone so suddenly, horribly wrong.

———

When I woke up at eight, I felt physically exhausted but mentally invigorated. Sleep had brought with it resolution. I would not be a third wheel. I would not be a bystander to my own future, either. Not when I had the ability to do something about it. Michael's and my relationship might still be uncertain, but it would *not* include Gabriella. If money would unbraid our three lives, I'd get the money. Rene had offered to help. She could easily help. Fifty thousand dollars was a fortune to me, but to her and Sam...

Honestly, if our roles were reversed, I'd give her the money in a heartbeat.

The three of us had a long talk over breakfast, during which we came to an agreement: Rene would give me a fifty-thousand-dollar loan, legally secured by my house, and at market-rate interest. She balked at the formality, but I insisted.

Dad always said that mixing money and friendship was a surefire way to lose both. But Dad had never met Michael, and he underestimated me. I'd sell myself on the streets before I defaulted on that loan. We agreed that the first six months' payments would be made in free dog supplies and unlimited babysitting. If Michael and I couldn't make regular payments after that, I'd sell the house. The thought made my heart hurt, but if the yoga teachings were right, attachment—to a two-bedroom Ballard bungalow, for example—led to suffering. In some twisted way, maybe selling my childhood home would ultimately help me find peace.

The next impossible challenge would be getting Michael to agree.

I tried to call him, but the call went directly to voicemail, so I left a vague message saying that I had a solution to our problem and asking him to call me back.

Sam and Rene decided to take their two- and four-legged kids on a day trip to Tillamook. I stayed in Cannon Beach and waited for Michael to return my phone call. Forty-five minutes after they left, I checked my cell phone for the third time. No messages. Full battery. Five bars.

"This is ridiculous," I said to no one in particular. I glanced at my bored-looking dog. "Come on girl, let's go to the beach."

At the sound of the B-word, Bella leaped to her feet and charged the door, jumping in circles and whining. "Okay already, I get it," I said, laughing. "I'm coming."

Bella and I descended the property's steep staircase to the beach, serenaded by the constant, rumbling white noise of the ocean. At ten in the morning, Haystack Rock's bell-shaped outline was softened by gray morning mist. The beach was desolate, populated primarily by light green foam, beached tubers of seaweed, and broken sand dollars. Most of the town's tourists were still hitting their snooze buttons or standing in line at the Bloated Boar, a local eatery famous for waffles, pancakes, cinnamon rolls, and other carbohydrate-rich indulgences.

I waved at a teenager playing fetch with an off-leash pit bull, pointed at Bella, and yelled, "This one's not friendly!" He waved back and threw a tennis ball in the opposite direction.

"Come on, Bella. Let's see if we can find a stretch of sand all our own."

I turned left and walked away from the town, inhaling the salty breeze and allowing the ocean's lullaby to soothe my frayed nerves. As we continued walking, hotels and houses disappeared, replaced by tall sandstone bluffs and boulders made of black basalt. Driftwood logs littered the sand. Some were the size of telephone poles, others small enough for Bella to carry. All were powerless against the coast's powerful storms.

After about twenty minutes, Bella and I reached a sandstone bluff that extended into the water at high tide, effectively bisecting the beach. I rolled up my pants and took off my shoes. "Come on, girl. Let's see what's on the other side."

We waded through ankle-deep water…

To our version of paradise.

The stretch of sand before us was as gorgeous as it was desolate. Imposing cliffs made of sandstone and red clay bordered the left, traversable only by an impossibly steep wooden staircase and a crude path dotted with orange traffic cones. The staircase led to a wooden building, a small grassy area, and a mostly empty parking lot with a sign labeled *Arcadia Beach State Recreation Site*. To the right, there was nothing but flat sand and bright blue water.

I smiled. There wasn't a person (or, more importantly, a dog) in sight. I shaded my eyes and peered at the parking lot. It was empty, except for an older, dark blue sedan that was barely visible through the evergreens. Bella whined and danced at the end of her leash, begging me with her eyes. *Please? Can I?*

Michael wouldn't have approved, but then again, Michael hadn't returned my phone calls. Worst case scenario: if a group of bearded men and their wild pack of dogs were in the car, I could easily call Bella back before they made their way down the staircase. I picked up a stray piece of driftwood and unhooked Bella's leash.

"Okay, girl. Fetch!"

Each time that glorified stick flew through the air, the rest of the world evaporated. Bella pushed her athletic body to full capacity, conquering the surf and coating her tongue with wet sand. The warm sun melted knots of tension from my shoulders. My dog's unfettered joy melted achy worry from my heart.

A half hour of playful bonding later, we reached another sandstone bluff. Bella collapsed happily in the sand, panting. I sat on a basalt rock and called Michael again. My stress level climbed with each unanswered ring. Why wasn't he picking up?

I tried to drown out my worried thoughts by chanting *So Hum*— the ancient mantra of the breath. I barely made it through four repetitions before I picked up the phone to call Michael again.

Dad's voice chided me. *Desperate much?*

I shoved the evil device back into my pocket. If Michael were available, he would have answered one of the last five times I'd called.

Maybe a movement practice would distract me.

I didn't have a yoga mat, but that didn't matter. Yoga—at least the kind I practiced—could be done anywhere, without any equipment. I tied Bella to a shaded log and ambled to an area of firm, wet sand. Bella expressed her displeasure by barking and play bowing.

"In a minute, sweetie," I promised. "You got to exercise on the way down here. It's my turn now."

I faced the ocean and touched my palms together in the Anjali Mudra, often called Prayer Pose. The simple, symbolic gesture soothed me. My heart rate slowed; my breath deepened. A few breaths later, I began the sequences of poses known as Surya Namaskar, or the Sun Salutation.

I mentally coached myself, just as I would one of my students. *As you inhale, reach your arms up toward the sky. As you exhale, fold forward. Bring your ribs toward your thighs and your hands to the earth.* Achy tension released from my lower back. Cool, wet sand moistened my palms. *With your next inhale, step your right foot back. On exhale, place your left foot next to it. Press your hips toward the sky and your heels toward the sand in Downward Facing Dog.* The pose was a wonderful symbol of strength (in my upper body), flexibility (in the backs of my legs), and grounding (every place my body touched the earth). *On your next inhale—*

A huge wave crashed into me, drenching me in freezing, salty water. I tumbled to the ground in what I would forever think of as Ass-in-Sand Pose.

Bella's eyes chastised me. *I tried to warn you.*

I let loose my first true belly laugh in days. "So much for that idea, huh, girl?"

Time to utilize the next tool in my yoga toolbox: meditation. I sat cross-legged in the sand next to Bella and tried to cleanse my mind while she covered my face in sloppy German shepherd kisses.

No use.

Each time my mind stilled, it flashed on Gabriella. What hold did that gorgeous woman have over Michael? Michael claimed that he loved me, and I believed him. So why did I still feel so jealous? More importantly, why hadn't he returned my phone calls?

I felt trapped, torn between irreconcilable longings. I longed to shove Michael away. I longed to grab onto him and never let go. I longed to go back to Dad's favorite Barbra Streisand movie: *The Way We Were*.

I shuddered. That story didn't exactly end happily ever after.

Ten minutes of breath-focused distraction later, I checked my cell phone for the five hundredth time. Still five bars. Still fully charged. Still no messages.

I frowned toward Bella. "No wonder one of the eight limbs of yoga is abstinence."

Bella withheld comment.

I untied her leash and unclipped it from her collar. "Come on, sweetie. Let's head back."

We followed the shoreline back toward Cannon Beach. I swung Bella's leash in my right hand while she herded waves on my left. By the time we reached the rock wall near the stairway to the parking lot, the tide had gone out enough that we could walk around it without getting wet. Now that it was almost noon, small groups of matchstick-sized people wandered the beach. Some of them were walking toward us.

I reached for Bella's collar, but stopped. A few hundred feet ahead, a colony of seagulls—dozens of them—dotted the shore. Bella's eyes begged me.

Please? Just one more run?

Why not? One of us should be having fun. "Okay, girl. Go get 'em!"

Bella galloped after those birds like a cheetah after a gazelle. It was ridiculous, really. All of us—human, canine, and seabirds included—knew that Bella would never catch them. But that didn't diminish anyone's fun. When Bella was about fifteen feet away, the birds took off in unison, flew a hundred feet down the beach, and landed, still in formation. Bella skidded to a stop, let out a single loud bark, and tore after them again.

May as well give up, hunter dog.

I reached out my arms and yelled, "Bella, come!"

As trained, Bella turned a one-eighty and ran back to me at full steam.

Three hundred feet ... two hundred ... one hundred ... "Bella, slow down!" I yelled. I repeated the command three more times in a rapid-fire panic. "Slow down! Slow down! Slow down!"

Bella didn't hear, didn't understand, or—more likely—chose not to listen. She launched through the air, collided with my chest like a hundred-pound bowling ball, and knocked me flat on my sitting bones for the second time in thirty minutes. A quick German shepherd chin nibble later, she ran a quick circle around me and chose a new destination: a Jenga-like stack of driftwood piled up against the cliff.

I spit out a million tiny particles of sand. "Bella, come!" I commanded.

No response.

I stood, brushed the wet sand off my bottom, and trudged toward my dog. "Bella, knock it off and get over here! Leave it!"

Bella pretended to be deaf.

What on earth was she so interested in? Half-eaten hotdogs? Urine from a particularly studly Golden Retriever? A seagull corpse?

Bella stopped sniffing and commenced digging.

I groaned. It had to be a dead creature of some kind. Bella couldn't digest *real* food unless it was incubated in expensive prescription enzymes; I imagined scooping up undigested seagull parts and groaned louder.

"Bella, I said come!"

Not even an ear twitch. This level of disobedience was unusual, even for her.

I broke into a jog. When Bella wanted something this badly, it was a sure bet that I didn't want her to have it. I skidded to a stop next to my recalcitrant canine and clipped the leash to her collar. "That's enough girl. Leave it."

She ignored me.

I tightened the leash and made my voice especially stern. "I mean it."

Bella refused to move.

Whatever she'd found, it was infinitely more interesting than a five-foot three-inch yoga teacher.

Bella, channeling her inner Ricky, grabbed onto something and pulled, exposing a woman's tennis shoe.

"Seriously, Bella?" I grumped. "This much drama over a shoe?"

I looked closer and gagged.

The shoe was attached to a foot. A foot that was attached to a caramel-skinned ankle. A caramel-skinned ankle wearing a starfish ankle bracelet.

Oh God, no.

Bella had unearthed a body—a woman. She was buried, facedown, in an obviously man-made mountain of driftwood, seaweed, and sand.

I wish I could say I was horrified. I wish I could say I screamed like a scared little schoolgirl. I wish I could say I vomited like I did the night I found my friend George's body.

But I didn't. I simply stood there, thinking the same words over and over: *not again.*

I clawed through the rocks, unearthed the broken body's left wrist, and forced myself to feel for a pulse. Her fourth finger was bare except for a band of lighter skin where a wedding ring used to be. I suppressed the urge to run off to warn Michael, pulled out my cell phone, and dialed 911.

"Hi. My name's Kate Davidson. I found a woman's body. I think she was murdered."

SEVEN

I SPENT THE NEXT fifteen minutes in a weird sort of attached avoidance. Bella and I huddled close enough to the body to protect it from unsuspecting beach walkers, but far enough away that I couldn't examine it closely. The dead woman had to be Gabriella, but I chose to live firmly in the land of plausible denial. I'd checked her pulse without excavating the rest of her body. If the police asked me about it later, I could say that I was afraid to tamper with the crime scene. Which was true, but only part of the story.

I didn't *want* to know for sure that the body was Gabriella. Not identifying her might slow down the police, at least for an hour or two. An hour or two during which I could locate Michael and warn him. I wasn't positive that Gabriella had been murdered, but it sure looked that way. She certainly hadn't buried herself, and I suspected the tide hadn't either. Not in a single night. Someone had purposefully covered her.

Someone who wasn't Michael.

I knew that instinctively, the same way Bella knew when a cat had invaded her territory. Michael would never hurt—much less kill—

anyone, and especially not Gabriella. As I'd painfully realized last night, he cared about her too much.

Unfortunately, my girlfriend's intuition wouldn't sway the police. Wasn't the spouse—especially an estranged spouse being denied a divorce—the most logical suspect? Last night's altercation between Michael and Gabriella wouldn't help, either. Even the most seasoned police officers jumped to obvious—and sometimes dreadfully wrong—conclusions. Who could blame them? I'd made more than a few incorrect inferences myself.

Which left me with my current dilemma: how could I keep the police off of Michael's trail until I had time to talk to him? I would never lie to the police, not exactly. Doing so would go against everything Dad had ever taught me. But I didn't have to volunteer unsubstantiated guesses, did I? My identification of Gabriella was based on a common skin tone and a cheap piece of costume jewelry. For all I knew, those ankle bracelets were sold all over the coastline, worn by every woman in the area under the age of seventy.

I was deluding myself, of course, and Dad's disapproving glare scalded the back of my neck all the way from the afterlife. He'd been a cop, after all. Withholding evidence in a murder investigation ranked high on his list of cardinal sins. But I was exhausted, overwhelmed, and in shock. I couldn't possibly think clearly. Or at least that's what I'd have my attorney argue at my accessory-after-the-fact trial.

I buried my face in Bella's fur and groaned. How could I be involved in another murder investigation? Dharma, my recently non-estranged mother, would have asserted that my stumbling across Gabriella's body had been preordained. That the universe was once again helping me to fulfill my life's purpose. That my dharma—my life work—was to bring killers to justice. For all I knew she was right. Still, in that moment I felt like giving the universe a "universal" hand gesture. The kind you give to motorists who cut you off on the freeway. Why couldn't my dharma be something less traumatizing? Like dog paddling naked through an ocean of starving barracudas?

Bella whined and strained against her leash, clearly wanting to go back and dig up the rest of Gabri—oops, I mean the rest of *the unknown stranger's* body. I ignored her complaining, tried to call Michael, and checked voicemail. No messages. Mostly charged battery. Still five bars.

I rubbed my hands up and down my arms, shivering in spite of the early afternoon sun. Bella stopped whining and howled.

Finally. Sirens.

As the wails grew closer, I whispered a prayer: *Please, God. Please. Just this once, let me be wrong.*

An ambulance arrived first. It drove onto the beach and parked next to the *No Vehicles Allowed* sign, causing the formerly oblivious passersby to pause, crane their necks, and whisper. Two paramedics—one male, one female—emerged from the vehicle carrying red medical bags. I tied Bella to the ambulance's bumper, told her to stay, and led them to the body. An insane, delusional part of me hoped that they'd try to revive her, but they came to the same conclusion I had. It was too late. Much too late. They ordered me to wait for the police and stood grimly to the side. I untied Bella and moved her away from the scene, hoping distance would calm her.

What felt like two centuries but was likely two minutes later, a police car pulled next to the ambulance. A female patrol officer climbed out of it. She spoke with the male paramedic, who showed her the body, shook his head no, and pointed to me. She wrote something in a spiral notebook and strode resolutely toward me. Disembodied voices crackled from the microphone clipped on her shoulder, causing Bella to sit at attention, ears pricked forward with interest.

Officer Alex Lewis (who asked me to call her Officer Alex) stood an inch or so taller than my five-foot-three-inch frame, had an athletic, swimmer's build, and wore her hair in a jet black crew cut that made her blue-black uniform look navy. Her energy felt masculine and feminine at the same time. Yin and yang, strong and compassionate. Flexible and competent. I instantly trusted her.

Evidently, Bella did, too. She abandoned her stay with an enthusiastic woof and greeted Officer Alex with full-body wiggle. For the briefest of moments, the officer's grim expression lifted. She gave Bella a quick head scratch, then addressed me.

"I understand you found the body."

The next hour floated by in a foggy haze, punctuated by strobe-like flashes of the commotion around me. I vaguely noticed two more police vehicles and a coroner's van join Officer Alex's patrol car, but I didn't meet the people who emerged from inside them. Officer Alex was the only person who interviewed me.

She jotted notes in her notebook and peppered me with questions, none of which were too pointed. For the moment, at least, she believed my story: I was simply an innocent bystander. A tourist who had been in the wrong place at the wrong time. A tourist who needn't be traumatized any further.

I answered her questions honestly, more or less. I told her my name (Kate Davidson), how I'd found the body (Bella's digging), and why I was in Cannon Beach (visiting friends). All the while, I avoided the overwhelming fear pounding my head. Was Michael's radio silence related to Gabriella's death?

A full ten minutes after I thought my heart would explode, Officer Alex said I was free to go. She jotted down my contact information and told me that she might be in touch again later. In the meantime, she hoped that I'd enjoy my vacation in Cannon Beach.

She had to be kidding, right?

I grabbed Bella's leash and staggered back to the rental house, amazed at how normal the rest of the world appeared. How could it not have stopped spinning? A woman was dead. A daughter. A sister. For all I knew, a mother. Probably murdered. Somewhere out there, a family's life had been changed forever.

But to the people vacationing on that gorgeous beach, today was simply another twenty-four hours in paradise. Dogs ran after seagulls. Children built makeshift sandcastles. Parents sunbathed and drank bottled water. Their greatest dilemma was deciding which gourmet restaurant they'd choose for dinner.

How did life just "go on"?

Bella, too, seemed unaffected. Like all dogs, she lived in the moment. And any moment spent loping along a sunny beach was, by definition, perfect.

There was a yoga lesson in that somewhere.

But not for me.

Not today.

For me, this was a horrible, terrifying day. A day filled with fears of the past, traumas in the present, and unanswered questions about the future. Questions only Michael could answer. I needed to find him, but how?

Bella and I opened the door to a completely empty house. No infant cries filled the silence. No adolescent puppies skidded across the floor to torment Bella. No best friends waited to ask me unanswerable questions.

"Anybody here?" I called.

No response. Nothing but upscale furniture, glossy bamboo floors, and ultra high ceilings. Not even an errant dust bunny to keep me company. Gorgeous *Architectural Digest* beach house be damned. I missed my cluttered Ballard bungalow. I missed my life.

I sank onto the plush couch. Bella jumped up next to me, turned a quick circle, then flopped down and rested her head on my thigh.

I pulled out my cell phone to call Rene, but I couldn't bring myself to dial her number. She and Sam were enjoying a day of family picnics, scenic drives, and tours of the Tillamook Cheese Factory. If I called her, she'd come back in a heartbeat. But what could she do when she got here? The person I needed to speak with was Michael.

So I dialed his number instead.

Again.

The phone went to voicemail.

Again.

Where in the hell was that man?

My body felt tight; my skin, itchy. I stood and paced, muttering expletives under my breath. Bella sat up and whined. "It's okay, girl. You're not in trouble. Michael is. If he doesn't call me back soon, *his* body will be the next one buried on the beach."

I froze and sucked in a quick breath.

Oh no.

Michael couldn't be … He wasn't … he wasn't lying hurt somewhere, was he?

Time to up my game. If I couldn't reach Michael, I'd try his sister. Only one problem: I didn't know her number. I called information, but Shannon's personal number was unlisted, and I had no idea which real estate agency she worked at. I considered calling Michael's parents, but what would I tell them? "Your cheating son disappeared. By the way, did it never occur to you to tell me that he was married?"

No good. Instead, I tried every other way I could think of to track down Michael. I called Tiffany at Pete's Pets. Voicemail. I emailed. I texted. I messaged him on Facebook. I stalked him on Twitter. I was about to give up and call Rene for ideas when I remembered: *Shannon's check!* In all of the craziness last night, I'd forgotten to give it to

Rene. I pulled it out of my billfold. No phone number, but it listed an address in Manzanita. I had no idea if it was Shannon's home or her business, but at that point, I didn't care. It was a lead. I gave Michael's phone one more try, then grabbed my keys off the counter and strode to the door.

"Come on, Bella, we're going on a road trip."

———

When I pulled up to the check's address—which was obviously a home, not a business—Shannon's orange Mini Cooper was parked in the driveway. I saw no sign of her Chevy, ancient or otherwise.

I clipped on Bella's lead but hesitated at the garden path, torn by conflicting emotions. Fear over Michael's well-being; anger that I hadn't heard from him; dread at the news I was about to deliver.

I stalled by taking in my surroundings. Everything I saw screamed Shannon.

The tiny, bright yellow cottage was accented by royal blue shutters and a candy-apple-red door. A coco fiber mat at the entrance read *If You Forgot the Wine, Go Home* in bold black letters. The large, plant-filled yard added to the oasis of color. Dusky pink hydrangeas bloomed to my right. To my left, a vegetable garden overflowed with yellow crookneck squash, bright orange pumpkins, and dark leafy kale. A trellis of late blooming roses scented the air with a sweet, almost wistful fragrance. Stone pavers at the yard's entrance spelled out an invitation: *Welcome Friends*.

Bella announced our arrival by squatting and peeing on them.

"Seriously, Bella?"

She didn't reply. She was too busy dragging me to the front door.

Shannon answered before my third knock. "Kate, I'm so glad you're here." The thin line of her lips contradicted her words.

"I'm looking for Michael. Do you know where he is?"

"Asleep, the dumb-ass."

Dumb-ass? In the brief time I'd known Shannon, I'd never heard her say anything negative about the "baby brother" she so clearly adored. I ignored the expletive and looked at my watch. "Asleep? Why is he asleep after five in the evening? Is he sick?"

Shannon opened the door wider and gestured me inside. "I'll wake him up. He can tell you himself." I followed her into a cozy living room crowded with a comfy-looking couch, two overstuffed chairs, and a freestanding wood stove. Shannon crossed the room and opened the blinds, drenching the space in early evening sunlight. She resolutely marched up to me, grabbed Bella's leash, and issued an order to my canine best friend. "Come on, you're with me."

She pulled my bewildered-looking dog down the hallway, pounded on the door at the end, and then flung it open, yelling, "Time to get up!" No response other than a low groan. "Fine," Shannon said. "Don't say I didn't warn you." She dropped Bella's lead, clapped four times, and pointed into the room. "Bella, go get him!"

My hundred-pound cannon ball let out a single loud bark and tore inside, no doubt leaping for the bed. If the resulting thump, cry, and vociferous swearing were any indication, she landed solidly on Michael's stomach.

"Shannon, what the hell!" Michael yelled.

"Get up," she barked in return. "Now. You have company."

The corpse that staggered out of that bedroom with Bella barely resembled my boyfriend. The skin around his eyes was puffy and bruised-looking, unlike the rest of his face, which was a sickly shade of greenish yellow. His hair was flattened on one side of his head. Any claims to a five o'clock shadow had passed at least twenty-four hours ago. Sprinkles of sand adhered to the hems of his jeans.

He covered his eyes with his elbow. "Geez, Shannon. Close the drapes!"

Shannon crossed her arms and scowled. "Deal with it."

Michael stumbled past me to close them himself, and I got a good whiff. Bourbon and body odor, with a slight hint of vomit thrown in for good measure. The man was clearly hung over.

Hung over? Michael?

Michael wasn't a teetotaler, but he rarely drank more than a couple of beers. I considered asking him who he was and where he'd taken my boyfriend, but I figured he wasn't in the mood for humor.

I stated the obvious. "You've been drinking."

Michael sagged against the wall and stared at his sand-covered socks, refusing to make eye contact.

I should have told him about Gabriella then, but I was too stunned. This wasn't the man I'd been dating for over a year. Not even close. I stood there, staring, stuck at the intersection of dread and disappointment.

Shannon frowned at Michael, then at me, and then back at Michael again. Her eyes softened. She dimmed the lights, moved next to her brother, and placed her hand on his shoulder. "Go take a shower. And for goodness sake, brush your teeth. I'll get Kate some coffee." Michael didn't move. "Go on now," she urged him. "We'll be fine."

Michael trudged back down the hall, opened the second door on the left, and closed it. Bella curled up outside, waiting for him.

Shannon led me to the kitchen, poured coffee from a glass carafe into two royal blue mugs, and handed one to me. She gestured toward the kitchen table. "Have a seat. Do you want sugar or cream? Sorry, I don't have soy milk."

I shook my head no. "Black is great." I thunked heavily into the chair and stared at my coffee, feeling much too overwhelmed to drink. I wanted to tell her that I'd found Gabriella's body, but I needed to talk to Michael about it first. I made meaningless small talk instead. "How did your meeting go?"

Shannon looked confused. "Meeting?"

"The one you had this morning. You know, the planning meeting."

Her cheeks reddened. "Oh, that one. I slept through it." She lowered herself into the chair opposite me. "It was a long night."

I was about to ask why, but she changed the subject. "While we're waiting for Mr. Stinky to wash off his hangover, I have a huge favor to ask."

"A favor?"

"Remember Susan, the woman wearing the knee brace last night?" I nodded.

"She tore a ligament in her knee. She was supposed to teach the warm-up and cool-down classes for the fun run Saturday afternoon, but there's no way she can do it in that brace."

She paused as if waiting for me to say something. I remained silent.

"I found someone to do the warm-up class, but they're not available after the run. Can you teach a yoga class at four-thirty? I hear yoga's great for post-run stretching."

Ugh. Shannon wanted me to teach. Even the thought made me feel exhausted. Typically I'd have been delighted to help, but nothing about this trip had been typical. At this point, all I wanted to do was hightail it back to Seattle and pretend the past few days had never happened.

"I don't know, Shannon. It's not a good time..."

"I know, and I normally wouldn't ask, but I'm really in a jam. I made such a big deal about the run this year, and the schedule has already been printed and distributed all over town. I'll be mortified if I don't find a replacement."

How could I say no? I nodded grudgingly. "As long as we're still in town, yes, I'll do it."

Shannon's face split into a smile. "Awesome. You just saved my butt. We'll talk about the details later."

I smiled back, but I doubt it looked genuine.

The shower turned on in the bathroom, and I waited for Michael to belt out an off-key show tune, his inexorable bath-time ritual. No singing, tone deaf or otherwise. Just water cascading over bath tiles. I brought the coffee mug to my nose, inhaled the bitter scent of full-bodied caffeine, and took a tentative sip. "I'm concerned about Michael. I've never seen him like this."

Shannon frowned toward the bathroom. "Honestly? Neither have I."

"Why didn't you call me?"

She shrugged. "I didn't have your number."

Naturally.

"And I knew Michael wouldn't want you to see him this way." She wrapped her hands around the mug and stared at the fluid inside. "I feel guilty. This is at least partially my fault."

"Your fault?"

"Michael's completely freaked out about this divorce nonsense. He's convinced that he's going to lose you unless he finds a way to pay off Gabby. Frankly, I still think he should tell her to go to hell. Gabby has a lot more to lose than Michael in all of this. If the feds figure out she committed marriage fraud, they'll plop her on the fast train back to Mexico before she can say 'frijoles.'" She frowned. "Michael won't do it, though. He's convinced she's in trouble. After everything she's done, the numbskull still wants to help her."

I shook my head, confounded. "I have to admit, Shannon, I don't get Gabriella's hold over Michael. He claims he doesn't love her, yet ..." I didn't know how to finish the sentence.

Shannon rolled her eyes. "What can I say? Baby Brother has some sort of messiah complex when it comes to that woman. He thinks he's the only man in the world who can save her." She shoved the mug to the side. "I call bullshit. Like I told him last night, Gabby's a big girl now. She can take care of herself. I flat-out called him a fool."

I cringed. "How did that go over?"

"It wasn't pretty. He got pissed. Frankly, I wasn't all that happy with him, either. But I never expected him to grab the keys to the Chevy and drive off drunk."

"Michael drove drunk?" My uber-responsible boyfriend would never get behind the wheel intoxicated. Never.

Shannon hesitated. "Drunk may be overstating it. He had two beers after we got home."

Two beers after three glasses of wine at dinner. Enough alcohol to push him past tipsy for sure. "Where did he go?"

"Honestly, I don't know. When the cab dropped him off a few hours ago, he staggered into the guest room and passed out before I could ask him."

"He was gone all night? Why didn't you call the police?"

"And tell them what? That a fully grown man stayed out after midnight?" I didn't reply. "When he didn't answer his cell, I figured he'd either gone back to Seattle or driven to the beach house and made up with you. Baby Brother may not have shown it just now, but he needs you. Talking to you will make him feel better."

I flashed on Gabriella's flaccid wrist. "Somehow I doubt that."

Shannon grabbed my forearm. Hard. "Kate, no. You can't break up with him. Not today. It will kill him."

I shook my head and gently pulled away. "That's not what I mean. Not even close." I was about to break down and tell her that I'd found Gabriella's body when the bathroom door opened. Michael emerged, wearing clean jeans, a Pete's Pets T-shirt, and sand-covered tennis shoes. In spite of the wet ringlets surrounding his ears, he didn't look refreshed. His eyes were clouded. Dull. Deadened.

I shuddered.

"Feeling better?" Shannon asked.

Michael's reply was interrupted by three loud knocks. Shannon, Michael, and I jolted in unison.

Bella took action.

She charged across the room and planted her paws on the front door, barking and snarling in her best impersonation of a rabid wolverine.

"Are you expecting someone?" I asked.

Shannon's brows furrowed. "No." She strode across the room and peered through the blinds. "What's Alex Lewis doing here?"

My heart froze. Alex Lewis? As in *Officer* Alex Lewis?

Shannon glared over her shoulder at Michael. "What did you do last night?"

Crap, crap, crap, crap, crap.

I jogged next to Shannon and peered out the window. As I'd feared, the female officer I'd spoken with earlier stood on the doorstep. Officer Boyle huddled next to her, wearing a grim expression.

"Don't answer it," I said.

Michael gaped at me as if I'd gone nuts. "Don't be ridiculous, Kate." He grabbed Bella's collar, pulled her away from the door, and opened it. "Can I help you officers?"

Boyle opened his mouth, but his reply was drowned out by a series of deep, throaty snarls. Bella lunged against Michael's grasp, clearly putting the bearded officer on notice: *This house protected by German shepherd.* Boyle's upper lip twitched.

I rushed to the door and blocked Boyle from Bella. "Sorry, she doesn't like men with facial hair."

Officer Alex narrowed her eyes quizzically. "Ms. Davidson? I didn't expect to see you again so soon."

"Again?" Shannon's gaze shifted back and forth between us. "You two know each other?"

The female officer's expression was deadpan. "Yes. We met earlier today."

Gulp.

This wasn't good. It wasn't good at all.

My mind spun, trying to come up with a believable reason to get Michael alone.

Immediately.

As in now.

I needed to warn him about Gabriella's death so he wouldn't be sucker-punched. He already seemed so vulnerable. So likely to say something stupid. Something stupid that could land him in prison.

In that moment, I only knew one thing for certain: I had to protect Michael. "Give Bella to me," I said.

I grabbed my snarling monster-dog's collar with both hands, kicked the door open wider, and forced on a toothy, completely fake smile. "Come on in, guys. Shannon, pour the officers some coffee while Michael and I take Bella to the bedroom for a time out."

I didn't fool anyone, least of all the two police officers. "Hold on a minute," Officer Alex ordered. "Don't go anywhere. Either of you." She narrowed her eyes at Michael. "Sir, are you Michael Massey?"

Michael's face grew serious. "Yes. Is there a problem?"

Officer Alex stepped through the door.

Or at least she would have if Shannon hadn't body blocked her.

"Stop right there, Alex," Shannon ordered. "I'm the homeowner here, and I didn't say you could come inside. What is this about?"

Officer Alex held up her palm. "Shannon, don't do this. We know each other. We're friends."

Shannon crossed her arms and stepped her feet wide. "I mean it. You are *not* coming into my house without a warrant or a damned good explanation."

"Shannon!" Michael snapped. "What is wrong with you?" He glared at me, at Bella, and then back at Shannon again. "What's wrong with *both* of you? Shannon, get out of the way and let the officers inside."

Shannon looked even less happy than Bella, but she took a step back.

"I'm sorry, Officer," Michael continued. "My sister gets a little overprotective sometimes. Please come in."

Bella growled, clearly objecting.

Michael's objection was louder. "Kate, lock Bella in the bedroom."

"But—"

"Now." His tone left no room for argument.

Bella and I both whined our protest all the way down the hall. By the time I returned, the two officers were standing in the hallway.

Michael gestured toward the living room. "Maybe we should have a seat."

Officer Alex gave her male counterpart a let-me-handle-this look. "We're okay standing, thanks."

Shannon glared at her but said nothing.

I knew where this was going, and I didn't like it one bit. Michael would like it less. I nudged him with my foot, trying to get his attention.

No response.

"I have a feeling I know why you officers are here," Michael said.

"That makes one of us," Shannon grumbled.

I bit the inside of my cheek and tried surreptitiously poking Michael in the back.

Michael ignored us both. "I got a little out of control last night. I'm sorry if you received some complaints."

I poked him again. And again. And again.

His cheeks reddened. "I rarely drink like that. Of course, I'll pay for any damage I caused, and—"

I pinched Michael's arm.

He whipped around and snapped, "Kate, knock it off!"

Officer Alex narrowed her eyes at me suspiciously. "How do you two know each other?"

Michael and I replied simultaneously.

"She's my girlfriend," he said.

"I'm his friend," I said, louder.

Officer Boyle leaned toward Michael and snarled, "Girlfriend? I thought you were married to Gabriella Massey?"

"Michael, I really need to talk to you," I whispered.

He ignored me and kept talking. "Gabby and I are separated."

"That's interesting." Officer Boyle flipped through a notebook. "Ms. Massey still had you listed as her emergency contact. When we called the number in her wallet, we got a place called Pete's Pets." He pointed at the logo on Michael's T-shirt. "A woman named Tiffany Kobrick told us we could find you here."

Tiffany. I should have known. Why couldn't the police have gotten voicemail like I did? Over two hundred miles away, and Tiffany still managed to foil me.

Michael's face flashed from confused to alarmed. "Emergency? Gabby's wallet? Has something happened to Gabby?"

Shannon stepped between Michael and the officers. "I'm sick of these games. Why. Are. You. Here?"

Officer Alex's lips tightened, then she closed her eyes and let out a deep sigh. "I'm sorry, Mr. Massey, but I'm afraid we have bad news.

As you probably know, Ms. Davidson found a body near Arcadia Beach this morning."

Michael's face blanched. "Kate found a body?" He peered at me incredulously, as if I'd somehow betrayed him. Maybe I had.

Officer Alex continued. "We regret to inform you that we believe the body is that of your wife, Gabriella Massey."

"G-Gabby's dead?" Michael's knees buckled.

"Please, can we go into the living room?" I asked. "He needs to sit down before he passes out."

Shannon guided Michael to the couch, where he collapsed and buried his face in his hands. When I reached out to hug him, he jerked away as if my touch scalded.

"I was going to tell you about it, Michael, I swear, but I didn't get the chance." I looked at Officer Alex, feigning shock. "Are you saying that the woman I found this morning was Gabriella? How horrible." I shuddered. "I never saw the body's face."

Officer Alex's expression clearly indicated that she wasn't fooled, at least not entirely. "We don't know the victim's identity for sure, but we suspect it's Gabriella Massey."

Michael laced his fingers together as if hoping—praying—that this was all a huge mistake. "You don't know for sure?"

Officer Alex's voice softened. "I'm sorry, Mr. Massey, but she was beaten, we suspect with a piece of driftwood. Her face . . ." She swallowed. "I'm afraid the injuries to her head and face were severe. We're hoping you can make a positive identification."

"We only need confirmation," Boyle added gruffly. "The victim had ID in her wallet."

"Can't you use dental records or something?" Shannon asked. "If her face was destroyed, how do you expect Michael to identify her?"

"She has a rather distinctive tattoo on her left breast," Officer Alex replied.

"Of a Mexican woman. With a monkey." Michael's voice sounded hollow. Distant. His eyes stared vacantly at the floor.

Officer Alex spoke softly. "We need you to come with us to Seaside."

"Seaside?" I asked. "Why Seaside? That's almost twenty-five miles away."

Michael didn't look up. "It's the closest town with a hospital large enough for a morgue."

"Be reasonable," Shannon chided. "My brother is obviously in no condition to identify anything right now. Can't it wait until tomorrow?"

"Given the circumstances," Officer Alex replied, "we would like to confirm the victim's identity as soon as possible. To do that, we need Mr. Massey to look at the tattoo."

She didn't fool me. If all they wanted was for Michael to look at a tattoo, they could have shown him a photo. They were trying to get him alone, hoping he would say something self-incriminating.

And he very well might.

I flashed on the vomit green inquisition room I'd been detained in the day of Monica's murder on Orcas Island. I'd been innocent—I'd tried to save her, in fact—but in the stress of the moment, it didn't matter. I would have said anything to get out of that suffocating space. Loitering in a morgue with your dead wife's faceless body couldn't be any easier. Michael needed protection—from himself. He needed an attorney.

"Michael is obviously in shock," I said. "I'll bring him to Seaside tomorrow. He'll make the identification and answer all of your questions." That would give me the rest of the evening to strategize with our friend and attorney, Dale Evans.

Michael blinked as if coming out of a trance. "No. I want to go tonight. I need to know if it's Gabriella."

"Michael, no. Before you go anywhere, we should call Dale." I glanced at Officer Alex. "He has the right to an attorney, right?"

Shannon replied with a high pitched squeak. "An attorney? Wait a minute. Is Michael under arrest?"

"Who said anything about him being under arrest?" Boyle leaned forward, looking suddenly friendly. "Mr. Massey can consult with an attorney, of course, but I'm not sure why he'd want to. Unless he's hiding something..."

Michael's shoulders squared. "No. I'm not waiting. Gabriella is my responsibility. I owe her that much."

I'd seen that stubborn expression before. Michael would accept no argument. I picked up my purse. "Then I'm going with you. You're in no condition to drive."

"There's no need for that, Ms. Davidson," Officer Alex assured me. "We'll drive Mr. Massey to Seaside and bring him back home when we're done. That will give us a chance to talk on the way."

Which was exactly what I was afraid of.

I nudged Shannon, hoping she'd insert reason into Michael's insanity. She shook her head and mouthed the words, *Let him go.*

I placed my hand on Michael's shoulder. "Promise me you won't say anything until I call Dale."

Michael shrugged on his jacket and spoke to his sister. "Take care of Kate for me." He trudged behind the police officers. The door clicked hollowly shut behind them.

I plastered my palms against the window and stared through the glass, overcome by a deepening sense of dread. Why on earth would Shannon need to take care of me? The request felt ominous. The words of a man expecting to be gone for a very long time.

My breath fogged the window. The police car swallowed Michael and carried him away.

EIGHT

I SPUN TO FACE Shannon. "How could we allow Michael to drive off alone with the cops like that? We should have forced him to call a lawyer."

Shannon shook her head. "That would have been a colossal mistake, Kate. Alex Lewis is sharp."

"How do you know her?"

"She's one of my real estate clients."

I gaped at her, incredulous. "You're trusting your brother's freedom to someone you only know as a customer?"

"Believe me, realtors—good ones, anyway—spend a lot of time getting to know their home buyers. We learn secrets even their families don't know. She and that Boyle character don't always see eye-to-eye, but she's a good cop. I trust her."

"It sure didn't seem like it when you blockaded her from your house."

Shannon glared at me. "I didn't have all of the information then, now did I? I thought she and Boyle were here to harass Michael about public drunkenness. Lots of people get stupid during Sandcastle Week.

I figured if I made getting to him hard enough, they'd move on to the next drunken idiot. I'd never have made such a fuss if I'd known Gabby was dead. Murder is serious. If Michael didn't go with them to identify her body, it would have looked suspicious."

"It already looks suspicious! Don't you get that?" The frustration in my voice covered my fear. "Let me spell it out for you." I counted off the points on my fingers. "One: Michael was planning to sue Gabriella for divorce, and she was fighting him on it. Two: He didn't come home last night. Three: Boyle saw Michael and Gabriella fighting less than twenty-four hours before her death. Four: I found the body." I groaned and buried my face in my palms. "Why did Bella have to sniff out that damned body?"

"Five," Shannon added, sounding a little testy herself. "You lied to the police. You knew the dead woman was Gabby all along, didn't you?"

I didn't reply. Then again, I didn't have to. The shame on my face spoke volumes.

"Kate, why didn't you tell the police it was Gabby? Don't you see how guilty that makes Michael look?"

Tears burned the backs of my eyes. "I wanted to warn him before the police questioned him."

Shannon's sarcastic smirk matched the tone of her voice. "How's that working out so far?"

I had to admit, my decision to withhold Gabriella's identity seemed pretty stupid in hindsight. Nothing had gone the way I had planned. I hadn't been able to forewarn Michael, and my caginess provided one more reason for the cops to suspect him. To suspect both of us, actually. At the rate things were going, Michael wouldn't be the only one who needed a lawyer.

I pulled out my cell phone. "I'm calling Dale."

"Dale's your attorney?"

"Yes."

"Is he any good?"

I didn't reply. The answer was too complex for a ten-second explanation. Dale was more than a "good" lawyer. He was practically legendary. Or at least he had been, until he abandoned his high-profile Seattle law firm to "retire" in the country. He was also Michael's and my friend, and, as of recently, my mother's life partner. She lived with him on Orcas Island, where they ran a rescue for goats and donkeys. He'd represented me over a year ago when I was suspected of murder. There was no one I trusted more to get Michael out of this mess.

He answered on the third ring. After a quick hello, I jumped right to the problem. I skipped both the niceties and the details about Michael's relationship to Gabriella. That was a story for a less urgent time. Instead, I told him that I was calling from Oregon, that I'd found another body, that Michael was a logical suspect for her murder, and that he was currently riding in a police car on his way to identify the body.

Dale interrupted. I could almost feel his white whiskers tremble through the phone line. "Wait a minute. You think Michael's under suspicion for murder, and you let him ride along with the police?"

My mother, Dharma, spoke in the background. "Dale, is that Kate? What's going on?"

Dale shushed her, a dangerous move with a woman as hot-tempered as my mother. He was taking the situation seriously. Good.

"Tell Dharma I'll fill her in later," I said. "I tried to reason with Michael, but he wouldn't listen. He insisted on going to Seaside with the police and—"

Dale shushed me, too. "Kate, I'll call you back and get the details in a few minutes. We don't have time to waste." The line went dead.

Shannon's eyes begged for good news. I shrugged. "He said he'll call back."

We stared at each other in uneasy silence for what felt like a century. Ten real-time minutes later, my cell phone rang.

Dale's muffled voice spoke on the other end of the line. "I'm in my office. Your mother's pissed because I won't tell her what's going on, and I'm sure she's trying to listen through the door, so I'll need to keep my voice down." He sighed. "I suspect I'll be sleeping with the donkeys tonight. Everyone believes in attorney-client privilege until it applies to someone they love."

He wasn't wrong. I'd hated it when Dale had withheld information from me about Dharma's case. I guess turnabout really *was* fair play.

Dale continued. "Michael didn't answer his cell, but I got hold of an attorney buddy of mine in Seaside. He's going to intercept Michael and those police officers at the morgue. My friend doesn't generally practice criminal law, but he knows enough to order that man of yours to keep his mouth shut. Did the police Mirandize him?"

"No. At least not before they left."

"Then we may be in luck. They won't ask him too many questions until they read him his rights. As long as they don't do it before my friend intercepts them, Michael shouldn't get himself into too much trouble."

I hoped he was right.

"Now tell me, Kate. What in tarnation is going on? Why are you in Oregon, who was this murdered woman, and why do the police suspect Michael of killing her?"

I filled Dale in on everything, starting with Michael's marriage, continuing through his confrontation with Gabriella, and ending with the police officers' visit to Shannon's house. Dale was silent through the entire ten-minute monologue. When I finished the story, he asked a single question. "Michael's married? Are you kidding me?"

Make that two questions.

I surprised myself by jumping to Michael's defense. "It wasn't a real marriage. Gabriella was in the US on a guest worker visa. Michael married her so she could get a green card."

Dale grumbled under his breath. "The idiot. That's a felony."

So was murder. And a much more serious offense than marriage fraud. "Their marriage seems pretty irrelevant right now, Dale. What do we do?"

Dale replied after five interminable seconds of silence. "For now, we wait."

"Wait?" The word came out sounding more like an accusation than a question. I'd been waiting all day. Waiting had eaten a hole in my stomach. Waiting had pushed Michael into that police car. Waiting could easily bisect my carotid artery.

The tone in Dale's voice brooked no argument. "Until we get more information, waiting is the best we can do. My attorney friend said he'd call as soon as he knew anything. If we're lucky, Michael's situation won't be nearly as dire as you think."

Lucky?

If Dale needed luck, Michael was in more trouble than I thought. When Dale represented a client, he never relied on luck. He relied on experience, sharp wit, and a genius grasp of the law. Then again, we were in Oregon, not Washington. Dale might not even be licensed to practice law here.

My mouth went dry. "Dale, I'm scared."

His voice softened. "Kate, you have to trust me. I'll help Michael, I promise. Have him call me tonight." Softness amped up to sternness. "And don't you go quizzing him without me present, either. You're his girlfriend. Not his wife."

"I know that, Dale. You don't have to remind me. His wife is the one who's dead."

"I wasn't referring to your complicated relationship. Since you're not married to Michael, you can be compelled to testify against him in court. The less you know, the better."

The thought sobered me silent.

Dale continued. "I'll assess everything tonight. If I need to, I'll head on out to Oregon tomorrow."

"You're willing to consult with Michael's attorney?"

"Heck no. I'll *be* his attorney, if he'll let me.

Relief washed through me. "You'd do that? Come all the way to Cannon Beach and represent Michael?"

"Of course," Dale chided. "Did you think I wouldn't? You're family. Besides, I kinda like that boyfriend of yours." He paused, and I imagined him frowning. "I used to like him, anyway. I'm beginning to wonder about his character, or at the very least, his common sense. I mean seriously. Not telling you he was married?"

"He made a mistake, Dale, but he's still the same Michael." My voice softened. "And I still love him."

"I know you do, Kate-girl. We all do. Don't worry yourself. I'll be his attorney. Unless you think he can find someone better?"

The question, of course, was rhetorical. There was still one potential barrier, however. A barrier I was almost afraid to ask about. "Can you practice law in Oregon?"

Dale chortled. "You think I'd volunteer to be Michael's attorney if I couldn't? The bar association part's easy. Washington and Oregon have a reciprocity agreement. The bigger hurdle is the travel. I'll need to arrange coverage for the farm, and it's a ten-hour trip from Orcas to the Oregon coast. The earliest I can get there will be late tomorrow afternoon. Hopefully this is all a big false alarm, and it won't come to that."

"Dale, you're a gem. I can see why Dharma fell for you."

Dale affected his fake southern drawl. I imagined him blushing underneath his white, Santa-like whiskers. "Well, shucks, Missy Kate. Aren't you as sweet as a petunia?" His voice grew serious again. "Try not to worry until we know there's something to worry about. But make sure Michael calls me. Tonight."

I clicked off the phone and turned to Shannon, who'd been standing over my shoulder for the entire conversation.

"I couldn't tell from my end," she said. "Was that good news or bad?"

"Both." I absently drummed my fingers against the cell phone's case. "Dale says all we can do right now is wait."

Shannon frowned. "I'm not very good at waiting."

"Neither am I, which is why we're not going to do it." Dale had told me not to quiz Michael, but he didn't say not to do *anything*. I'd spent the past several days refusing to let anyone tell me about Michael and Gabriella. Time for that to change.

I lifted my cell phone again and pressed the autodial button for Rene.

———

Forty-five minutes later, Rene, Shannon, Bella, and I huddled around a glass-topped table in Shannon's living room. Rene had laid out a buffet of multicolored tortilla chips, four kinds of dip, and gooey peanut butter chocolate chip cookies. I sat on one end of the couch, notebook and pen at the ready. Rene sat on the other, smothering blue chips with hummus. The rich, garlicky smell would have made my stomach growl if I'd had any appetite. Bella curled between us, delightedly chewing on an extra-large ostrich tendon Rene had brought for her.

Michael wasn't back from Seaside yet, so our information-gathering session was happening without him. Since it was past the twins' bedtime, Sam had opted to stay at the rental house with the girls and the puppies.

Frankly, I was glad. As much as I loved spending time with Rene's family, tonight my monkey mind was swinging on hyperdrive. I could barely muster the attention to put together a complete sentence. I'd never have been able to focus in the midst of sleep-deprived infants and mischief-making labradoodles.

Shannon handed Rene an oversized glass of Chardonnay and perched on the edge of a guest chair. "Okay, Kate. Now that you've called this meeting together, what are we doing, besides binge eating and waiting for Michael?"

Rene dipped a yellow chip into a vat of deep red salsa. "Oh, honey, this is no binge; it's a light snack. And isn't it obvious? We're creating our sleuthing plan."

"Sleuthing plan?" Shannon asked.

Rene cocked her head and eyed Shannon curiously. A textured smear painting of salsa and corn crumbles decorated her chin. "You don't know, do you?" She leaned over the table, grabbed a cookie with one hand, and pointed at me with the thumb of the other. "Kate here is the yoga equivalent of Sherlock Holmes. I'm her sexy Watson. Kate tracks down killers all the time!"

"That's a gross exaggeration, Rene," I said.

"You've solved four murders in the past two years. That's one hundred percent of your cases. The Seattle Police Department doesn't come close to that solve rate."

Shannon leaned away from me, body stiff, mouth open. I couldn't tell if she was impressed, horrified, or a little of both.

"I've been peripherally involved in a couple of murder investigations, that's all," I assured her. "My mother says it's some sort of…" I hesitated, trying to figure out how to describe the yogic concept of dharma (life work) without going too deeply into yoga philosophy. "Some sort of gift, I suppose."

"A gift? Do you mean you're psychic?" Shannon asked.

"I wish. More like I'm dumb enough to stick my nose into other people's problems." I shrugged. "I've mainly been lucky in the past. I doubt I can do much to solve Gabriella's murder, but I'd like to at least wrap my arms around what happened. Otherwise I'll drive myself nuts pacing the hallway."

I deliberately downplayed my intentions. Gandhi would take up gunslinging before I'd let Michael get charged with a crime he didn't commit. But if Shannon was anything like her brother, she'd try to talk me out of getting involved. That was an argument best saved for later. With Michael.

Shannon's expression was dubious, but she played along. "Okay then, how do we start?"

"Good question," I replied. "Honestly, I'm not sure. Why don't you fill me in on the history between Gabriella and Michael?"

Shannon stiffened. "History? Like what?"

"Like how did they meet and why did Michael end up marrying her?"

Shannon took a long, slow sip from her wine glass, as if trying to decide whether or not to answer. When she spoke, she avoided eye contact. "What has Michael told you about their relationship?"

"Not much," I replied. "Actually, I wouldn't let him. I wasn't ready to hear his side of the story."

Shannon set the glass on the table and frowned. "I don't think I should talk with you about it behind Michael's back. It seems disloyal."

Rene interrupted. "Kate's trying to help him, remember?"

I nodded. "And I can't do that if I'm flailing around in the dark. Besides, if the police arrest Michael for murder, our relationship woes will be the least of his problems."

Shannon's brow furrowed. "Fine. But when Michael gets pissed at me—and he will—I'm blaming you." She picked up her wine glass and drained it. "I need more alcohol. Anyone else?"

"I'm good," I said.

"Me too," Rene replied. "I'm driving, so one is my limit."

Shannon returned a few seconds later, picked up a corn chip, and absently swirled it in green salsa. "It's a long story. Before Michael moved to Seattle and met you, he lived in Cannon Beach and worked at Puppies in Paradise."

"Michael told me about that place," I said. "It's the local pet supply store, right?"

Shannon nodded. "Yes, at least sort of. It sells more tourist trinkets than dog food."

"He told me that, too. That's why he moved to Seattle and opened Pete's Pets. He wanted to specialize in healthy pet supplies."

Shannon grunted. "What he really wanted was a fresh start. As long as he lived in Cannon Beach, he had to keep up the façade."

"Façade?" I asked.

"I'm getting to that. Like I said, it's a long story." She abandoned the corn chip without eating it and took another long drink from her wine glass. "Michael's pretty mellow since he started dating you, but he used to be quite the player. He and Von hit the bars every weekend."

I picked up the notebook and wrote down the name Von. "Von's the guy you pointed out at the spaghetti dinner, right?"

"Yes. Von Russo. He worked with Michael at Puppies in Paradise. They had this whole bromance thing going on. Anyway, one weekend Crystal, the owner of the hair salon upstairs, invited herself to join them. I think she was hoping that Michael would finally notice her."

"Sorry," I said. "Another question. Is that the same Crystal who was outside of the community center with Gabriella?"

96

"That's her. Her last name's Buchanan." I added her name to my list. Shannon continued. "Michael wasn't interested in Crystal, but he didn't want to hurt her feelings, either. So he asked me to go with them. I guess he thought I'd be some sort of romance buffer. Oddly enough, we all had a blast. We started going out every weekend. We called ourselves the Fearsome Foursome."

"So Michael ended up dating Crystal and you ended up with Von?"

Shannon grinned. "Hardly. Von had a bigger crush on Michael than Crystal did. We were more like that TV show *Friends*. A group of singles who hung out together."

I didn't point out that most of the characters in that series ended up sleeping together.

"Anyway," Shannon continued, "Cannon Beach rolls up the sidewalks pretty early, even on weekends, so we usually drove to Seaside and hit the tourist bars there. Gabriella waitressed at Sunbathers."

"Sunbathers?" I looked at her curiously.

"The bar at the Sea Baron hotel. Michael and Gabby took one look at each other and fell into lust at first sight."

My throat tightened. "Lust? Michael and Gabriella were together? As a couple? I thought the marriage was a sham." Bella must have noticed the change in my voice, because she stopped chewing and stared at me.

Shannon cringed. "You didn't know? Sure, the marriage was fake, but that didn't mean …" Her face turned bright red. "Oh, criminy. I really should have let Michael tell you this."

Rene reached over Bella's back and took my hand. Her eyes clearly telegraphed the words, *I'm so sorry*.

I swallowed. Hard. "It's okay. Please keep going."

"Michael and Gabby *did* date for a while, but not for very long. They were all hot and heavy for a month or two. Then the infatuation wore off, and they realized that sex was all they had in common. Their relationship quickly devolved from casual dating to friends with benefits. They were never in love. Not real love, anyway."

Michael wasn't exactly my first lover. I'd held no illusions that I was his first, either. But the image of Michael having "benefits" with Gabriella made me want to go down to the morgue and revive her, just so I could bludgeon her all over again. "I still don't understand how they ended up married."

Shannon sighed. "For the record, I was against it, and Michael knew it. I never liked Gabriella. She was a skilled manipulator, and she pulled Michael's strings like a puppet master. He showed up at my house one night begging for a favor. He said Gabriella's H-2B guest worker visa was about to expire and she was afraid to go back to Mexico."

"Afraid? Why?" I asked.

"She claimed she'd come to the US to escape an abusive boyfriend."

I wrote the words "domestic violence" and "boyfriend" in my notebook. If Gabriella was a domestic violence survivor, her abuser might be a suspect.

Shannon continued. "I doubt her sob story was true, but it worked. My idiot brother offered to marry her so she could stay in the States."

"He offered? The sham marriage was his idea?" The news surprised me.

"So Michael claimed. I didn't believe it for a second, though. Gabriella was a con artist. I'll bet she started scamming to get that green card on their first date. Making Michael think it was his idea was simply part of her plan."

Rene interrupted. "You said Michael begged for your help. Why?"

"To perpetuate the con. Michael and Gabby could fool the Cannon Beach locals easily enough; Gabby didn't know anyone there other than Crystal and Von. But they needed family to fool the feds. Baby Brother knew I'd never believe their marriage was real, and he didn't want our parents involved. He had no choice but to convince

98

me to play along with the charade. I argued with him about it—a lot—but ultimately, I agreed." She shrugged. "I can never say no to him."

Shannon drained her wine glass again, stared at the bottom, then set it on the end table. "The rest was simple. Gabriella and Michael had a small ceremony, got the paperwork in order, and moved into an apartment above the pet store. A few months later, Michael left Cannon Beach, and Gabby pretended to be the long-suffering wife, waiting for him to come home again. The truth was that they were biding time until Gabby got citizenship. As soon as that happened, they planned to get a quiet divorce."

Rene pushed her plate next to Shannon's glass and leaned forward. "Here's what I don't get in all of this. You say Michael and Gabriella lived together for a few months before he moved to Seattle."

"That's right."

"Wasn't that three years ago?"

Shannon frowned. "Almost. Does it matter?"

"My husband, Sam, has been doing some research. Gabriella would have gotten her conditional green card when they married, and assuming they followed the appropriate procedures, she got a permanent one two years later. Why didn't they divorce after that?"

"She claimed she wouldn't feel safe until she had citizenship, which realistically wouldn't happen until they'd been married for four or five years," Shannon explained. "Michael promised her that they'd stay married until then." She shrugged. "Like I said, she was his puppet master."

I tapped the pen on the edge of my notebook and scanned what I'd written thus far. My eyes stopped at the words "domestic violence." I flashed on the man skulking near the children's play area. "Gabriella was afraid of someone back in Mexico?"

"That's what she told Michael."

"He mentioned that she seemed scared of something last night, too."

Rene cocked her head curiously. "What are you thinking, Kate?"

"I saw this creepy guy hanging out near the children's play area last night. He had his hat pulled low over his face, so I couldn't see his features, but he had dark hair and dark skin. He could have been Mexican. He sure disappeared fast when the police showed up."

"You think it's her ex-boyfriend?" Rene asked. "Gabriella left Mexico over three years ago. Why would he show up now?"

I wrote the words "camo hat" followed by a long line of question marks. "I don't know. It doesn't make much sense when I say it out loud, but it's worth noting. Shannon, can you think of anything else she might have been afraid of?"

"How would I know? I avoided Gabriella back when she lived with Michael. We certainly didn't stay in contact after he left."

I would have continued quizzing her, but I was interrupted by the sound of tires crunching on gravel. Bella abandoned her spot on the couch and trotted to the front door. Shannon and I ran to peer through the window next to it. An exhausted-looking Michael climbed out of a white SUV and staggered to the door. When he walked through it, he absently reached down and rubbed Bella's ears. Shannon gave him a hug.

I touched his hand. "Who brought you home?"

"A lawyer. Some friend of Dale's."

I wasn't sure I wanted to know, but I asked the question anyway. "How did it go?"

"Not good. The body was Gabriella." His chin trembled. "Kate, the police … they think I did it."

I pulled out my cell phone. "I'm calling Dale."

"No need. I talked to him before we left Seaside. Dale's coming tomorrow."

NINE

I DESPERATELY WANTED TO quiz Michael about what had happened with the police, but he begged off, claiming that Dale had ordered him not to answer questions from anyone—including me—unless he or his attorney friend were present. It was probably for the best. Michael was so exhausted, he could barely remain standing. He'd never have withstood the barrage of questions Shannon, Rene, and I would have thrown at him. But that didn't mean that I liked it.

Dale planned to catch the early morning ferry off Orcas Island the next day and then drive from the ferry terminal directly to Shannon's house in Manzanita. Barring traffic issues, he'd arrive around four in the afternoon. Michael asked for some alone time until then, which meant he'd have almost sixteen hours to sleep and gather his thoughts. Sixteen hours during which I could have sleuthed out more information to help with his defense.

Could have, but wouldn't.

Dale had also told Michael that I shouldn't do any sleuthing until he arrived and assessed Michael's situation. He was afraid that I might inadvertently do or say something to compromise Michael's case. I hated to admit it, but he might very well have been right.

So I reluctantly gave Michael his coveted space and agreed to return to Shannon's at around three-thirty the next afternoon. The bright side to Michael's dilemma—if there was a bright side—was that I would get to spend some unanticipated time with Dale, Dharma, and Bandit (their precocious Jack Russell terrier). In the meantime, I vowed to write down everything I knew about Gabriella's murder, and then get some sleep myself.

It seemed like a reasonable enough plan.

Documenting what I knew about Gabriella's life and subsequent death took all of five minutes, which made sense, since I knew essentially nothing. By the time I'd finished adding to and reviewing my notes, I had a grand total of one suspect: the suspicious-looking, camo-cap-wearing stranger I'd seen skulking outside of the community center. I sighed and tossed the notebook on the nightstand. Suspicious or not, the stranger was a weak suspect at best. Whatever he'd been up to, it likely had nothing to do with Gabriella.

So much for my supersleuth superpowers.

Likewise, sleep proved elusive. A trickster, tiptoeing close to my grasp, then scampering out of reach. I stared at the ceiling until two, then crawled out of bed and tried a short yoga practice designed to promote relaxation. At three, I got up and helped Sam soothe his fussing children. At four, I practiced Kate's Sleeping Pill, my favorite breath practice for insomnia. At five, I attempted to quiet my mind through meditation. Nothing worked. My mind raced on anxiety's squeaky hamster wheel. Louder, even, than the ear-piercing screams of unhappy infants.

I got up for good at six and helped Sam for another hour, then called and woke Tiffany to ask how the studio was doing. When I hung up the phone, I felt worse than I had before. The studio was fine—thriving, even. Tiffany was not. Michael had called to warn her that he might be gone longer than anticipated. She was worried about him, feeling guilty about telling the police where to find him, frantic about what to do with Pete's Pets if he got arrested, and bursting with reasonable questions I wasn't allowed to answer.

By the time Rene tottered down the staircase at nine, I'd progressed well beyond stir-crazy to practically crawling out of my skin. I paced back and forth across the living room, which provided the perfect hunting game for Ricky and Lucy. They stalked me like kittens wearing curly-haired dog costumes. They dive-bombed my feet. They tugged on my shoelaces. They growled, punctured my ankles with needle-sharp canines, and pinned my shoes to the floor.

"Ouch! Knock it off, Lucy!" Cranky from lack of sleep, I snarked at Sam, who was in the kitchen making Rene's breakfast smoothie. "What's up with the shark attack, Sam? I thought you were training these little monsters to stop shoe diving."

Sam sounded pretty cranky himself. "I'm trying, but you're not helping. Stomping back and forth like a human dog toy just encourages them. Stand still until they lose interest."

Yeah, like that was going to happen.

I ignored his advice and started pacing again, resigned to wearing fur-covered ankle weights. Bella snoozed next to the fireplace in post-breakfast bliss, grateful that she wasn't the object of the fur balls' torture.

"Sam, stop arguing with Kate and come grab Amelia," Rene said. "She's getting squirmy."

Sam turned off the blender, poured a chunky, disgusting-looking beige concoction into a glass, and took it to Rene. He plucked the brunette infant off Rene's breast with one hand and handed her the glass with the other.

She held it up to the light and suspiciously tipped it left to right. "What is this?"

"A peanut butter apple oatmeal lactation smoothie. Stop eyeballing it and drink it."

"Well, aren't you a grumpy crab bucket?" Rene lifted the glass to her lips, took a tentative sip, and handed it back to him. "Not enough peanut butter." She narrowed her eyes and peered at her husband. "You look as awful as Kate does. What did you two do last night, go out partying without me?"

"Hardly. The twins fussed all night," he replied.

"Is it too early for them to be teething?" I asked.

Rene shrugged. "They're only three months old, and teething usually starts at six months. It's unusual, but not impossible."

"Well, something was up with them last night," Sam grumped. "I barely got two hours of sleep. Honestly, Rene, I don't know how you slept through it."

"It must be the ocean air. I haven't slept this well in months!" Rene arched her back into a deep stretch. "I feel great." She paused. "But honey, if the girls fuss again tonight, wake me. Parenting is a team sport, remember?"

Mollified, Sam carried the rejected smoothie back to the kitchen, poured it into the blender, and added three heaping tablespoons of peanut butter. Once the blender was whirring again, he placed Amelia in the crib and extracted Alice from Rene's other breast.

I shook my head, bewildered. "I don't know how you do that."

"Do what?" Rene asked.

"Breastfeed both twins at the same time."

"It's easy, once you figure out the balancing act. It's all in the pillows." Rene stood, reached up her arms, and stretched side to side. Sam returned to the kitchen and spooned the now browner, thicker brew into the glass. Rene added a huge dollop of honey, stirred, and took a deep drink. She sighed "Perfect."

Momentary distraction over, I recommenced pacing. The puppies abandoned my shoelaces and attacked Bella. Lucy, the gold one, pulled at her ear; Ricky pounced on her head. Bella leaped to her feet in a flurry of teeth, fur, and vicious-sounding vocalizations. Her teeth snapped a half inch from Ricky's nose. She pinned Lucy with her paws. The puppies screamed as if being slaughtered. With any other dogs, I would have scrambled into the fray. Then again, I wouldn't have let any other dogs get within five feet of Bella.

In this case, no intervention was necessary. Bella was *teaching* the pups, not traumatizing them. She loved Ricky and Lucy as if they were her own puppies, which in a way, they were. She'd raised them from when they were six weeks old. Five seconds after the scolding began, the puppies scampered off to the bedroom, completely unscathed. Bella dropped back to the floor, rested her head on her paws, and went back to sleep.

"You tell 'em, Bella," Rene said. She grabbed my arm and pulled me to the couch. "Sit down already. You're wearing a canyon in the floor with all of that pacing." She yelled to Sam, "Honey, why don't you make Kate a smoothie? Be sure to blend in a Valium or two."

Sam peaked from the kitchen. "You want something, Kate?"

"No thanks. I can't eat." He nodded and disappeared again.

I obeyed Rene's command and flopped on the couch. "This waiting around for Dale is killing me. I can't just sit here. I should be doing something to help Michael."

"Then why aren't you?" Rene asked. "It's not like you to be so obedient."

"I'm not being obedient, or at least not *just* being obedient. I'm being smart. I already screwed up once. Until Dale arrives and gives me some guidance, I can't risk making things worse."

"Well, all of this pacing is driving you to Bonkersville, and you're taking Sam and me with you." Rene set her glass on the end table with a decided thunk. "You know what they say..."

I internally cringed, but I asked anyway. "What's that?"

She flashed me a lopsided grin. "When the going gets tough, the tough go shopping. We're heading to town."

———

Which is how, forty-five minutes later, Bella, Rene, the twins, and I found ourselves hoofing it down S. Hemlock Street, Cannon Beach's main drag. Sam stayed at the beach house to take a much-needed nap with the puppies. Rene carried the twins in their tandem baby carrier with Amelia nestled against her chest and Alice against her back.

Two days before the Sandcastle Festival, the town was already teeming with tourists, many of whom had traveled a great distance to see the renowned competition. I recognized a few locals as well: the woman who'd been selling raffle tickets at the spaghetti dinner; the banjo player from the bluegrass band; one of the teenagers—the girl—who'd been making out in the parking lot.

If I'd been visiting Cannon Beach for another reason—*any* other reason—than to distract my mind from murder, I would have been enchanted. Playful orange nasturtiums, dark purple petunias, and deep red geraniums burst from containers. The colors were so vibrant, I could almost delude myself that it was late spring, not early fall. Bustling storefronts offered anything I could want in a vacation destination: organic bakeries, art galleries, designer clothing stores, wine shops. There was even a private label distillery that advertised hourly vodka tastings.

None of it mattered. All I wanted was to leave so I could start clearing Michael.

Bella immersed herself in new scents while Rene tried to distract me with mindless prattle. "You know, this business with Gabriella isn't all bad."

"Which part? The part where she was married to my boyfriend or the part where she's dead?"

"The murder, of course," Rene replied, sounding unaccountably glib. "Now that Michael's a widower, he's free to marry you!"

I groaned.

Rene flinched, uncharacteristically chagrined. "That was a dumb thing to say, wasn't it?"

I didn't reply.

In her own, admittedly perverse way, Rene had been trying to make me feel better. But her words weighted my shoulders like a wet wool raincoat. Michael's newfound freedom gave him more motive.

We turned right at a stone fountain and entered a courtyard. Zoey, the mother of the rampaging toddler, slumped at an outdoor table, reading a romance novel and sipping stimulants from a white paper cup. Jimmy ran in circles around her, a bright red balloon attached to his wrist. She slowly wiggled her fingers at me and smiled.

I would have waved back, but Rene abruptly stopped walking, causing me to collide with her back. "Ouch!" I yelled.

Alice screwed up her face and burst into tears.

"Sorry," I cooed to the gorgeous, unhappy infant. "Your mom needs brake lights. Rene, be careful with the sudden stops. You're going to give the twins whiplash and me a concussion."

Rene ignored me and pointed at a sign. *Puppies in Paradise.* "Isn't this the place Shannon mentioned last night? The one Michael used to work at?"

"Yes…"

Rene grabbed Bella's leash and reached for the door handle. "We're going in."

I gripped her arm. "No way, Rene. I told you: Dale said not to snoop around until he gets here, and I'm listening to him. I've already done enough damage."

Rene rolled her eyes. "Who said anything about snooping? It's a pet food store. Bella needs a cookie."

Before I could stop her, she pulled open the single glass door. Bella (whose favorite word was cookie) charged through it, dragging Rene and the babies inside. The gentle *woof woof* of an electronic motion sensor announced their arrival.

Dogs. A pet store. Oh no!

Visions of saliva-covered fur, shattered glass, and visits with stern animal control officers crashed through my mind. Bella had never harmed another dog, but that wouldn't stop her from causing a ruckus. "Rene, wait! There might be dogs inside!" I pushed through the door behind them.

I needn't have worried. The small retail space was empty, except for a man holding a phone to his ear with one hand and typing at a computer with the other. I recognized his dark beard and sultry, chocolate eyes.

Von.

He smiled up from his phone conversation, held up an index finger, and mouthed the words *one minute*.

"That's Michael's friend Von," I whispered.

"Wow! He's gorgeous," Rene replied, a little louder than I would have preferred.

"Don't get any ideas, Rene," I grumbled. "Remember what Shannon said last night. He's gay. Your feminine wiles won't work on him."

Rene sighed. "The cute ones always are." She shrugged. "You'll have to interrogate him then."

Part of me—the intelligent part—wanted to grab my dog and tear back out the door, but the sleuth inside of me couldn't. I leaned toward

Rene and whispered, "No one's interrogating him. We'll just look around the store. Behave yourself and find Bella that cookie you promised her."

Rene gave me a lopsided grin. The kind that grade school boys flash when they're about to do something naughty. "Behave myself? Don't I always?"

"I mean it," I growled.

She handed me Bella's leash and wandered to a display of pet toys. I took in the rest of the small space. It was even more of a tourist trap than I'd imagined. A tourist trap masquerading as pet food store.

I'd obviously been spoiled by Pete's Pets. When I'd first fostered Bella, I'd been shocked at the sheer number of items owners could purchase for their companion animals. A dozen different cat litters, toys by the thousands, and racks upon racks of pet foods ranging from kibbled to canned to dehydrated to sausage-like ready-to-cut rolls. I'd been as frozen as the raw foods stocked in the store's freezers. Without Michael's guidance, Bella would have starved long before I figured out which food to purchase.

No such dilemma here.

Puppies in Paradise was overwhelming, but in a completely different way. The store's tiny selection of pet food was tucked away in a small, dark side room, like an unseemly stepchild they hoped to hide from the neighbors. What the store lacked in basics, however, it made up for in the superfluous. One corner held an upscale assortment of stuffed toys, colorful tennis balls, and a selection of individually priced dog cookies. The sign on the shelf declared *Fresh Baked Daily on Cannon Beach!*

Bella took one whiff of the bone-shaped morsels and dragged me toward them, clearly on a mission to search and devour. I picked one up, gasped at the five-dollar price tag, and quickly put it back. "Maybe next time." Bella chided me with mournful, deep brown eyes, but allowed me to drag her to the next display: a selection of waterproof jackets, knit sweaters, and all-weather coats that no self-respecting German shepherd would ever be caught dead in.

The most valuable shelf space was dedicated to Rover's owner. Magnets proclaiming everything from *You Had Me at Woof!* to *Back Seat Barker* decorated a revolving display. Underneath them, pet-themed doormats implored guests to *Wipe Your Paws* and *Ring Doorbell and Run*. I grinned. That one might have to be mine.

I'd almost convinced myself to buy it when Von hung up the phone and moved in my direction. I wrapped Bella's leash around my wrist and gave her the "down" command. Miraculously, she complied.

A huge, hairy smile lifted the corners of his mouth. "What a gorgeous dog! Can I give her a treat?"

"She doesn't like men with beards," I replied. "You probably shouldn't get within striking distance."

"Really?" he replied. "Could have fooled me."

Bella whined, thumped her tail against the floor, and crawl-walked toward him. I couldn't help but laugh. "Those must be some pretty amazing treats. Okay, Bella, up!"

Bella leaped to her feet and nudged her new friend's hands.

"Just give her a little one. She has a digestive disease. She'll get sick if she eats too much food without added enzymes."

Von cocked his head toward Bella. "This dog has EPI?"

I nodded, surprised. "Not many people know about it."

"A pit bull with EPI comes in here sometimes. He's a lot skinnier than your dog, though. She looks fantastic!" He pocketed the treat in his hand. "Hang on, I've got something special." He went back to the desk, opened a drawer, and pulled out a sandwich bag filled with dark green hearts. "These are from my private stash. Bubble's owner says EPI dogs shouldn't have grain. We don't sell any grain-free treats here, so I buy these in Seaside." He put an index finger up to his lips. "Shh … don't tell my boss. She'd pop an aneurism if she knew I was supporting the competition. But I think Bubbles deserves a goodie or two when he visits, don't you?"

I grinned. I could see why Michael had been friends with this man.

Von kneeled next to Bella and held out his fist. His shirtsleeve lifted, exposing a large bandage. He must have noticed my stare, because he said, "My newest war wound, courtesy of a twelve-week-old puppy that came in this morning."

"Yikes."

He shrugged. "Puppy teeth. Occupational hazard." He turned back to Bella and opened his fist. Bella snarfed up the green goodie with one quick swipe of her long, black-spotted tongue, then nudged the plastic bag, clearly asking for seconds.

Von ruffled her ears and smiled up at me. "One more?"

"Sure, why not?"

Bella inhaled the second treat, then expressed her gratitude by nibbling Von's beard. He gave her a final, friendly pat and then stood and addressed me. "Can I help you find anything?"

I grabbed the doormat. "Bella's not great with other dogs, so I shouldn't press my luck. I'll buy this and get going."

Rene and the babies appeared behind me at the checkout counter. She tossed one of the five-dollar dog biscuits on top of the mat. "Bella says to get this, too." I would have argued with her, but I was distracted by the package she held in her hand: a four-pack of tiny, light pink doggie tennis shoes.

"These are adorable," Rene said to Von, "but you only have one set in extra-extra small. I need two, preferably one pink and one blue." She eyed him expectantly. "You know, because I have two dogs."

"Sorry, all of our stock is out."

Rene flashed Von an innocent smile filled with perfectly straight, ultra-white teeth. The smile of a reality TV host, and almost as genuine. "Can you please check for me, just in case?"

He shrugged and disappeared through a door marked *Employees Only*.

I narrowed my eyes at Rene and whispered, "What are you up to? Even if you managed to survive putting sneakers on Ricky and Lucy with your hands still attached, those are two sizes too small!"

"I needed to get rid of Mr. Tall, Dark, and Gorgeous for a minute. Are you seriously going to leave the shop without asking him any questions?"

"I told you. No sleuthing until I talk to Dale."

"You didn't have any qualms about digging around in Michael's past last night."

"Talking with Michael's sister is one thing. Chatting up a total stranger is completely different."

Rene would have hounded me further, but she didn't get the chance. Von emerged from the back room, shaking his head. "Sorry, like I said, all of our stock is out. If you'll still be in town next week, I might be able to special order a second pair."

"Bummer. We're leaving after the Sandcastle Festival." Rene affected disappointment, but her scheming, beady little eyes sparkled. I had to get her out of this store. Pronto.

I slid the doormat and cookie across the desk. "We'll take these and get out of your hair."

Rene pushed them aside. "Kate and I were going to vacation here longer, but not now. Not with a killer on the loose." She leaned forward and lowered her voice to a stage whisper. "A woman was murdered on the beach yesterday."

The energy between Von and us shifted. His face darkened. His jaw hardened. For a moment, I thought he was going ask us to leave.

But he didn't. The storm cloud vanished almost as quickly as it had appeared. So quickly, I might have imagined it.

"Believe me, I know," he said. "The murder is all anyone's been talking about. It didn't happen yesterday. It was the night before."

Dale's grumpy voice screamed through my psyche, *Retreat!* But now that Rene had started this conversation, I couldn't figure out how to stop it. To be completely honest, I didn't want to. How much trouble could I cause if I limited myself to listening?

"She was killed Tuesday night? How do you know that?" Rene asked.

"The police told me. They've been interviewing everyone who knew her."

"You knew her?" The words popped out before I could stop them. I knew Von was acquainted with Gabriella, of course. He'd been Michael's friend. But I couldn't help but jump at such an obvious opportunity to extract more information.

"She was married to a friend of mine."

The shock in Rene's eyes seemed so genuine, she almost convinced me. "Oh no. I'm so sorry. How terrible. For both you and your friend." She lowered her voice again. "Do you think it was a stalker? I heard she was a famous model. They can attract all kinds of crazies."

Confusion spread across Von's face. "Gabby? A model? Where did you hear that? As far as I knew, she was a waitress." He frowned to the side. "She was attractive enough to model, I suppose. I didn't know her all that well."

I spoke again. "I thought she was a friend of yours."

Von shook his head adamantly. "I didn't say that. I said she was *married* to a friend of mine."

An interesting distinction. Perhaps Von hadn't approved of Gabriella any more than Shannon had. I kept pressing. "You didn't like her?"

113

Von hesitated again. He picked up the dog cookie and scanned its code into the register. "I didn't get a *chance* to like her. Michael had only been dating her for a couple of months when they got married." His expression grew bitter. "I thought he was smarter than that."

Rene gave him a wry smile. "I hope you didn't volunteer that opinion to your friend."

Von's cheeks reddened. "Actually, I did."

"Ooh … not bright." Rene wagged her finger. "Never tell a friend that you don't approve of his marriage."

"No kidding. I apologized later, but it wasn't enough. Michael basically stopped speaking to me."

Rene seemed to be connecting with Von, so I faded into the background and let her continue to lead the conversation.

"One ill-conceived comment ended your friendship?" she asked.

"Yes, which surprised me. It wasn't at all like Michael to hold a grudge. He wouldn't admit it, but I always suspected that Gabby encouraged him to stay away from me. From all of his friends, for that matter."

Rene nudged me with her foot, clearly asking if I wanted her to continue. I gave her a tiny nod.

"So you hadn't seen your friend and his wife for a while?" She asked.

"Michael, no. At least not until recently. I still saw Gabby pretty regularly. She lived in the upstairs apartment here."

"Just her? Not her husband?"

Von shrugged. "He left town a few months after they got married. Gabby kept their apartment."

Rene lifted her eyebrows. "Sounds like trouble in paradise."

"I always assumed so. They must have been separated, but Gabby would never admit it."

"Did you see her out with other men?" Rene asked.

Von hesitated. "No."

I flashed on the camo-hatted stranger. "How about someone hanging around her, then, someone suspicious?"

Von seemed surprised—and not all that pleased—to have me re-enter the conversation. "No." He pierced me with not-unintelligent eyes. "Why do you ask?"

I was about to hem and haw my way to an explanation when Rene widened her eyes in an expression of coquettish innocence. "Seriously? Two women, traveling alone..." She shivered. "What if the murderer is some crazed, sex-killer psychopath!"

"You two are traveling alone?" Von glanced at Amelia. "I mean, except for the babies."

Rene pinched my leg, clearly warning me not to contradict her. "Well, not alone, exactly. We're *together.*" Her inflection implied that we were much more than traveling companions.

Von cradled his forehead in his palms. "Of course. I should have known. You two are a couple! For a gay man, I have terrible gaydar."

"That's why we're so concerned about stalkers," Rene continued. "We have no man to protect us."

Von pointed at Bella. "I doubt you have anything to worry about as long as she's with you. Besides, I don't think anyone knows why Gabby was killed yet, but I doubt she had a stalker. At least not one she was aware of. Crystal would have told me."

"Crystal?" Rene asked.

"Another friend of mine." He gestured with his chin to the ceiling. "She owns the hair salon upstairs, on the floor below Gabby's apartment. I don't hang out with her that much anymore, but I see her at Jitterbug Java pretty regularly. She would have told me if anything weird was going on with Gabby."

"She and your friend's wife were close?"

Von smirked. "That's one way of putting it. After Michael left, Crystal glommed onto Gabby like a baby possum hanging onto its mother. My boyfriend thinks they might be—" He shuddered. "He thinks they *might have been* closeted lovers. Andreas says Michael probably split because he found out that Gabby was gay."

"That would suck, for your friend at least," Rene said.

Von shrugged. "Making Michael her beard would have been cruel, but I can't really judge her about that. I didn't come out until I was twenty-five."

The front door opened, admitting a burly man and a white tea-cup poodle, both wearing spiked leather collars and matching jackets. Bella lifted her lip and flashed a mouth sparkling with sharp, jacket-shredding teeth. The man scooped the tiny fluff ball up to his chest and scurried to the dog shoe aisle.

I handed Von some money and tucked the doormat under my elbow. "That's our cue. Thanks for talking with us. I'm sorry for your loss."

I was halfway to the door when I heard a low grumble. "That manipulative, man-stealing poser was no loss."

I turned to look back, but Von was already heading toward the poodle owner wearing a huge, hairy smile. "How's Bruiser today?"

The door closed behind us. "Did you hear that, Rene?"

"Hear what?"

I frowned at the door. "Nothing. I thought Von mumbled something as we were leaving." I gestured to the outdoor seating area. "Come on. Let's have a seat."

We grabbed a wrought-iron table nestled between Puppies in Paradise and the Jitterbug Java coffee shop next door. A red arrow labeled *CB Cuts* pointed up a narrow stairway between the two businesses. Crystal's hair salon, I assumed. Jimmy's mother was still immersed in her paperback two tables away.

Rene turned her back to me. "Take Alice so I can sit down, would you?" I fed Bella her five-dollar cookie, then pulled the adorable blonde sweetheart out of the backpack and snuggled her against my chest.

My sitting bones had barely touched the chair when Jimmy spied Bella. "Puppy!" he yelled. Bella leaped to the end of her leash, hoping to drown his cheeks in warm, sloppy kisses. This time, Zoey prevailed. She grabbed his plump little wrist and pulled him onto her lap. "Not now, Jimmy. You have to stay with Mommy." She gave me a wan smile, ignored the toddler's tearful complaints, and returned to her book.

Rene flopped into the chair next to me and flashed a happy smirk. "I was pretty good with Von in there, don't you think?"

"You were, indeed. But was the lovers-in-paradise charade really necessary? I mean, seriously." I put my voice solidly in singsong. "'Us poor helpless females have no man to protect us'? What is this, the 1950s?"

"It kept him talking, didn't it? If I'd left it up to your bumbling interrogation, Von would have clammed up as soon as you asked him why he hated Gabriella." That wasn't my actual question, but I let it slide. "Thanks to me," Rene continued, "he told us plenty." She ticked off the points on her fingers. "One: Gabriella and Crystal stayed in contact after Michael left town. They may have been lovers. Two: Crystal still works upstairs in this building. The very same building, might I remind you, that Gabriella called home." Her smirk deepened. Sharp canine teeth sparkled in the sunlight. "He even gave me an idea for a cover story you can use to talk to Crystal."

I glared at her through narrowed eyes. "What cover story?"

Rene ignored me and kept talking. "Three: If Gabriella was afraid that her ex-boyfriend was stalking her, she didn't tell anyone about it."

"That one's a stretch," I countered. "Von didn't hear about it, but that doesn't mean Gabriella didn't tell anyone. I do have a fourth, though. Von wasn't exactly a fan of Gabriella."

"He blamed her for losing Michael's friendship."

"That was certainly part of it. But I have a feeling it was more than that."

"Like what?"

"I don't know. Something Von wasn't willing to admit. Maybe Shannon was right and Von was in love with Michael. If so, he might have been resentful about a lot more than losing touch with a friend. Jealousy can be a powerful motive."

Rene clapped her hands together, clearly delighted. "We've already found a new suspect! Not bad for our first undercover op."

"I agree, but why lie and tell Von that we're traveling alone? I wouldn't volunteer that information to a stranger even if it were true."

"My options were limited. He's gay, so my feminine wiles would only go so far. I was forced to tap into his protective caveman instincts instead. Besides, I figured he might open up to us more if he thought we were gay, too." She shrugged. "Something in common."

"I'll admit, your ruse seemed to work. But Rene, I promised Dale that we wouldn't ask any questions about the murder."

"You did?" Rene winked. "Well, that was silly of you, wasn't it?" She looked annoyingly proud of herself.

"Fine," I grumbled. "But you're in charge of telling him about this, and he's not going to be happy." I stood and wrapped Bella's leash around my hand. "Come on, let's head back. I need to get some enzymes into this beast or I'll regret giving her all of those treats around midnight."

I put Alice back into the carrier and followed Rene to the sidewalk. I would have kept chiding her all the way to the car, but when we were a few steps away from the street, Bella froze, halting my forward motion and practically dislocating my shoulder. "Bella, knock it—" I stopped mid-sentence.

Something was wrong.

Bella stared straight ahead, teeth exposed, ears pricked forward. The guard hairs along her spine stood on end like the quills of an angry porcupine. Low growls rumbled from deep in her chest.

"What is it, sweetie?" I kneeled next to her and followed her gaze. She'd locked on a man who was standing—or rather skulking—in a dark, narrow alley across the street. He wore a camouflage baseball cap.

"It's him," I whispered.

Rene glanced left to right. "It's who?"

The stranger looked up and we made eye contact. For the first time, I got a good look at his face. Dark hair. Tan, weathered skin. Light blue, almost icy, eyes. He turned and bolted down the alley.

As to what happened next, I can only plead temporary insanity.

"Rene, stay here." I ordered. I thrust Bella's leash into her hand and broke into a run, determined to catch the suspicious stranger.

"Where are you going?" Rene yelled to my back.

I ignored her and shoved past an elderly woman. "Excuse me." I dodged to the right and twirled past a young mother pushing a stroller. "Sorry!" I leapt over a low bench and landed—hard—on the edge of my right foot. Pain jolted from my ankle to my knee. I recovered my balance and kept running, but the camo-capped man ran faster. He was getting away!

I didn't think. More importantly, I didn't look. I acted on pure instinct. I darted off the curb and into the busy street. The driver of a black pickup truck slammed on his brakes.

The next three seconds passed with petrifying clarity. The horrified expression on the driver's face; the ear-piercing screech of locked tires against pavement; the chemical smell of burning rubber; the sour taste of adrenaline. I gaped down at my knees, or more accurately at the truck's bumper, which had stopped an inch from my legs. The driver leaned out his window and yelled, "Jesus, lady! Watch where you're going!"

"My fault!" I yelled. I started running again.

Across the street, down the alley, and out to the sidewalk on the other side. I skidded to a stop, lungs heaving, and whipped my head back and forth.

The suspicious stranger had vanished.

TEN

By the time I arrived at Shannon's later that afternoon, I was dying to hear everything. About Michael, his relationship with Gabriella, and what had transpired with the police the night before. I considered trying to nudge the information out of Michael, but I'd already broken Dale's no-sleuthing order once today and Rene wasn't present to veto him this time. Dale had insisted on meeting with Michael and me in private. Meaning that Shannon, Rene, and Sam had to make themselves scarce.

Rene and Shannon were less than pleased, but they eventually acquiesced. What choice did they have? Rene and Sam opted to go to Seaside for dinner and then relax in the rental house. Shannon used the time to make sure the final plans were in place for the Sandcastle Festival fun run and yoga class.

Ugh. The yoga class.

Lord how I wished I'd never agreed to teach that yoga class. I hadn't found an instant of inner peace since I'd learned that Michael was married. How on earth was I supposed to create it for others?

Still, like Dad always told me: a promise is a promise is a promise. Shannon needed my help, and I would not let her down, at least not intentionally. I would show up at her event on Saturday afternoon, and I would teach. What and how effectively? That was a problem for another day. Today's problem was Michael.

Michael and I waited for Dale in Shannon's living room, making meaningless small talk and avoiding eye contact. Neither of us had an appetite, and we'd opted to avoid alcohol to keep our minds clear, so I sipped coffee while Michael busied his hands playing with a glass of ice water. Sweat beaded both the glass and the back of my neck. The sour stench of anxiety emanated from underneath my armpits.

"It's almost four. Shouldn't Dale be here by now?" I asked.

"Be patient, Kate. It's a long drive."

As if I didn't know that.

Bella tried to diffuse the tension between us the best way she knew how. She brought Michael her red rope toy, dropped it at his feet, and barked, clearly saying, *Hey you! Stop sulking and play with the dog!*

Michael picked it up, offered it back to her, and gave it a halfhearted tug. "Don't worry, sweetie. Everything's okay."

Liar.

What felt like a thousand years—but was actually thirty minutes—later, an ancient engine growled through the open window. Bella abandoned the living room and charged the door, barking notice to ax murderers and UPS drivers everywhere: *Beware! German shepherd on duty!*

I peeked through the blinds at Dale's orange rattletrap Plymouth pickup, which was parking on the street behind a car that I assumed was Shannon's Chevy. Dale sat in the driver's seat. The passenger's seat was empty. "Michael, put Bella in one of the bedrooms. I don't see Dharma or Bandit, but we should lock her up, just in case."

Bella and Bandit, Dale's incorrigible Jack Russell terrier, had a love-hate relationship. As in Bandit loved to terrorize Bella, and Bella hated every hair on Bandit's black-spotted body. Thus far, their scuffles had been more symbolic than physical, but I didn't want to take any chances. One murder was enough to deal with this weekend.

I flung open the front door as soon as the bedroom door clicked shut behind Bella. "Dale, I'm so happy you're here!" I gestured toward his outfit. "You look fantastic!"

I barely recognized the man standing on Shannon's doorstep. Instead of his normal attire of jeans, flannel shirt, and goat-dung-encrusted work boots, Dale wore a three-piece suit, red silk power tie, and a short, recently trimmed beard. The only hint of the goat farmer I adored was the *Stubborn Old Goat* baseball cap he held between his hands.

"Kate-girl, it's good to see you, too!" He wrapped me in a huge hug, then leaned back and peered at me intently. "You look exhausted. I'd ask how you've been, but we both know the answer to that, and it ain't good."

Michael appeared beside me. His eyes flicked to Dale, then down to the floor. "Thanks for coming."

Dale acknowledged him with a single, curt nod.

I pointed at his pickup. "Where are Dharma and Bandit? Did you already drop them off at Rene's?" With all of the hotels in town booked, Dale would never have found lodging, so Rene had texted him, inviting him to bring his entourage and stay at the beach house.

"Sorry, Kate. Dharma's back on Orcas, taking care of the critters."

"She didn't come with you?" I'd assumed that if Dale came to Cannon Beach, Dharma would be right beside him. Until that moment, I hadn't realized how much I wanted to see my mother. Needed to see her, even. To lean on her. To draw from her strength. This insight surprised me. Until a few months ago, I hadn't known—hadn't wanted to know, for that matter—that my mother existed. Now I couldn't imagine life without her.

Dale gave me a squeeze. "Dharma wanted to be here, Kate, believe me. She couldn't."

"Couldn't?" Michael's voice sounded skeptical.

Dale's sounded downright cranky. "Think it's easy to find someone to take care of sixty-three donkeys and thirty-four goats on short notice? We were lucky to get coverage for my duties. Believe me, Dharma has her hands full. Besides, the last jenny is due this weekend. Dharma won't feel comfortable leaving her until the colt is born."

Dharma and Dale were still adjusting to the "asses" part of their animal rescue, Dale's Goats and Dharma's Asses. They had recently rescued fifty donkeys from a Mexican meat packing plant, many of them pregnant. Fourteen, by my calculations.

"Can she take care of the farm by herself?" I asked.

"She'll be okay for now. Your mother's a hard worker. We have volunteers, and the young'uns who helped out with the petting zoo this past spring agreed to work a few hours after school. If I'm still here in Oregon next week, Dharma will hire some temporary farmhands and join us." He pointed to the door. "Are you two going to invite me inside, or do you want to talk about your legal troubles in front of the neighbors?"

I opened the door wider. "Of course, please come in."

Michael reached out his hand, but stopped when Dale didn't grasp it. Dale frowned, then steeled his shoulders. "Before we start, I need to get something off my chest." He pointed at me with his thumb. "Kate here is like a daughter to me. You, well, I always thought of you as a friend." He paused, whiskers trembling. "But man, Michael, what in the *holy hell* were you thinking? Not telling our Kate-girl that you were married? As my granddaddy would've said, that's lower than lice on a rattlesnake's belly."

Michael flinched but remained silent.

Dale continued. "When all of this is over, you and I are gonna have ourselves a little talk about how to treat a woman. And there'd better be whiskey involved. Lots of it." He scratched his chin hairs and slowly shook his head left to right. "As for Kate's mother, well, that woman has a temper. You'd best be avoiding Dharma until she calms down. Maybe in a century or two."

I instinctively jumped to Michael's defense. "Why's Dharma so quick to judge? She wasn't exactly perfect when she was married to my father."

"Indeed," Dale replied. "A juicy little tidbit I mentioned to her last night." He shuddered. "Which was a mistake I will never repeat. Getting kicked in the head by one of those donkeys would have been significantly more pleasant."

Michael finally spoke. "I screwed up, Dale. Believe me, I know. Someday I hope to make it up to Kate. To everyone. That will never happen if I spend the rest of my life in prison." He hardened his jaw. "I understand why you're angry, and I appreciate your taking the time to drive down here. You're the best defense attorney I know. Hell, you're the only defense attorney I know." He swallowed. "But I'm not sure you should represent me."

He had to be kidding. No one in their right mind fired Dale. Dale was a legend. He rarely lost, even when his clients were guilty. Drinking himself into oblivion and now this? Had Michael gone from reckless to self-destructive?

"Michael, I think you should—"

He held up his hand. "Please, Kate, let me finish." He turned back to Dale. "You don't have to respect me. You don't even have to like me. But if you're going to be my lawyer, you have to believe in me. Be honest: should I look for another attorney?"

I hoped against hope that Dale's answer would be a firm no.

Dale met Michael's gaze, unflinching. "I won't lie. I'm disappointed in you, Michael. Frustrated. Furious on behalf of Missy Kate here. It would be disingenuous of me not to say so."

I started to interrupt, but Dale gave me a *shush now* look, stopping me.

"But I still like you. I wouldn't be here otherwise. And of course I believe in you. There's no way you're guilty, at least not of murder. You're not capable of that kind of evil." The right side of Dale's mouth lifted into his trademarked southern grin. "Frankly, that makes you infinitely more appealing than most of my clients." He scratched his fingers along the sides of his beard. "If you want another attorney, well, that's up to you. But rest assured, if you allow me to represent you, I'll do my level best to get you out of this mess." He gestured to me with his eyes. "What Kate here does with you after that is up to her. So, what do you say?"

Michael held Dale's gaze for several long seconds, then reached out his hand again. "Then I say I want to hire you, if you'll have me."

This time, Dale shook it.

I released the breath I'd been unconsciously holding. "Okay, boys. Glad we got that out of the way. Now that you're both done swaggering, let's go to the living room."

Michael released Bella from her bedroom prison. She did a quick happy dance around Dale before settling at his feet next to the guest chair. Michael and I claimed opposite ends of the couch.

Dale pulled out a legal pad. "Okay, Michael. Tell me what happened, from the beginning."

I remained silent while Dale took copious notes. Michael's story began three years earlier and covered familiar ground, including everything he and Shannon had already told me: how he'd met Gabby when she was working as a waitress at Sunbathers, how she'd been brought to the States on a guest worker visa, and how he'd agreed to marry her so she wouldn't be forced to go back to Mexico.

"You married her when her H-2B visa was set to expire?" Dale scolded. "Talk about raising a red flag. Do you have any idea how stupid that was? Marriage fraud is a felony. Even if we get you off on the murder charge, you could still do prison time."

"Only if Immigration finds out that their marriage was illegitimate," I said. "And I don't see why they would, if they haven't already. The reason Michael and Gabriella got married isn't relevant to her murder."

"Not relevant?" Dale asked. "Seems mighty relevant to me."

"Wanting a divorce gives Michael motive, I get that. But why does it matter if the marriage was legit or not?"

"It matters," Dale replied, "because it proves that Michael isn't afraid of breaking the law when it suits him."

Michael flushed. "It was a victimless crime, Dale."

"Tell that to the people who've been waiting for over a decade trying to get into the country legally."

Michael scowled. He opened his mouth as if to say something, then closed it. For a moment, I thought he might be about to fire Dale.

"Look," Dale said. "All I'm saying is that nothing about illegal immigration is simple. There are victims on all sides and enough anger to fill up the Superdome, especially toward illegal immigrants from Mexico. Look at what happened during the last presidential election."

Michael didn't reply.

"Plenty of people would love to see you rot in prison until your prostate swells bigger than your head for marrying that woman. You need to take your crime seriously."

"I *do* take it seriously, Dale. If my life had a rewind button, believe me, I'd press it. Marrying Gabby wasn't worth it. Not given what it's done to Kate and me. When it comes to Gabby's murder, though, I agree with Kate. It's a nonissue. Until I told Kate last week, no one but Gabby, my sister, and I knew that the marriage was fake."

"People always know." Dale's expression was certain.

"Not in this case," Michael replied. "We were careful. We combined assets—not that we had many. We lived together. We had a real wedding, complete with pastor, dinner, guests, and a photographer. To the outside world, Gabby and I looked like a happily married couple. We made sure of it. Anyone we couldn't fool, we avoided."

"Is that why you stopped speaking to Von?" I asked.

"Yes, I was afraid—" Michael stopped. "Wait a minute. How do you know about that?"

I glanced guiltily at Dale, whose eyes had narrowed into suspicious slits. "Who in tarnation is Von?" he asked.

"An old friend of mine," Michael replied. The look he flashed my direction matched Dale's. "Kate?"

"Well…um…Rene and I might have spoken to him this morning."

Dale slammed his legal pad onto the coffee table. Bella abandoned his feet and took refuge next to me on the couch.

"Dammit, Kate," Dale grumped. "I told you not to—"

I held up my hands in surrender, then lowered them and began quietly stroking my dog. "It was innocent, really. At least it started that way. I was driving Rene crazy this morning, so she forced me to go to Cannon Beach with her. While we were walking around the town, we came across Puppies in Paradise."

Michael groaned and buried his face in his hands.

"Puppies in Paradise?" Dale asked.

"The local pet supply store. Michael used to work there with Von. Rene snatched Bella and went inside. I warned her that you wouldn't approve, but honestly, we didn't do anything that would hurt Michael's defense. As far as Von knows, we're just a couple of tourists in town for the Sandcastle Festival. Rene made up some stupid story about her and I being a couple, but other than that, she just asked a few generic questions about the murder."

Dale didn't look convinced. "If your conversation was as innocent as you claim, how did Michael's name even come up?"

"It wasn't difficult. Von's pretty bitter about Michael and Gabriella." I turned to Michael. "He thinks you shut him out after you got married, and for basically no reason."

Michael frowned. "I'm not surprised he's still hurt. Von's pretty sensitive, and we were close. Gabby thought he might be secretly in love with me."

"Is that why you ditched him?"

Michael looked affronted. "No. Not at all. I felt cornered. Von asked too many questions about Gabby's and my marriage. I was afraid that the first time we went out drinking, I'd blurt out something stupid and he'd figure out the truth. So I pretended to be furious with him over some lame, throw-away comment he made." Michael grew smaller. "Abandoning my friendship with Von was only the start. I had to lie to everyone. My friends, my family, the world. Life grew very small." His eyes begged me to understand. "I'm not a liar, Kate. Truly I'm not. Keeping up Gabby's and my story took too much energy. That's why I left town and started over. I knew that as soon as I left, people would start gossiping that Gabby and I were having marital problems, but she said she could handle it. She was used to putting on a public facade. I wasn't. It almost killed me. It's *still* almost killing me."

"Here's what I don't get in all of this," Dale said. "You had to know that marrying this woman would turn your life upside down. Why did you do it?"

Michael paused. "I loved her."

My hands clenched, causing my fingers to dig deeply into Bella's skin. She jumped off the couch, shook her entire body, and trotted off to the bedroom, presumably so she could rest in peace.

"Not *that* kind of love, Kate. Gabby and I dated for a couple of months, but she wasn't my soul mate and I certainly wasn't hers. But I cared about her. From the stories she told me about her life, I may have been the only person who did." He placed his hand on my shoulder. "She wasn't strong like you are, Kate. She was damaged."

I shook off his touch. Jealous frustration bubbled up from my stomach and erupted through my vocal chords. "Fine. Gabriella was damaged. Why not act like a normal person and get her some counseling, for God's sake. Why marry her?"

Michael hesitated, but he didn't flinch. For the first time since he'd told me about his marriage to Gabriella, he didn't look guilty. "It was the only way I could think of to keep her safe. She was terrified of going back to Mexico."

Dale leaned forward. "Terrified? Of what?"

"Her ex-boyfriend. He was an asshole. Obsessive, controlling, and not afraid to use his fists." Michael's entire body tensed. "He sent her to the hospital. Twice. Once with a badly broken arm, once with a punctured lung. The only thing he never damaged was her face." His expression hardened. "As if that made it better somehow."

"Why didn't she have him arrested?"

"Why does anyone stay with an abuser? At first Gabby thought she deserved it. When the violence got worse, she didn't think anyone would take her seriously. Her dad used to beat her and her mom. Reporting her dad made the next beating worse."

"It doesn't surprise me," Dale interjected. "Mexico has one of the highest domestic violence rates in the world."

Michael nodded. "She didn't find the strength to leave him until the second time he sent her to the hospital. As soon as she got out, she secretly started making plans to escape. She thought that the only way she could get away from him would be to give up her modeling career and come to the US to take that temporary crap job."

"Crap job?" I asked.

"The job at the Sea Baron hotel. They work their H-2B workers like slaves." He wrinkled his lips, as if the words in his mouth tasted bitter. "They pay minimum wage and force their immigrant workers to surrender their tips. What little money Gabby did make, she had to pay back to the hotel's parent company in exorbitant rent. She lived with four other women in a tiny one-bedroom apartment and paid over half of her income for the privilege. They all knew it was wrong, but they were too terrified to speak out."

Dale frowned. "Her story isn't uncommon. Temporary foreign workers are often victimized."

"That doesn't make sense, Dale. Surely they have rights."

"What good are rights without options? They're tied to the company that brought them here. If they quit, they're deported." Dale shrugged. "Like I said, victims on all sides."

"No options is right," Michael said. "Gabby told me that as tough as her life was here, it was a thousand times better than going back to that psycho in Mexico."

Dale's expression grew grim. "I've heard similar stories from domestic violence survivors before. I'm not sure how getting a temporary work visa kept him away from her, though. In my experience, abusers don't give up their victims that easily. Your friend's name and work assignment would have been in the system. A few hundred dollars in bribe money and he could easily have found her. What made her think he wouldn't follow her here?"

Michael smirked. "The guy was a real winner. He had an outstanding warrant in the US. Drug smuggling. She didn't think he'd risk crossing the border."

I flashed on the stranger I'd seen twice now. Could he be the mysterious ex-boyfriend? "What if she was wrong? About him crossing the border, that is?"

"What are you thinking, Kate?" Dale asked.

"I noticed this creepy-looking guy lurking outside the community center the night Michael confronted Gabriella. I don't know for sure what he was doing there, but he could have been watching Gabriella. I saw him again today near her apartment."

Dale buried his face in his hands. "Oh lord, don't tell me you went to the victim's apartment, too."

"No, just the pet store."

"They're in the same building," Michael explained.

Dale gave me a stern look. "Well, don't. Go to the apartment, that is. The last thing we need is for the police to find you snooping around the victim's apartment before they search it."

"You mean they haven't already?" I asked.

"Michael's name is on the lease. Without his permission, they'll need a search warrant." Dale gave Michael a sharp look. "You didn't give them permission to search her apartment, did you?"

"I would have, but your lawyer friend said not to."

"Good. Requiring a warrant won't stop them, but it will slow them down." Dale picked up his pen. "Back to this guy you saw, Kate. Can you describe him?"

"I only got a quick look at his face." I closed my eyes, trying to remember. "He was five-ten or so, mid-thirties. He had darker skin. At first I thought he was Hispanic or Middle Eastern, but I'm not sure anymore. He has these creepy light blue eyes..."

"Any tattoos, scars, or other obvious markings?"

I shook my head. "Not that I saw."

Dale looked at Michael. "Ring any bells?"

Michael frowned. "No, sorry. But Gabby's ex was originally from Spain, so he could easily have blue eyes."

Dale tapped his pen on the yellow pad. "Kate's suspicious stranger may have nothing to do with this woman's murder, but the idea is certainly worth pursuing." He gave me a grudging smile. "Good work."

Michael spoke for several more minutes about his move to Seattle and how he'd promised Gabriella that he would stick with their fake marriage until she got citizenship. He'd helped her get a decent job at an Italian restaurant in Cannon Beach, and she seemed to be settling in on her own. Then he moved to Seattle. He finished by recounting her demands for a payoff when he'd asked for a divorce. Fifty thousand dollars' worth.

Dale whistled. "That's a nice chunk of change for a waitress."

"For a pet food store owner, too," Michael replied. "The thing is, she knew I'd been saving to buy a house, so she probably thought I could easily come up with it. And I could have, a year ago. I told her that I'd drained my savings and invested everything in Kate's house, but she wouldn't budge."

"Any idea what she needed so much money for?" I asked.

"None. When I asked her, she said it was none of my business. I suppose she might have started using cocaine again…"

"Could she have been trying to smuggle someone else into the States?" I asked.

Dale interrupted. "We could spend all night theorizing. Better to hold off on blind guesswork until we get more facts." He made a note. "I'll look into her financials and find out if anything came back on the autopsy's tox screen."

Michael's story ended the night of Gabriella's death. "Seeing Gabby really upset me. I came home and had a couple of beers. Then Shannon started picking at me. She went on and on and on about Gabby and how stupid I was to let her keep using me. I had to get out of there before I blew my stack and said something I'd regret, so I grabbed her old car and drove to Cannon Beach. My memory's pretty hazy, but I think I got a little crazy. When I came to, I was parked in the lot above Arcadia Beach, covered in sand, puke all over my shirt. There was half a bottle of whiskey on the seat next to me."

My breath stopped. "Arcadia Beach?"

"Yes. At some point I must have wised up and decided to get off the road. I spent at least part of the night passed out in the parking lot."

I flashed on the dark blue sedan I'd seen parked above Arcadia Beach, then on the similarly colored Chevy on the street out front. "Michael, where is Shannon's car now?"

"Parked out front. We picked it up this morning. Why?"

"Arcadia Beach isn't far from where I found Gabriella's body."

Michael's skin turned gray. "I spent the night passed out close to where she was killed? You mean, if I hadn't been a drunken idiot, I might have been able to save her?"

I placed my hand on his arm. "You can't think like that, Michael. I could barely see the car from the beach, and she was a ten-minute walk from there."

"But if she screamed..."

"You wouldn't have been able to hear her. Not over the surf."

Dale stood. "Let me get this straight, Kate. You found the body *and* you saw Michael's car parked near the scene?"

I swallowed. Hard. "Yes. Do I have to tell that to the police?"

Dale walked to the window and stared through it for several seconds. When he turned back around, his expression was carefully neutral. "I can't counsel a witness to lie if the police ask a specific question."

"So you mean—"

Dale waved his hand through the air. "Think about my words, Kate. Think about my *specific* words."

I took that to mean no. Not unless the police asked me something *specifically* related to seeing the car.

Michael finished his story. "When I woke up, it was almost noon. I was too hung over to drive, so I walked into town, grabbed a cab, and headed back to Shannon's."

"Why didn't you call Shannon or me?" I asked. "One of us would have picked you up."

"I didn't have my cell phone." Michael gestured around the living room. "I thought I left it here, but I haven't been able to find it. I tried calling the number but it goes to voicemail. I'm betting the battery's dead. Have you seen it?"

"No." That explained why he hadn't returned any of my calls. He hadn't gotten them.

As if on cue, Dale's cell phone rang. "Dale Evans." His greeting was businesslike. Not a trace of affected southern twang. Michael and I stopped talking and watched him intently.

"I see." He looked at his watch. "We'll be there in thirty minutes. Yes, I understand. I owe you one. Thank you." He clicked off the call, wearing a grim expression. "My lawyer friend came through for us again. The police got that warrant we were talking about. They're heading over to search Gabriella's apartment now." He picked up his keys. "We need to get going."

"I'll follow behind with Bella," I said, preparing to grab my own.

Dale's reply was firm. "Not this time, Kate. You already know too much. Given everything you've seen, it's best if we keep you in the dark from here out."

Michael's eyes, when they met mine, were stricken. "I'll call you later tonight, Kate. I promise."

The door clicked behind them, enveloping me in silence. Bella emerged from the bedroom, looking confused.

"Looks like it's you and me again, pup."

Waiting.

ELEVEN

It took me less than two minutes to come to a firm conclusion. *Screw waiting.*

The thought wasn't my most Zen, but I'd had enough waiting to last three lifetimes. It was time for action.

I'd promised not to sleuth until Dale arrived in town, and I hadn't, for the most part. Dale didn't want me to go with them to Gabriella's apartment. Fine. Bringing your girlfriend to the search of your murdered wife's home was undoubtedly poor form. But I had to do something to help, even if it was futile.

I left two notes on the kitchen table: one updating Shannon, the other imploring Michael to call me as soon as he got back. Then I loaded Bella into my car and headed for the beach. Or more specifically, to the section of beach where I'd found Gabriella's body.

I don't know what I expected to accomplish. The police had already combed the area for clues, but it was the best idea I could come up with on almost no sleep and not nearly enough caffeine. I pulled into Tolovana Beach's main parking lot at ten minutes to seven, turned off the car, and clipped on Bella's leash. I would have parked at Arcadia Beach, but I wasn't sure if I could get from there to where Bella had found Gabriella's body at high tide. The sun had begun its descent into twilight, so I grabbed my emergency flashlight from the glove box and checked it. Full beam, bright light. For once, luck was with me.

"Come on Bella, let's go."

Bella emerged from the car, but not with the joyful exuberance I would have expected from a dog about to cavort in the sand. She slinked beside me, ignoring the tantalizing scents, pausing only briefly to do her business. Perhaps she still felt the tension from my meeting with Michael and Dale. That made two of us.

As the twilight darkened, so did Bella's mood. Every shadow became danger; every person, a potential threat. Leading her was like walking an unexploded ordnance, apt to go off at any second. She snapped at a man with a goatee and lunged after a beagle. She body-blocked me from a dozen perceived evils, including a downed piece of driftwood, a man on a bicycle, and a white plastic grocery bag floating along the shore. I shortened her leash and wrapped it tightly around my wrist. "No off-leash time for you tonight, Missy Girl."

After fifteen minutes spent avoiding imaginary threats, we arrived at our destination: the rocky cavern that had enshrouded Gabriella's body. The area seemed unaccountably normal, as if nature had reclaimed her territory. All crime scene markers were gone, supplanted by wet sand, broken shells, and tubers of dark green seaweed. If Bella's reaction was any indication, the scent of death was gone too, replaced by the aromas of the ocean: salt, seaweed, and a hint of burning cedar courtesy of a distant campfire.

Like many yoga teachers, I'd become attuned to life's subtle energies. The imprints, if you will, of recent history. The traces left behind. Sometimes those traces told stories, though I often didn't understand them at the time. Did this place have something to tell me? And if it tried, would I be able to hear?

According to *The Yoga Sutras*—yoga's key philosophical text—we each have the ability to see the world clearly, but our vision is clouded by filters. By our attachments, our ego, our fears, our doubts. Once we wash those away, the truth can emerge. At that moment, I wasn't sure I believed in yoga—or much of anything else—anymore, but it was worth a try.

I sat on the sand next to Bella, closed my eyes, and settled into my favorite breath-centered meditation, hoping to clear my mind. As I inhaled, I focused my mind on the cool, salty air entering my nostrils. As I exhaled, I relished the breath's warm, soft release. Every time my mind wandered—which it did often—I invited it back to the air moving in and out of my body, just as I'd taught my yoga students hundreds of times before.

Twenty minutes later, I'd realized nothing. Except that meditating sometimes felt an awful lot like being waterboarded.

I stood and sighed, frustrated. Maybe I was trying too hard. Maybe I was too emotionally close to the crime to tap into its energy. Maybe it had been too long since Gabriella's death. Then again, maybe the teachings were all a bunch of woo-woo garbage, no more real than the dangers Bella sensed behind every shadow.

"Come on, Bella," I said. "This was a waste of time."

Then, in a moment of startling clarity, I saw it: Gabriella's body.

In my mind, she was positioned precisely the way she'd been when I'd found her, but the image was crisper. Sharp with detail. The bright red of her starfish ankle bracelet. The untied laces on her right tennis shoe. The unadorned fourth finger on her left hand.

I sucked in a breath. *Gabriella's wedding ring.*

What had happened to her wedding ring? I'd noticed it was missing, of course, but I hadn't realized the significance until now. The married women I knew hardly ever took off their wedding bands. Gabriella could have been an exception, but somehow I doubted it. Wearing the ring would have been integral to her deception.

So where was it? Stored securely in her apartment or tucked deep inside the killer's coat pocket? And if the killer *did* take Gabriella's wedding ring, why? The simple gold band was worth a few hundred dollars at best. Enough to kill over? Doubtful.

Perhaps it had come off in the struggle. I turned on my flashlight and played its beam across the rocky beach. I looked underneath every log and filtered through the surrounding sand. I rearranged driftwood and moved aside long tendrils of seaweed. It wasn't there. Either someone—likely the police or the killer—already had it, or it was never here to begin with.

The missing ring was the first of three post-meditation revelations. The second was that how Gabriella had been killed might be important. From what I could tell, her body had still been fully clothed, so hopefully she'd been spared at least one violation.

Her beautiful face, however, had been destroyed. Beaten so severely that Michael had been forced to identify her body based on a tattoo.

According to Michael, Gabriella's abusive ex-boyfriend never touched her face, even though he seemingly had no reservations about breaking the rest of her body. If he'd never damaged Gabriella's face during her life, why would he do so now, in her death?

On the other hand, if the murderer wasn't her ex, why had Gabriella been beaten so severely? Didn't obliterating a victim's face connote rage? Was the killer destroying her beauty? Erasing her personhood? Acting in a frenzy of pure, unmodulated fury? I shuddered. Murder was never nonviolent, but this seemed exceptionally brutal.

The third realization was that Gabriella had been killed at night. I didn't know the time of her death, but we'd seen her leave the spaghetti dinner at seven-thirty. Unless she was killed and buried the following morning—which seemed unlikely, given there were no witnesses—it had to have been pitch black when she came to this place. I couldn't imagine her hanging out in such a secluded area by herself. She must have been with someone she trusted.

Gabriella's killer was no random stranger.

Bella's whine broke my reverie, and I glanced across the horizon. Twilight's pinks had darkened to navy. Bella or no Bella, I shouldn't be here alone after dark, either. "You're right, sweetie. Time to go home."

We were halfway back to the car when my cell phone rang. I glanced at my watch. Eight o'clock. I didn't recognize the number, but the voice was Michael's.

"Hey, I'm so glad to hear from you. How did it go at Gabriella's apartment?"

"It went." Michael's voice sounded as heavy as the knot forming in my stomach.

"That good, huh?"

He ignored my comment. "Dale says to thank Rene for her offer, but he's going to stay here with me at Shannon's. He'll take the guest room; I'll sleep on the couch. Dale thinks he should stay nearby in case the police decide to—" His voice broke. "In case they arrest me."

"Oh, Michael. Is it that bad?"

"It's not good." I imagined him running his hands across his scalp, the way he always did when he was stressed. "How did this get so messed up?" His voice wasn't simply heavy anymore; it was defeated.

"Michael, don't give up. Dale's great at his job. He won't let you get convicted of a crime you didn't commit."

"That might not be in Dale's control, Kate."

Not just defeated; empty. Dead already. Like the noose had been tightened and he was waiting for the stool to be kicked out from under him.

"Michael, talk to me. Did the police find something at Gabriella's?"

He sighed. "I don't know. They copied her computer files onto a flash drive. They also took some old clothes I kept in the closet, but I haven't worn them in years."

"What about the ring?"

"What ring?"

"Gabriella's wedding ring. Did they find it?"

Michael sounded confused. "What does her wedding ring have to do with anything?"

"While you were at Gabriella's apartment, I went back to the beach where I found her body. Being there sparked some memories. Gabriella was wearing a wedding band when we saw her outside the community center. She didn't have it on when I found her body.

"So?"

"So it struck me as odd. Was it valuable?"

"Hardly. The gold content was so low, I'm surprised her finger didn't turn green. You don't think she was killed over that worthless piece of jewelry, do you?"

"Probably not. But it's odd, don't you think?"

He didn't reply. In fact, he was so quiet, I was halfway convinced that he'd stopped breathing. It was as if he'd already started to leave. To retreat so deeply inside himself that I might never find him again.

"Michael, you're scaring me. What aren't you telling me?"

"Kate, I didn't kill Gabby, but it may not matter. The police have something. They were different tonight. The female cop barely looked at me. The male one acted like he wanted to kill me. When no one else was listening, he told me that he was planning to put the needle in me himself."

"Don't read too much into that, Michael. Officer Boyle wasn't exactly friendly to you at the community center, either."

Which, now that I thought about it, was odd. Why was Officer Boyle so aggressive toward Michael? He'd seemed to know Gabriella that night, too. Not surprising in a small town, but still…

Michael's voice interrupted my thoughts. "I'm exhausted, Kate. I'm heading to bed."

"Hang on for a second. I have one other question. Have the police said what time Gabriella died?"

"No, and I didn't ask. Why?"

"It was dark when Gabriella and Crystal left the community center. If she was killed that night, the beach would have been pitch black."

"So?"

"So why would she go to the beach alone in the dark?"

He didn't reply.

"The answer is, she wouldn't. No sane woman would. If she went with someone, she had to have known them."

"Kate, I can't think about this anymore right now. I can barely stand up. Can we talk tomorrow?"

"Yes, of course. But can you put Dale on the phone? I'd like to ask him some questions."

"He's in the shower right now." Michael didn't give me time to argue. "I love you. I'll call you tomorrow." The phone clicked to silence.

I whispered into the darkness, "I love you, too."

———

By the time Bella and I got back to the beach house, it was almost nine. Sam was upstairs, putting the twins to bed. The puppies snoozed in their playpen. I ground Bella's kibble, added water and enzymes, and set the kitchen timer for twenty minutes. Bella—who was well aware of the routine—curled up under the kitchen table and waited like Pavlov's dog for her dinner bell.

Rene poured two glasses of Chardonnay, gave one to me, and sat across from me at the table. "How's Michael?"

"Not good. He's convinced that the police are going to arrest him. I almost think he wants them to. Some crazy penance."

"For what?"

"I don't know. For marrying Gabriella? For not saving her? For disappointing me? Whatever it is, at the rate he's going, he may well flagellate himself all the way to the electric chair."

"Oregon uses lethal injection," Rene said.

I gave her a dark look.

"What does Dale say about all of this?" she asked.

"I don't know. He's not telling me." I took a slow sip of oaky tranquilizer, more to give myself time to think than because I actually wanted it. "Michael gave some lame excuse about Dale being in the shower, but I think Dale's stonewalling me. He's shutting me out."

"Why would he do that?"

"He said I already know too much that could hurt Michael, but I think that's a ruse. He doesn't want me involved in the investigation."

"Dale wasn't opposed to your sleuthing on Orcas Island. If I remember right, he even encouraged it."

"True. But that was different. I was the client in that case."

Rene reached down and scratched the soft spot behind Bella's ears. "There's a second possible reason Dale might be avoiding you."

"What's that?"

She stopped scratching Bella and solidly met my gaze. "Michael," she said.

"Michael?"

"Michael may not want you involved in the case, either. He loves you. You endangered yourself for Dharma. For your student Rachel, too. Michael probably figures that if he keeps you in the dark, you'll be safer."

The instant the words hit my eardrums, I knew she was right. Dale might be encouraging Michael to keep silent, but Michael sure wasn't arguing. "*I* might be safer, but Michael won't be. If either of them thinks I'll sit back and let Michael fry, they don't know me nearly as well as they think they do."

The timer beeped. Bella charged out from under the table and did a happy dance near the counter as if she hadn't eaten in weeks. I set her bowl on the floor. She snarfed down the oatmeal-like gruel in thirty seconds flat.

I picked the dish up again and rinsed it out in the sink. "I've got news for both of them. They can't stop me. Every hour they shut me out is an hour I'll spend investigating on my own."

"That's my girl." Rene winked. "And I'll be right next to you. The Hardy Girls ride again. Where do we start?"

"By having a chat with Gabriella's friend Crystal."

The right side of Rene's mouth lifted into her trademarked I'm-one-step-ahead-of-you grin. "I was hoping you'd say that. I've already built you the perfect cover story." She handed me a slip of paper with a phone number and a time. "Your haircut is scheduled for tomorrow morning at nine."

TWELVE

AT EIGHT FIFTY-FIVE THE next morning, Rene, Bella, and I trudged up the stairwell to Crystal's hair salon, only to be thwarted by a burgundy wooden door. Its rectangular window sported a handwritten sign: *Welcome to CB Cuts. Please keep door closed. No dogs allowed.*

"Darn," Rene grumbled. "I told you we should leave Bella at home."

"Sam has his hands full with the twins, not to mention the puppies. Besides, Ricky and Lucy have been driving Bella bonkers." I frowned down the stairwell, imagining the temperature in the Honda's interior. "I didn't park in the shade, so Bella will have to stay with you. Why don't you grab some coffee and wait for me in the courtyard? I shouldn't be more than a half hour or so."

Rene's lips pursed into an unhappy pout. "But I'll miss out on all the fun! Besides, you need me. What good is Sherlock without Watson?"

Truthfully, Rene was right. This whole haircut ruse was her idea in the first place. I wanted her to be with me. I needed her. As annoyed as her antics made me sometimes, Rene's no-nonsense advice kept me sane. And she'd managed to extract some pretty useful information out of Von...

Of course, Von.

I could sic Rene on Von again. Who knew what juicy tidbits she'd charm out of him without the twins and me weighing her down?

"Tell you what," I said. "Maybe we can divide and conquer. If you promise to stick to our story and not act too suspicious, you can stop in at Puppies in Paradise and ask Von some more questions."

Rene grinned, exposing a mouth full of sparkling white, mischievous teeth. "Ooh, that sounds like fun. What do you want me to ask?"

"Michael said last night that Von may have been in love with him. Shannon mentioned something similar. See if you can get him to admit to it. An infatuation with Michael would give him a motive for wanting to get Gabriella out of the picture."

"Got it. Anything else?"

I thought for a moment. "Nothing specific, but when we saw Von yesterday, he said everyone had been talking about Gabriella's death. See if he's heard anything new. Someone around here has to have information about the killer."

"And they're going to blurt it out to the local pet store guy?"

"Emphasis on local. It's a small town. Insiders gossip. I'll admit, it's a long shot, but who knows? Maybe we'll hit something."

"I'm all over it." Then Rene's face fell. "Damn. I'm out."

"Why?"

"I just remembered, the pet store doesn't open until ten."

I sighed, frustrated for both of us. "Well then, get a latte and grab a table in the courtyard."

"So I'm back to sitting around waiting for you again."

"Not necessarily. Bella's an attention magnet. People are bound to ask if they can pet her. When they do, ask them if they've heard about the murder." I spoke faster, warming to the idea. "Bella will have witnesses glued to your table in no time."

Rene grabbed Bella's leash, grumbling. "You hear that, sweetheart? Kate thinks *you're* better at finding witnesses than I am." She grumped down the stairwell, obviously not pleased, but acquiescing nonetheless.

I placed my hand on the doorknob of CB Cuts and mentally rehearsed my cover story. Rene and I had decided to stick with our gay-lovers-in-paradise ruse, figuring that Crystal might be more open about a closeted relationship if she thought we were gay, too. I saw no reason to change that strategy now.

There was a single, not-insignificant risk: Crystal had seen me with Michael outside of the community center the night of the spaghetti dinner. But only briefly, and her focus had been on *Gabriella* and Michael. To her, I was an invisible stranger, not worth the brain cells required to remember.

Or so I deluded myself.

After a minute of mental rehearsal, I took a deep breath, turned the knob, and walked inside. A bell chimed softly, announcing my entrance.

A female voice called from an open doorway to the right, "Close the door behind you so the kitten doesn't escape."

Kitten?

Thank goodness Rene hadn't stayed. One sniff of cat dander and she'd have sneezed so hard, she'd have blown out her eardrums. Which might have been a blessing if Bella was with her. Bella, a kitten, and a confined space could be a loudly explosive combination.

I glanced around the small room, simultaneously searching for the kitten and checking out the space. The salon was bright, orderly, and surprisingly spotless. Not a single strand of hair—feline or human—decorated the floor. I took a quick sniff. No trace of the eau de cat box I'd come to associate with indoor felines, either.

Impressive.

A single haircutting station sat in front of a large, rectangular mirror, which was framed by evenly spaced snapshots. The workspace beneath it held a hand mirror, a jar filled with combs soaking in liquid disinfectant, and a flourishing potted ivy bathed in sunlight courtesy of a courtyard-facing window.

The wall to the right contained a perfectly arranged makeup display, a hooded hair dryer chair, and an open doorway that led, I assumed, to either a storage room or an office. The wall to the left featured a long, built-in base cabinet topped by a shelving unit that was stocked with shampoos, conditioners, hair sprays, and lotions, all neatly lined up like soldiers in formation. A shampoo bowl angled out from the corner.

An approximately six-month-old calico kitten curled up underneath the shampoo bowl's chair. Fluffy black ears matched its long black tail, which was tipped in white. An orange spot covered its right eye.

I crouched in a perfect rendition of Utkatasana (also known as a Full Squat) and held out my hand. "Hey there, kitty." The kitten backed against the wall, flattened its ears, and hissed.

Crystal emerged from the side room, drying her hands on a towel. She looked attractive, though not classically beautiful, in the salon's forgiving light. Her makeup was still overdone for my tastes, but the pink tones in her blonde hair glinted with sophistication, and every strand of the asymmetrical cut fell precisely in place.

Then again, what did I expect? She was a hairdresser, after all.

"You must be my nine o'clock." She nodded toward the kitten, who was now growling and exposing her front claws. All fourteen of them. "Mouse is semi-feral, so you probably shouldn't get too close to her. She might bite your finger off."

"My gosh, her feet are huge!" I exclaimed.

"She's a Hemingway cat."

"A what?"

"A polydactyl. A cat with extra toes. Some people call them Hemingway cats. Most cats have eighteen toes—ten in the front and eight in the back. Mouse is an overachiever. She has twenty two. Seven on each front paw."

She handed me a clipboard and pen, then pointed to the styling chair. "Have a seat and fill that out." She kneeled in front of the shampoo bowl and made soft clucking noises. The kitten leaned forward and sniffed her fingertips.

I stared at the page labeled *Client Intake Form*. My first dilemma: make up information or write down the truth? I stalled for time by making light conversation.

"You named your cat Mouse?"

She pointed to a hole in the sheet rock. The shampoo bowl's water line snaked through it. "When she gets scared, she crawls into the wall and disappears, like one of those cartoon mice. The name seemed appropriate."

Meanwhile, back on the form, I wrote down my real name and cell phone number, but opted for Serenity Yoga's address.

"She's cute," I said.

"Isn't she? She'd been living off scraps in the courtyard for months. I finally trapped her a week ago. I've been trying to tame her, but it's slow going."

I stared at the form. *Approximately when was your last haircut?* The truth—a week ago—would never do. I screwed up my face and chewed on my lower lip.

Crystal looked at me oddly. "It's not a test, you know."

I smiled. "Sorry. I was trying to remember my phone number. I never call myself." *Eight weeks.* Next question: *What are your expectations for your appointment today?* Expectations? I considered writing *gather clues to track down a murderer* but settled for *trim ends*

150

instead. I finished the form by listing *allergies* (none), *medications* (none—my birth control pills were none of her business), and *tools used on your hair on a regular basis* (rubber bands and a comb).

I handed the form back to Crystal. "This is thorough."

"I pride myself on taking great care of my clients. I can't do that without information."

Crystal scanned my answers, then cocked her head to the side as if first truly noticing me. "Hey, wait a minute. Don't I know you?"

Crap. Crap, crap, crap, crap, crap.

"I…I don't think so." I tried to distract her by changing the subject. "Does the CB in your business name stand for Cannon Beach?"

She frowned and replied absently, "Crystal Buchanan." She tapped her index finger against her lips. "I never forget a face." The finger kept tapping. Tap, tap, tap. Tap, tap, tap. Pummeling my nervous system like a hyperactive woodpecker.

I made another attempt at diversion. "I'm pretty happy with the general shape of my cut, so—"

"Just a second. This is going to bug me until I figure it out." She glanced down at the form, then back up at me again. "It says here you're from Seattle…" She lowered her hand and snapped her fingers. "Seattle. That's it! You're that woman with the crazy German shepherd."

I suddenly wished she'd start tapping again.

"You were with Michael Massey at the spaghetti dinner. Are you a friend of his?"

Gulp.

"Yes." I didn't volunteer that said friendship included benefits, such as cohabitation.

She leaned back and crossed her arms. "Friends, huh? And you two just happen to be visiting Cannon Beach at the same time?"

I winced. "Yep."

That's when we began the dance. The chicanery cha-cha. Two con artists, each conning the other. Each wondering who had the upper hand.

Crystal frowned slightly, then shrugged. "Fair enough. Friends it is. None of my business, anyway." She pressed against the foot pedal and raised the chair several inches. "What would you like me to do with your hair today?"

"Just a light trim to take off the split ends."

I was afraid to ask too many questions, so while Crystal examined my hair, I tried to glean information about her—and her supposed relationship with Gabriella—from the photos she had taped around the mirror. My favorite was a recent shot of Mouse curled into an orange-and-black ball, fast asleep amidst an avalanche of overturned shampoo bottles. Several photos were of people I didn't recognize. The one top and center showed Gabriella and Crystal, arms wrapped around each other, smiling in front of Haystack Rock. Next to it was a shot of the group Shannon had called the Fearsome Foursome: Shannon, Michael, Von, and Crystal. Von stood at one end of the photo; Shannon, the other. Michael and Crystal smiled from the center. The two women both leaned toward Michael, who looked uncomfortable—almost trapped—between them.

"Your ends look pretty clean to me," Crystal said. "Are you sure your last haircut was eight weeks ago?"

"Maybe it was only six." *Days.* "If I don't need a cut, maybe you could just do a shampoo and style?"

"That hardly seems worth your money. This isn't a good cut for you, anyway." She stepped back and assessed me. "A short, layered look would bring out your eyes better. Are you up for something completely new and different?"

The answer was a firm, resounding no. Any style I wore had to be controllable by ponytail. "Maybe next time. Today, just take off a quarter-inch or so." I smiled. "I'm not a great fan of change."

She held several strands of my hair up to the light as I continued scanning the photos. The one bottom-center made my heart drop to my stomach.

Shannon, Michael, and Gabriella.

At Gabriella and Michael's wedding.

I stared at my boyfriend and his bride, trying to imagine the day. Relaxed body language, bright smiles, joyful energy. Michael and Gabriella seemed happy. Heartbreakingly happy. If they were faking, they should have won Oscars. Shannon, on the other hand, looked tense. Her smile, forced. Kind of like mine at the moment.

I pointed at the photo with trembling fingers. "Who's that woman with Michael?"

Crystal's face remained carefully neutral, but I could have sworn she was suppressing a smirk. "That's Michael's sister, Shannon."

A sane person would have given up then. I leaned forward and touched Gabriella's image. "Not Shannon, this woman."

"Michael's wife, Gabriella. Or at least she *was* Michael's wife. She was murdered two days ago." The glint her eyes said, *But you already knew that.*

Yep. Dancing away. One, two, three, cha-cha. One, two, three, cha-cha.

Crystal dropped my hair and motioned to the shampoo bowl. "Have a seat over there."

Mouse retreated into the hole behind it. I wished I could join her. I sat.

Crystal draped a towel over my shoulders, ordered me to lean back, and lathered up my hair. I closed my eyes, as much to avoid eye contact with Crystal as to keep out the soap. The sweet scents of pine-apple, coconut, and hibiscus seemed incongruous with the sour energy between us.

"So you claim you're a friend of Michael's, but you didn't know his wife?" Crystal turned off the water and firmly—a little too firmly—massaged my scalp.

"I'd never met her, at least not until the other night. I didn't know he was married until last week."

Crystal stopped scrubbing, turned on the water, and rinsed. Boiling liquid scalded my scalp.

"Ouch! That's too hot!"

"Oh, sorry," she said, not sounding sorry in the slightest. With a flick of her wrist, the steaming hot water turned freezing cold. I didn't complain. Ice water might ease the pain of my third-degree burns.

She finished rinsing, wrapped the towel around my head, and pushed me to standing. When I sat back down at the haircutting station, Mouse peeked out from inside the base cabinet underneath the retail shelving unit.

"When did she get in there?" I asked.

Crystal shrugged. "She hangs out in that linen cabinet sometimes. Hopefully the health inspector won't find cat hair on all of my towels." She pulled a comb out of the blue solution and started yanking the tangles out of my hair. "I can't believe Michael didn't tell you he was married. How do you two know each other again?"

"We own businesses in the same building." Which was true, if incomplete.

"You may not know this, but Gabby was my friend. Michael was too, for that matter, before he moved to Seattle. She and Michael were inseparable. Soul mates." She yanked on a particularly large knot, jerking my head back.

"Ouch!" I yelled. "Did you use conditioner?"

154

Crystal looked at me drolly. "I must have forgotten." She kept ripping the comb through my curls. "Anyway, that's why I was so shocked when I heard that Michael had taken up with some slutty home wrecker. I don't suppose you know anything about her?"

I unconsciously grasped the heart-shaped locket at my throat, as if holding it would make me less guilty. When I glanced in the mirror, my face was bright red. My shoulders, stiff as a statue. "I...uh...I..."

Crystal slammed the comb on top of the styling station's cabinet. "All right, I've had enough of this nonsense. You're *her*, aren't you? You're the slut who stole my friend's husband."

I remained uncharacteristically composed in spite of Crystal's insult. I didn't blame her for lashing out at me. If Sam cheated on Rene, I'd flatten his mistress's nose. The question was, what should I say to her now? Gabriella obviously hadn't told Crystal that she'd married Michael for a green card. I wasn't about to volunteer that information either. As for the ruse about Rene and I being lovers? Well, that had just flown south for the winter.

In the end, I decided to tell the truth. Sort of.

"You're right. Michael and I ..." My hand unconsciously fingered the locket again. "We're close."

Crystal picked up the scissors and started cutting. Her tone was as sharp as her shears. "So you *are* his mistress."

I cringed at the word. "Not mistress. More than that. Closer. And our relationship was never an extramarital affair. Michael and Gabriella were separated."

Snip, snip, snip, snip. Wisps of hair falling to the floor. My hair.

"Separated?" she snapped. "Since when?"

I wasn't sure how to answer. "For always" would require an explanation I wasn't willing to offer. I settled for a vague answer instead. "For a while. A long while. Since well before Michael and I got together. She didn't tell you?"

155

Crystal palmed the scissors, for the first time looking unsure. "That's why Michael moved to Seattle, isn't it?"

I didn't reply.

"It all makes sense now. I could never understand why Gabby didn't go to Seattle with him. There's no way I would have let that one get out of my sight." She glanced toward the wedding picture. "The first time I heard that Gabby and Michael were having trouble was the other night at the community center. The night she was…" She looked away, but not before I glimpsed sorrow behind her crisp façade.

"The night Gabriella was murdered," I finished. "I'm in a relationship with Michael now, but I swear I didn't break up his marriage. I was as surprised to learn about Michael being married as you were to learn about me."

Crystal's eyes grew wet. "I don't get it. I thought Gabby was my friend. I thought they were *both* my friends. Why didn't she tell me?"

I didn't know how to answer, so I theorized out loud. "You *were* Gabriella's friend. As least as much as she had any." I'd only seen a brief glimpse of the two women together, but according to Von, they had been inseparable since Michael left town. If they weren't lovers—and unless Crystal was hiding something, they weren't—they must have been close friends.

"Michael told me that Gabriella was a very private person." I took a deep breath and continued. "That's why I'm here. You knew Gabriella better than anyone, at least recently. I'm hoping you can help me figure out who killed her."

"Isn't that the police's job?"

"Yes, normally, but they've been questioning Michael."

Crystal lowered her hand. Her brow wrinkled. "They think Michael killed Gabby?"

"Yes."

She didn't reply.

156

"They're wrong," I added.

"Of course they're wrong. Michael doesn't have a violent bone in his body."

I hazarded a glance in the mirror. So far, my hair was still attached to my scalp. That had to be a good sign, right?

I continued my newest subterfuge, which was an unholy combination of truth, inference, and lie. "Michael's lawyer, Dale, is a friend of mine. I've helped him solve cases before." That was the truth. "Dale thinks the police are building a solid case against Michael." Inference. Why else would Dale have objected to my being involved? "I promised to help him interview witnesses." And there was the lie.

"You're a private investigator?"

I avoided answering. "Look, I don't expect you to like me, but we're on the same side. We both think Michael is innocent. Will you help me?"

Crystal hesitated, but when she answered, her voice was firm. "No." I stood to object, but she pushed me back down. "I'm not finished. Do you want to look like you cut your own hair with toenail clippers?"

I sensed it was a rhetorical question, so I didn't reply.

She continued. "As I was saying, I won't help *you*. But I will help Michael. Michael's a good guy." Her cheeks warmed almost as pink as her hair. "I'll answer your questions, but I'm not sure how much relevant information I'll have. I'm beginning to wonder if I knew Gabby at all."

She ran her fingers down the left and right sides of my hair, making sure they were even. "Like I said, I had no idea their relationship was in trouble until Michael came back into town. I mean sure, I thought it was odd that he moved to Seattle without taking Gabby, but she always claimed it was temporary. It was obvious after that debacle in front of C-BAC that something weird was going on, so I cornered Gabby in the car on the drive home. She said she'd recently

157

learned that Michael was having an affair, and she was devastated. I told her to call him and work things out. Anyone with half a brain could see that he still loved her."

I flinched.

"Sorry, that was probably insensitive, but it's true. I hate to break it to you, but they would have gotten back together eventually."

She opened a drawer and pulled out a blow dryer. I raised my voice to be heard over the racket. "Did she do it?"

"Do what?"

"Did Gabriella call Michael?"

"Not while I was with her, but I assumed she was going to." Crystal closed her eyes and swallowed. "She probably got killed before she had the chance."

Or she tried, but Michael didn't have his cell phone. I didn't share that thought with Crystal. Instead, I said, "The last time Michael saw Gabriella, he thought she seemed frightened. Was she concerned about anything that you know of?"

"I already told you. She was upset that Michael was having an affair."

"That's not what I mean. Could she have been afraid of someone? Did you ever notice anyone suspicious hanging around her? Maybe someone who wore a baseball cap?"

"No. No one different than usual, anyway."

"What you mean?"

"Gabby always had men sniffing around her." Crystal shrugged. "I don't remember anyone with a baseball cap, though."

She turned off the blow dryer, wrapped the cord neatly around it, and laid it precisely in the middle of her workstation. "The only person who might have wanted to harm Gabby is Michael's sister, Shannon."

"Shannon?" She had to be kidding.

"Shannon comes off all sweet, but she's a terror if you cross her. And she's super protective of Michael. It's kind of creepy. Does she have to call him 'Baby Brother' every other sentence?"

Now that she mentioned it, that affectation did seem a little odd.

"Shannon hated it when Michael and Gabby got serious. She pretended to support their marriage, but anyone with an IQ higher than a postage stamp could see through it. If Michael wanted out of the marriage and Shannon thought Gabby stood in his way, she wouldn't have thought twice about clobbering her over the head." Crystal grunted. "Though running her down with that new Mini Cooper might be more her style."

"Gabriella was hit over the head?" I knew that already, of course. But how did Crystal?

Her lips tightened. "Yes, at least I assume so. Today's *Clatsop County Herald* said that according to the police report, the cause of death was 'severe head injuries.'"

I stared into the mirror, searching Crystal's eyes for disingenuousness. I didn't find any. "Do you know anyone else I should talk to?"

"Like who?"

"Gabriella's other friends."

She shrugged. "You're looking at them. Gabby mostly kept to herself. She didn't know anyone in Cannon Beach until she and Michael got married, and once they hooked up, they didn't have time for anyone else. Gabby's English wasn't that great and she seemed lonely after Michael moved away, so I took her under my wing. Other than me, I don't think she knew very many people."

"How about at work?"

"At Tuscany? You can go there, I suppose, but I don't think you'll learn much. Mona—the old biddy that owns the place—runs a tight ship. All work, all the time. No fraternization between employees. Frankly, I was surprised she hired Gabriella. For a woman whose grandparents immigrated from Italy, she's mighty bigoted. If she had her way, Trump's wall wouldn't stop at the Mexican border. She'd seal up the whole country in a big plastic dome, like in that Stephen King novel." Crystal examined my hair cut critically in the mirror, then picked up the scissors again for a few final touches.

"Is there anything else I should know?" I asked. "Anything unusual about Gabriella?"

"Not really." Crystal paused, scissors closed and pointing toward the ceiling. "Well, maybe one thing, but I don't know how important it is. Gabby asked me for a loan."

The hair on my arms vibrated. "When? And for how much?"

"A couple of months ago. I told her I didn't have anything to give her, so we never got to a specific amount."

"Did she say why she needed the money?"

"To pay off Michael's debts. Evidently business in Seattle was slower than he'd hoped." Crystal grimaced. "At least that's what she told me. I don't know what to believe anymore. Do you think money's what got her killed?"

I didn't volunteer the complete truth: that Gabriella hadn't been scaring up money *for* Michael; she'd been scaring it up *from* him. Crystal had experienced enough heartbreak for one day. Still, my response wasn't a lie. "I don't know."

Crystal grasped a large chunk of my hair and prepared to make a few final cuts.

Everything next seemed to happen at once.

The door behind me opened and Rene's voice called, "Aren't you about done in here? We're bored."

Bella—who stood on leash next to her—spied Mouse; or, more accurately, Mouse spied Bella. The calico kitten arched her back like a Halloween decoration, let out a loud yowl, and dove into the hole behind the shampoo bowl.

160

"Oh no, a cat!" Rene screamed. She broke into a sneezing fit and dropped Bella's leash.

Bella froze for a moment, torn. On the left was a delectable calico morsel, hers for the eating. On the right, a complete stranger who held a sharp cutting instrument close to her human's throat. For a self-proclaimed German shepherd guard dog, the decision was obvious.

Protect the one who feeds you.

Bella charged at Crystal, growling and snapping her teeth. Crystal screamed. Her hand spasmed. The scissors closed, cutting a three-inch-wide swath from my hair. "Help!" she yelled. "Keep that vicious dog away from me!"

"Bella, stop," I yelled in return. "This is our friend!"

Bella skidded to a stop beside me, then took off after the kitten. She sniffed back and forth between the shampoo bowl and the base cabinet, whining.

I gasped at my reflection in the mirror. "My hair!"

The left side of my hair floated down past my shoulders. The right ended at the top of my ear.

Rene's mouth dropped open in a wide O. She took three steps back toward the door, still sneezing.

"For God's sake, Rene," I yelled. "What are you doing here?"

She shrank to half her normal size and stared at me with wide, innocent eyes. "We were getting bored out in the courtyard. Bella saw you through the window and wanted to say hi."

Crystal pointed at my right ear and proclaimed, "This isn't my fault. The dog attacked me!"

I bared my teeth at Rene. She replied with a submissive grin. "At least asymmetrical haircuts are in style."

I pointed to the door. "Get out. Now."

Rene grabbed Bella's leash and scampered down the stairs. The door's slam echoed behind her.

Crystal chewed on her bottom lip, wincing. "What do you want me to do now?"

———

Twenty minutes later, Crystal and I joined Rene in the courtyard. Autumn's midmorning breeze felt uncomfortably cool against my bare neck. Rene sat at a table with Von, chatting. She looked up and flashed a smile so fake, it could have been carved out of wood. "You look adorable! You'll love how fast that cut dries."

We both knew she was lying. I looked like a boy. An unattractive boy. An unattractive boy about to strangle his best friend.

Crystal edged around the table, clearly trying to stay out of Bella's striking range. Rene kept talking, faster now. "Bella was just re-introducing herself to Von. He thinks he might be able to find me a second set of those shoes. Isn't that fabulous?" She lifted her eyebrows, clearly asking me to play along. "I told him that the twins are with the nanny."

If Crystal noticed Rene's awkwardness, she didn't mention it. "I didn't realize you'd already met Von. You two should talk. He might be able to help."

"Help with what?" Von asked.

I knew what was about to happen, but I was powerless to stop it.

"Kate is a—" Crystal paused. "A friend of Michael Massey. She's also a private investigator. She's helping Michael's lawyer investigate Gabby's murder."

Von's face split into a grin. "You didn't tell me that you knew Michael. How—" He stopped, midsentence, and scowled. "Wait a minute…" He clenched his fists and spit out the same words, this time as an accusation. "You didn't tell me that you knew Michael. What in the hell is going on here?"

"I'm sorry, Von," Crystal replied. "It was confusing for me at first, too. Kate isn't just Michael's friend, she's his girlfriend."

Cha cha cha.

"His girlfriend?" Von glared from Rene to me and then back to Rene again. "You told me you were gay. Are you two playing me for a fool?"

I didn't have a chance to explain. Von slammed his fist against the table, swept Rene's coffee to the pavement, and stomped away.

THIRTEEN

Rene begged for forgiveness all the way back to the rental house. "Seriously, Kate, you were taking *forever*. How was I supposed to know that Bella would react like that? And that scene with Von is one hundred percent on you. We had a plan. A plan that did not include you pretending to be a private investigator."

I ignored her, but not because I was angry. Rene was right, actually. I was as much to blame for the morning's fiasco as anybody. I ignored her because I was using each and every one of my brain cells to mentally debrief my conversation with Crystal. While Rene continued apologizing, I created a mental list of new information and the additional questions it created.

To my surprise, I'd learned quite a lot.

One: Gabriella had asked more people than Michael for money, which meant that demanding money in exchange for the divorce hadn't been solely a crime of opportunity. Why did she suddenly need money? She'd told Crystal that it was to help Michael, but that was an obvious fabrication. Was the real reason somehow related to her death?

Two: Gabriella and Crystal had probably *not* been lovers, at least not if Crystal had told me the truth. Frankly, Gabriella hadn't been much of a friend to Crystal, either. She'd asked her for money and lied to her about her fake marriage.

Three: Crystal thought Shannon could be the killer. Shannon had never occurred to me as a suspect, but it made a weird kind of sense. She'd threatened to "squash Gabriella like a cockroach" the night of her death. The comment had seemed like a poor attempt at gallows humor at the time, but what if it was more than that?

As far as I knew, Shannon didn't have an alibi for the night Gabriella was killed either, and she'd missed her meeting the next morning—supposedly because she'd had a "long night." A long night doing what? Stewing over her fight with Michael, or eliminating the source of their disagreement? She loved her brother, maybe a little too much. Would she have killed to protect him?

Four: I had a new person to question: Mona, Gabriella's boss at Tuscany. No-fraternization policies notwithstanding, Gabriella might have opened up to someone at the restaurant. If she—

Rene poked my arm, making me jump. "For goodness sake, Kate. Have you been listening to me at all?"

I gaped through the windshield. I'd obviously been driving on autopilot. When had I pulled into the beach house's driveway?

She continued chiding me. "Are you going to stay out here and give me the silent treatment all day, or are you coming inside?"

"Sorry, I wasn't ignoring you. I was thinking. Are you hungry?"

Rene looked at me askance. "What kind of question is that? I'm always hungry."

"Great. Let's go to lunch. We're having Italian."

I knew Dale and Michael would never approve of my plan, but I tried to call them anyway. Not to ask for permission to question Mona, but to beg them to level with me first. As far as I knew, Michael still hadn't found his cell phone, but I tried it anyway. Straight to voicemail, which was now full. No answer on Shannon or Dale's phones, either.

Tuscany was normally only open for dinner, but they served lunch during Sandcastle Week. Sam looked up the restaurant's address online while Rene bundled up the twins in matching teddy bear onesies. I incarcerated the puppies inside their crate in the living room and secured it with a Bella-proof carabiner. Bella had figured out how to break the puppies out of their crate when they lived with Michael and me. Fortunately, she couldn't open the carabiner. Yet.

I hated leaving Bella behind at the beach house. She still suffered from significant separation anxiety, and although the anxiety part of her neuroses was lessened when she had the puppies for company, their howling drove her stark raving mad. I wasn't sure I'd be able to find shade parking near Tuscany, though, and I didn't want to risk leaving her in the car in the noon-hour sun.

So I compromised by scratching behind her ears and giving her an extra-large ostrich tendon. "Sorry to leave you alone with the monsters, but we won't be gone long. If they bug you, go upstairs and hide in one of the bedrooms. It'll be less noisy up there." Bella—who understood a remarkable amount of English—snatched the tendon from my hand and trotted up the stairway.

Puppies incarcerated and Bella mollified, Rene, Sam, and I headed to Tuscany in a two-car caravan. Taking both cars wasn't the most ecologically sensitive option, but it was the most flexible. I needed my own wheels to join Dale and Michael should either of them ever return my phone calls.

Tuscany was housed in a tiny, pink stucco structure that had once been somebody's home. Nestled between multi-story hotels, the restaurant's energy was both charming and incongruous. The roof was missing a fair number of shingles, and the trim was faded and peeling. But well-kept rosebushes bloomed along the cement walkway, and pristine stained-glass windows sparkled with color. The entrance was crowded with people waiting for a table.

Sorry, Bella. We may be longer than I thought.

A half hour later, Rene, Sam, the twins, and I were shown to a table covered by a bright white tablecloth and decorated by a three-stem bouquet of fragrant, deep red roses. Pavarotti's honeyed voice dampened nearby conversations.

The delicious aromas of tomatoes and roasted garlic would normally have made my mouth water, but stress had quashed my appetite. Which was probably a good thing, since Rene appeared to be eating for four. She reached across the table, grabbed the last chunk of hot, fresh, rosemary sourdough, and lathered it with butter. She waved at an overweight, exhausted-looking waitress across the room. "Can you bring us more bread please?"

The woman nodded a single yes and shuffled into the kitchen.

Sam peered at me across the table. "Wow, Kate. I can't get over that haircut. It's short. I mean *really* short."

Rene wrinkled her lips and gave him a look. A look that indicated he'd better stop talking—and soon—or his twin-making privileges would be permanently suspended.

He winced. "I mean, your hair looks great and all, it's just different." He cocked his head to the side. "Maybe it takes a while to get used to." He jumped. "Ouch! Rene, stop kicking me!"

"Blame your wife," I said ruefully. "It was either this or a mullet."

"That haircut was Rene's idea?" He turned to his wife. "You're not planning to cut yours like that, are you?" This time Rene stomped on his foot.

The waitress reappeared, thumped a second basket of bread on the table, and handed us each a menu. "Sorry about the wait." She flashed a tired smile at the twins. "Well, aren't you a couple of cutie-pies." Amelia gurgled in reply, still deeply asleep. The waitress grinned. "Bet they keep you on your toes."

"Don't you know it," Sam said. "I wish we could get them to sleep like this at night."

I gestured toward the half-dozen people still waiting near the entrance. "You guys are busy today," I said.

"Sandcastle Festival," she replied. "Busiest weekend of the year. We're not this backed up normally. Doesn't help that one of my waitresses has the flu and the other one quit two days ago without notice. That leaves me, my chef, and my broken-down dishwasher to deal with this mess. I've been running my feet off."

Her waitresses? She must be the owner.

"Are you Mona?" I asked.

She stepped back and appraised me with cautious curiosity. "I am. Who's asking?"

"My name is Kate Davidson." I reached out my hand. Mona shook it without enthusiasm. "I'm here on behalf of a friend. I was actually hoping to ask you a few questions about one of your waitresses."

Curiosity changed to suspicion. "Which one?"

"Gabriella Massey."

Mona scowled. "Sorry, I don't have time to talk."

An elderly woman a few tables away waved her fingers in the air. "Ma'am, we've been waiting for over twenty minutes. I've got low blood sugar."

Mona nodded. "I'll be right there." Under her breath, she muttered, "Eat some bread, you old crone." She pulled out her order pad and turned to leave.

"Please," I said. "It's important."

"Like I already told you, today's not a good day." She showed me her backside and started walking away.

Sam stood and spoke. "We can make it worth your time."

Mona froze. Then again, so did I. What on earth was he talking about?

He gave Mona an engaging smile. The kind you see in toothpaste commercials. For a second, I would have sworn he was channeling Rene. "This is a gorgeous restaurant. I can see that you've poured your heart into it. Your website doesn't do it justice." He reached into his billfold, pulled out a business card, and handed it to Mona. "It's not mobile friendly, either."

She grimaced. "I don't have the time, the money, or the energy to work on a website. I have customers to feed. Which is what I should be doing right now."

Sam didn't give her a chance to leave. "*You* may not have time, but I do. As you can see on my card, I own a software company."

Sam owned a software company, all right. One that was about to go public. One that had no reason to scavenge for work on small business websites. What was he up to?

Mona glanced at the card and started to hand it back. "Sorry, like I said. No money either."

"I don't want money. All I'm asking for is ten minutes of your time to answer Kate's questions." Mona frowned at him skeptically. "I'm serious. Give her ten minutes, and I'll provide you with a new, mobile-friendly website. I'll even throw in an online ordering app."

Her shrewd eyes pinned Sam to the table. "Are you serious?"

He pointed his thumb at Rene. "As serious as the heart attack this one's going to get from eating all of those carbohydrates."

The elderly woman at the other table waved her hand furiously. "Excuse me, ma'am? We're still waiting."

Mona ignored her. She flicked Sam's business card with her thumbnail, then tucked it into her pocket. "It's one o'clock. We close for dinner prep at two. I can give you fifteen minutes then. In the meantime, take a look at the menu. I'll be back to take your order as soon as I can." She shuffled hurriedly to the other table.

The right edge of Sam's mustache lifted in a caterpillar-like grin.

"Did you mean that?" I asked. "Are you really going to redo her website?"

He shrugged. "I don't see why not. The one she has now is terrible. I can do it myself if she doesn't want anything too fancy. If she does, I have three floors filled with web developers. If I provide enough pizza and beer, one of them will have it done in an evening."

"I don't know what to say," I replied.

"You don't have to say anything. I used to work with small business owners like Mona all the time. They're stressed and cash poor. They barely have time to brush their teeth."

That certainly described Michael and me.

"She'll be more cooperative if we make it worth her while. Besides, I'm sick of sitting around while you and Rene get to have all of the fun. Michael's my friend, too."

I wrapped him in a huge hug, not even cringing when his mustache brushed my cheek. "I owe you. Michael and I both do." I leaned back and grinned. "I might even forgive you for that comment about my hair."

Rene bit off another chunk of steaming, freshly buttered carbohydrates and spoke between mouthfuls. When you two finish the love-a-thon, can you look at the menu? I'm starving!"

I cracked open the bound leather menu and tried not to cringe. The items ranged from fifteen-dollar side salads to forty-dollar lobster linguine, with not much below twenty-five in between. I settled for pumpkin ravioli and a bottle of sparkling water. Sam ordered vegetarian lasagna; Rene went for fettuccine primavera with extra fettuccine on the side. The twins slept like identically dressed angels inside their stroller.

Sixty minutes of intense but deeply satisfying gorging later, Mona sagged into a chair beside me. "The last tables haven't finished yet, but I can spare a minute or two now. Talk fast."

I didn't waste time. "Like I said earlier, I'm looking for information about Gabriella Massey."

"What are you, a reporter?"

"Not exactly. I'm a friend of her husband." The word *husband* still caught in my throat.

All exhaustion on Mona's face vanished, replaced by a huge, bright smile. "Michael Massey? Why didn't you say so?"

"You know him?" I asked.

"Know him? I adore him! He saved Pugsy." She pushed back her chair. "Wait here a minute." She disappeared into the kitchen and returned a few seconds later carrying a cell phone. "Pugsy is this sweet little thing here." She pointed at a photo of a black pug sporting pink lacquered toenails and a matching collar. Her tongue, also pink, lolled out the side of her mouth, reminding me of a geoduck clam. "Isn't she cute?"

"She's adorable," I said honestly.

"Pugsy started having kidney problems when she was just a puppy. Wouldn't touch the expensive prescription food the vet tried to push on me. Michael did some research and found a food that she loved. Not only that, he special ordered it for me at cost. I never could have afforded it otherwise."

That sounded exactly like Michael. When it came to animals in need, he was a big softy.

Mona continued. "He'd have gotten into a lot of trouble if his boss found out. Nearly broke my heart when Michael told me he was moving to Seattle. I thought that meant the end of my sweet little Pugsy for sure. But you know what? Michael still has that food delivered to me every two weeks from his store in Seattle, and still at his cost. Pugsy's vet said she should have died years ago. And she would have, if it weren't for Michael. That boy is solid. A good man."

I smiled. "He is indeed."

"Which is why I never understood why he hooked up with that…" She lowered her voice as if uttering a swear word. "That *Mexican*."

I deliberately kept my voice neutral. "You don't like Mexicans?"

Mona held up her hands. "Oh now, don't go getting the wrong idea. I'm not prejudiced or anything. I just wish they'd stay in their own country. They come here, sign up for welfare, and take all of our good jobs." I didn't point out that drawing welfare and working at "good" jobs were typically mutually exclusive. She tapped her chest with her index finger. "This employer hires Americans."

"Except for Gabriella," I said.

She waved her hand through the air. "Gabriella was an exception. I had to hire her, for Michael. She couldn't get a job anywhere in Cannon Beach except as a maid in a hotel, and she didn't want to work as a maid. After everything Michael did for me, how could I say no?"

I tried to imagine the challenges Gabriella must have faced when working for Mona, given her prejudices. It couldn't have been pleasant. "Did you and Gabriella get along?"

Mona looked surprised. "Of course. Why wouldn't we?"

I paused, working hard to keep the judgment out of my voice. "Given your views about immigrants, I'd have assumed it would be hard for you two to work together."

"Oh, honey, you weren't listening. Like I said earlier, I'm not prejudiced. I just think we should take care of our own problems before we let other countries saddle us with theirs. Mexico doesn't exactly send us their best and brightest, now do they? Gabriella was lucky I agreed to take her on." She nodded grudgingly. "I have to admit, though, she was a hard worker. I was pretty upset when she left me."

This time I couldn't hide my frustration. "You know that she didn't leave, right? She was murdered."

Mona made the sign of the cross. "Yes, God rest her soul. But that was after she quit."

The skin on the back of my neck prickled. "She quit? When?"

"The night she got herself killed." Mona's lips wrinkled. "Frankly, I was pissed. After all I did for that girl? I hired her when no one else would, and she up and quit on me without notice. And on the busiest week of the year!" She harrumphed. "She didn't even have the courtesy to tell me in person. I came in Wednesday morning to a voicemail message saying she was leaving town. No thank you. No two-week notice. No arrangement for coverage. Nothing."

"Where was she going?" I asked.

"She didn't say. Didn't say why she was leaving, either."

Sam interrupted. "Where were you supposed to mail her last paycheck?"

"She didn't tell me."

"Didn't that strike you as odd?" he asked.

"Nope. Like I said, I normally hire Americans." She shrugged. "How am I supposed to know what those people do?"

I was beginning to understand why Michael had been drawn to help Gabriella. Even with his assistance, her life in the States hadn't exactly been roses and sunshine.

"Did you tell the police that Gabriella was planning to leave town?" I asked.

Mona's expression remained blank. "They never asked me."

I made eye contact with Rene and Sam, clearly asking them, *Any more questions?* They both shrugged. I had a huge one. One that Mona couldn't answer.

Why did Gabriella decide to leave town?

As soon as the question zapped between synapses, I realized that I already knew the answer.

She was running again.

That's why she didn't give Mona a forwarding address. She didn't want to leave a trail someone could follow.

I wasn't sure if Gabriella's sudden departure worked *for* Michael's defense or against it. On the plus side, the person she was running from might be her killer. On the minus, the police would probably assume she was running from Michael.

"Did anything else about Gabriella's behavior strike you as odd lately?" I asked.

Mona replied with a disinterested shrug.

I flashed on the camo-hatted man again. "How about someone else? Did you see anyone weird or suspicious hanging around her?"

She thought for a moment. "Suspicious? No."

My shoulders slumped.

"Annoying, yes."

They lifted again. "Who?"

"I dunno. Some guy. He sniffed around that girl like a lovesick puppy." She pointed to a tiny table near the kitchen. "He monopolized that two-top at least twice a week, sucking down coffee and eating my bread. Never once ordered more than an appetizer. Just sat there and mooned. I finally told him that he had to start ordering full meals or take his sad sack routine somewhere else." She shrugged. "It must have worked, because he stopped hanging around a few weeks ago."

I leaned toward her, finally hopeful. This might be our man. "What was his name?"

"Heck if I know. He always paid cash." She lifted her eyes toward the ceiling and absently rubbed her chin. "Gabriella called him Broke once, so that might be his last name." She smirked. "It would make sense, since he never seemed to have any money."

The hair on the back of my arms prickled.

Broke.

I'd heard the name somewhere, but where?

Then it hit me.

From Gabriella, outside the community center. "Broke" wasn't her admirer's last name. It wasn't his first name, either. "Broke" was what the name "Brock" sounded like in Gabriella's thick accent.

Gabriella's admirer was named Brock. As in Officer Brock Boyle. One of the police officers investigating her murder.

This couldn't possibly be good.

"Do you think Gabriella and he were together?" I asked.

"As in having an affair?" Mona scowled. "I never considered that they might be sleeping together, but now that you mention it, maybe. Men were always buzzing around that woman. The affection seemed pretty one-sided, though." She shook her head, disgusted. "I'd have fired her on the spot if I'd realized she was cheating on Michael. That man took good care of her." She leaned back in her chair and crossed her arms. "If she and that loser were sleeping together, I suspect it was over. The last time I saw him, they were arguing out in the parking lot."

"What were they arguing about?" Rene asked.

"I haven't the slightest. Gabriella was speaking in Spanish." Mona's lips wrinkled. "Again. I'd told her before: 'You're in America now. Speak American.' Shouldn't they at least try to learn our language?"

By "they," I assumed she meant Mexicans. I didn't reply.

"Anyway, that Broke guy must be a cop. They were arguing next to a patrol car. I have no idea what Gabby said to him, but he didn't like it. Not one bit. He hauled off and started kicking the car. Broke the headlight and left some pretty decent dents in the bumper. Then he got in and drove away." She huffed. "Our tax dollars at work."

The elderly woman who'd complained earlier waved at Mona. "Ma'am we're ready to leave. Can we get some change?"

Mona placed her palms on her thighs and stood. "That's my line. Any last questions? It's time to lock up and start dinner prep."

"Only one," I said. "Gabriella was trying to raise money. Do you know why?"

Mona shrugged. "I haven't a clue. She shouldn't have been hurting for money, though. That girl was a looker. She made plenty in tips. You know how men are." She nodded at Sam. "No offense."

He nodded back as if to say, *None taken.*

"Maybe she was saving up for something?" Rene asked.

Mona chortled under her breath. "Saving. Now isn't that a novel concept? Sure wish I could do that. I pour my heart and soul into this business, and some Mexican waitress makes more money in tips than I do in profits. All because she has a nice booty."

Mona wrote a phone number in her notebook, ripped out the page, and handed it to Sam. "That's all I know. Call me on Monday and we'll talk about that website you owe me." She hurriedly shuffled to the other table.

Sam folded the paper in half and tucked it into his shirt pocket. He glanced over his shoulder at Mona, then lowered his voice. "Wow, she's some piece of work. Gabriella was murdered, and she's upset because she quit without notice and made decent tips."

Alice started fussing. Rene pulled a binky from a bright yellow pacifier purse and popped it in the infant's mouth. "Are you actually going to make a website for that woman?"

"I told her I would," Sam replied. "I wouldn't feel right if I didn't follow through."

"But she's a bigot!" Rene whispered.

He shrugged. "Honey, I work in high tech. Most of my customers are jerks."

"Jerk is right." I balled up my napkin and tossed it on the table. "Dale might be right."

"About what?" Rene asked

"Immigration is a hot button." I thought for a moment. "Do you think that might be why Gabriella was killed? Because someone thought she was an illegal immigrant, I mean."

"I doubt it," Rene replied. "First, why would anyone think that? You told me Michael and Gabby kept the reasons for their marriage top secret. Second, what moron would be angry enough to kill over it? Seems like a pretty weak motive."

I looked pointedly toward Mona.

Rene shrugged. "Not impossible, I suppose, but I don't see it."

She was right. Even if Mona had gotten angry enough about Gabriella's deception to commit murder, losing a waitress on the busiest week of the year wouldn't have been in her best interest. And I had a feeling Mona always acted in her own best interest.

I sighed. "Unfortunately, I don't see it either. I wonder why Gabriella decided to leave town all of the sudden. Who was she running from?"

"Maybe she wasn't running from anyone," Sam countered. "According to Mona, Gabriella's message only said that she was leaving town, not where she was going or why. For all you know, she was running *to* something."

My phone chirped. Shannon's home number flashed on the screen.

"Finally. It's Michael."

I was wrong.

"Kate, it's Shannon. I just got off the phone with Dale. Michael's back at the police station. You need to come to my house. Now."

FOURTEEN

ANGRY TEARS STREAMED DOWN Shannon's face as she marched up and down the narrow hallway of her Manzanita cottage. "I can't believe those idiots might actually arrest Michael." Her boots clicked staccato drumbeats against the hardwood floor, pummeling my skull like flies buzzing against a window. "This whole fiasco is my fault. I never should have allowed it to happen."

I'd arrived at Shannon's house five minutes earlier, but thus far hadn't gotten anything out of her except panicked grumblings that were frustratingly devoid of specifics. "What, Shannon?" I asked. "What shouldn't you have allowed?"

She stopped pacing and frowned, as if noticing me for the first time. "Did you get a new haircut?"

"Yes, but that's not important." I repeated my prior question: "What shouldn't you have allowed?"

"Michael's marriage to that bloodsucking leech. If he hadn't married Gabriella, she would have been shipped back to Mexico and none of this would have happened." She paused and threw her hands in the air. "I should have just killed her myself." She recommenced pacing.

Shannon was kidding, right? She was frustrated, of that I had zero doubt. The question was, why? Was she worried only about Michael, or was she stressed because her brother might be arrested for a crime that she had committed? Crystal had voted Shannon most likely to have bludgeoned Gabriella, and she knew both women better than I did. Which left me at an impasse: If Shannon was a suspect, I should keep my mouth shut. On the other hand, if she were simply a distressed loved one …

Clunk, clunk, clunk. Each heel strike hammering my head. Not like a fly anymore, like a goddamned jackhammer.

I cradled my forehead in my palms. Lord, I wished I'd brought Bella with me. I needed to calm Shannon, and nothing would do that better than a good dose of Bella therapy. Absent that, it would be up to me.

Then again, how hard could it be? I made my livelihood manufacturing peace.

I grabbed Shannon's hands, pulled her to the living room couch, and spoke in my softest, most soothing yoga voice—a low, rhythmic monotone designed to lull stressed-out students. "Shannon, you need to calm down." I lengthened my breath, making it long, smooth, and subtle. "Why don't we do some breathing exercises?"

She looked at me like I was bonkers, yanked her hands away, and jumped up to standing. "Breathing exercises? Are you insane? Michael's about to be arrested for murder and you want to sit around *breathing*?" She started pacing again. Back and forth, forth and back. Thump, thump, thump.

So much for that idea. Time to try tough love instead.

I grabbed her shoulders and forced her to stop moving. "You told me to get over here, and I came. Now I need you to stop pacing and tell me what in the hell is going on. Was Michael arrested?"

Shannon wiped tears from her cheeks with the back of her hand. "No. At least I don't think so. Not yet. But the police found something."

"What?"

Shannon averted her eyes. I squeezed her shoulders. Hard.

"I don't know," she wailed. "That stupid lawyer friend of yours wouldn't tell me. He got a phone call." She held up her hands. "And before you bruise me again, I don't know who called. But from the look on his face, whatever they told him wasn't good. All I got out of him was that the police had new evidence and they wanted Michael to come to the station. He loaded Michael into that beat-up old pickup truck and they took off."

The prospect of new evidence was concerning, but Michael had been summoned by the police before and Shannon hadn't gotten nearly this upset. She was holding something back. "Shannon, what aren't you saying?"

"Michael made me promise not to tell you. He doesn't want you to worry."

I gaped at her incredulously. "Not worry? Are you kidding me?"

Shannon turned away and squeezed her eyes shut. For a second, I thought she was about to start pacing again. She steeled her jaw and turned back to face me. "Fine. I told Michael it was stupid to keep you in the dark, anyway. The police told him last night that they found Gabby's cell phone on her body. They were able to crack her password and retrieve her stored messages yesterday."

"So?"

"Some of them were from Michael."

"That's not news. We already knew Michael called her." I sounded significantly more confident than I felt. True, I knew that Michael had left Gabriella several phone messages. I didn't, however, know if he'd said anything incriminating.

"You don't understand, Kate. They also retrieved her text messages. They found one from Michael at ten-thirty the night of her murder. He asked Gabriella to meet him on the beach."

I hesitated, confused. When I spoke, my voice quavered, like a child realizing for the first time that Santa Clause was a hoax. "That's not possible. Michael lost his cell phone. He couldn't have used it Tuesday night because he didn't have it. He thought he'd left it at home."

She didn't reply.

"You don't think he's lying?"

"Honestly, Kate, I don't know what to think anymore."

Shannon doubted Michael? Seriously? His own sister, who thought her "baby brother" could do no wrong? My confusion disappeared, replaced by righteous indignation. "What's wrong with you? You know better than that."

Shannon flinched and took several steps back.

Easy, Kate, Dad whispered. *Don't make this worse.*

I took a self-prescribed calming breath and forced my voice to be steady. "That text means nothing. Someone must have stolen Michael's phone. They're using it to frame him."

"Kate, I want to believe that as much as you do, but why would someone frame Michael?"

The obvious answer was, *so they can get away with murder*. But I didn't say that. Frankly, even thinking it made my stomach hurt. If Michael was being framed, proving his innocence might be a heck of a lot harder than I'd imagined. Especially if the person framing him turned out to be one of the investigating officers.

One thing didn't make sense in Shannon's story, though: the timing. "Michael told you about the police finding the text messages last night, right?" I asked.

"Yes."

"But the police called him in to talk about new evidence this afternoon."

"So?"

"Don't you see? They'd already spoken to Michael about the cell phone. They wouldn't have called him in again today for that. They found something else." I met her gaze. "After they searched Gabriella's apartment."

"Oh my lord, you're right. It's even worse than I thought. They have something more than the text message. Something they found in the apartment." Shannon sank onto the couch. "Kate, what do we do now?"

I slumped next to her. "I have no idea. Whatever the police found there, it's gone now."

After a few silent seconds, Shannon spoke. "What if it isn't?"

"What do you mean?"

"I mean, what if the evidence isn't gone?"

I stared at her with a blank expression.

She nibbled her lower lip. "Michael was in the apartment when the police searched it yesterday, remember?" I nodded. "He told me that the police took a few items but not many. Mainly they took lots of photographs and videos. They didn't take her computer, for example. They copied the files onto a flash drive."

"You think there's evidence on Gabriella's computer?"

"Probably not, but that's not my point. I'm just saying, it's possible that the police missed something, or that whatever they found is still there."

I shrugged. "I suppose that's possible …"

"What if we went to the apartment and looked around ourselves?"

"Nice thought, but I already got caught breaking and entering once. I have no desire to repeat the experience. We won't be much good to Michael if we're locked in the cell next to him."

"Who said anything about breaking and entering?" Shannon gestured toward the kitchen. "Come with me." She dug around in the top drawer of the cabinet next to the refrigerator, which was stuffed with a messy assortment of pens, playing cards, rubber bands, and Post-it notes. Three full minutes and a loud "gotcha!" later, she held up a single key attached to an elastic wristband. "Michael used to live in that apartment too, remember? He gave me a key to use in an emergency." She grinned. "Think this qualifies?"

"I'm not sure we should risk it. If we get caught, we might get Michael into more trouble."

"How? The police have already searched the apartment, no one told us to stay away, and I have a key. Besides, if we don't find anything, no one will ever know we were there."

The thought was appealing. We could look around, learn more about Gabriella, and scoot off without anyone being the wiser. Still, there were risks. Maybe get-you-arrested risks. Dad's frowning voice echoed in my head. *Kate, don't do it. Let the police do their jobs. No man is worth an accessory-after-the-fact charge.*

I mumbled under my breath, "Sorry, Dad. You never met Michael." Shannon frowned. "Did you say something?"

I snatched the key from her hand. "Yes. Are you driving or should I?"

———

Cannon Beach rolled up the sidewalks early, even on the Friday of Sandcastle Weekend. At six-thirty, all of the retail shops were closed, leaving only restaurants and the ocean to entice tourists out of their cabins. Shannon parked the Mini Cooper on South Hemlock. We strategized as we walked along the empty sidewalk toward Gabriella's apartment.

"What are we going to say if someone sees us?" I asked.

"Like who?" Shannon countered. "The pet store closes at five. I'm sure tourists will be out in the courtyard, but what will they care? As long as we look like we belong there, no one will think twice."

"What about Crystal's hair salon? It's right below the apartment. She might hear us walking around upstairs and get curious."

"Not a chance. She likes to party, remember? She locks up tight no later than four-thirty on Fridays."

"I don't know... She has a new kitten."

"Crystal's no crazy cat lady. At least she wasn't when I hung out with her. I sincerely doubt a kitten will keep her at work on a Friday night."

"And if you're wrong?" I asked.

"I won't be. But just in case, we'll stop at the salon before we go up to the apartment. If Crystal's there, we'll go home and come back later."

"What excuse will we have for stopping by?"

Shannon grinned. "I suppose saying you need a new haircut is out."

"Funny. Real funny."

She winked. "I'll tell her I'm short-staffed for tomorrow's fun run and ask if she's willing to volunteer. If she says yes, all the better. I could use some extra help."

We walked through the mostly empty courtyard and past the darkened storefront of Puppies in Paradise. Shannon marched confidently up the stairwell, making plenty of noise. I crept stealthily behind her, feeling distinctly uncomfortable.

Shannon stopped at the entrance to CB Cuts and rattled the doorknob.

Locked.

She framed her eyes with her hands and peered around the sign covering the window. "Crystal, are you in there?"

No answer.

"I told you. She always closes early on Fridays." Shannon continued marching upstairs without waiting for me to reply.

Dad chided me from the afterlife. *I have a really bad feeling about this.*

Frankly, so did I, but it was too late to back out now. I glanced down the darkened stairwell a final time to make sure no one was following, then hesitantly tiptoed behind her. When I reached the third-floor landing, Shannon stood outside Gabriella's front door, looking confused.

"No crime scene tape?" she asked.

I shrugged. "It's not a crime scene. Gabriella was killed on the beach, remember?"

"Huh. I'm kind of disappointed." She pulled the apartment key out of her pocket, inserted it into the lock, and jiggled it back and forth.

The door didn't open.

Disappointment-laced relief relaxed my shoulders. "Gabriella must have changed the lock."

"Give me a second," Shannon said. "The door sticks sometimes." She pulled the knob toward her and played with the key. A loud click later, she pumped her fist through the air. "Got it!" The door squeaked open and Shannon marched through it. "Hello? Anyone home?"

She took three steps inside, then froze. "Oh, man." She turned back to me. "I don't think you should come in. Michael wouldn't want you to see this."

"What? Did the police trash the place?" I pushed past her. Visions of upended papers, ripped-open couch cushions, and black fingerprint powder filled my imagination.

The reality was worse. Much worse.

The apartment itself was an adorable juxtaposition of shabbiness and charm. The air inside felt stale, but the homey living room was filled with light. The carpet was threadbare and the fixtures were dated, but the living space was painstakingly decorated. Gabriella had obviously made this place her own. In an odd yet comforting way, I felt like I was finally getting to know her.

She liked color. The room was painted in bright primary colors, and its worn purple couch had been accented by red throw pillows. The sofa faced a picture window with the same courtyard view as the one in Crystal's salon, only one story higher.

The walls were what drew my attention, however, at least at first. They were covered with framed posters, each of which was a gorgeous study in tragedy. They had all been painted by the same artist: Frida Kahlo.

I closed my eyes and sighed. *Of course. Gabriella's tattoo was of Frida.*

Frida Kahlo was the Mexican artist Gabriella had inked on her breast. Her connection to Frida made sense. Both had been beautiful, tragic, talented, and tortured. I walked around the room, examining each poster. The work over the couch was titled *The Wounded Deer*. In it, Ms. Kahlo's head was attached to a deer's body, which had been pierced by a hunter's arrows. An innocent destroyed by an unfair world. In the poster mounted above the fireplace, Ms. Kahlo's spine was broken; her body pierced with nails.

I felt unaccountably sad, as if the heartbreak depicted on each canvas were somehow my own. Had Gabriella simply been an admirer of fine Mexican art, or were her decorations symbolic? Was this how Gabriella saw her life? I reached up and touched the fractured spine, wishing I had the power to heal it.

Then I looked down at the mantle and realized what Shannon hadn't wanted me to see.

A shrine to a life that Michael claimed had never existed.

My own metaphorical spine shattered, slicing my heart into pieces.

In the eight-by-ten portrait farthest to the left, Gabriella smiled at the camera, wearing the white cotton dress she was wearing in the wedding photo taped to Crystal's mirror. She held a vibrant bouquet of yellow, orange, red, and pink Gerbera daisies. Michael gazed adoringly at her in a black tux with a yellow Gerbera daisy boutonniere. In the photograph next to it, the couple shared a wedding kiss so romantic it made my stomach churn.

Next up was a four-photo collage. Michael and Gabriella on the beach, cuddled next to a campfire, hiking in the forest, clinking champagne glasses. If Michael and Gabriella's life together had been the sham Michael claimed it was, why did it look so real?

The shot on the far right was a family one: Michael, Gabriella, and Shannon roasting marshmallows over a bonfire. I recognized the location. It was near the driftwood-strewn alcove in which I'd discovered Gabriella's body.

Shannon startled me from behind. "I'm surprised she kept all of this stuff."

I pointed at the photo of the bonfire. "Who took that?"

Shannon picked up the photo and examined it closely. "I don't remember anymore. Is it important?"

I pointed to the alcove. "That's where I found Gabriella's body. At least I think it is."

"We used to go to that beach all the time. It's less crowded than Haystack Rock." Shannon frowned. "I think this was one of the photo shoots Michael and Gabby staged after the wedding. If so, we used a tripod."

"Why?"

"So all three of us could be in the shot."

"No, I mean why stage a photo shoot?"

"It was part of the show. Proof that Michael and Gabby could show to the feds." She gestured to the mantle. "Gabby and Michael took tons of photos. Of the wedding, fake vacations, a honeymoon. This one was supposed to be of a family gathering." She placed her hand on my shoulder. "The pictures don't mean anything. The last time I was here, they were stored in a box in the closet."

Why didn't that make me feel any better?

She set the frame back on the mantle. "We should start searching. You take the living room and bedroom. I'll take the kitchen and bathroom."

"It would help if we knew what we were looking for," I mumbled.

Shannon shrugged. "Anything." She headed off to the kitchen. I turned to the living room.

The room was neat and organized, proof positive that Michael hadn't lived here for quite some time. I tried to forget about the photos, but Gabriella's eyes burned the back of my neck. Not like she was watching me, exactly. Not like she was mocking me, either. More like she was egging me on. Encouraging me to find something important.

I started with the desk in the corner. I booted up the computer, hoping that Gabriella hadn't used password protection. No such luck. I tried her name, then several iterations of Michael's. Next I tried Frida Kahlo and the titles I'd seen on the living room's posters. No luck there, either. I leaned back and drummed my fingers on the desktop. What else did I know about Gabriella? The answer was *unfortunately nothing*. The cursor blinked at me blandly. *Nice try, yoga girl.* I gave up and tried searching the desk instead.

The top drawer contained pens, papers, paperclips, and staples. The second held envelopes, stationery, and a rubber-banded-together collection of bills. The bill on the top bore a red stamp: *Final Notice*. I slipped off the rubber band and flipped through the rest. Gas, electricity, water, cable. All past due. At the bottom was a credit card statement in Michael's name, maxed out at eight thousand dollars. Minimum amount due, two hundred dollars. Payment due date, yesterday.

Did Michael know he was on the hook for all of this debt?

The answer, of course, was undoubtedly no.

I kept digging and found a checkbook register. If Gabriella's entries were accurate, the account had less than a hundred dollars. For the past three months, she had only recorded equal, biweekly deposits of around six hundred dollars. Her waitressing paycheck, I assumed. Where had all of that supposed tip money gone?

Shannon called from the kitchen. "Kate, come take a look at this."

I folded the credit card bill, tucked it inside my pocket, and joined her. "Find something interesting?"

She handed me a typed letter. "You could say that. This was on the refrigerator. Don't freak out."

I smoothed out the creases and quickly scanned from the top (dated three weeks ago) to Michael's signature on the bottom. I looked up and met Shannon's gaze. "What is this?"

"It looks like a love letter." She lifted her eyebrows apologetically. "I told you not to freak out."

My mouth filled with cotton, but I forced myself to read anyway, at least the parts that I could understand. Much of the letter was written in Spanish. It ended with a promise. *My darling, being away from you has been harder than I ever imagined. I promise, we will be together again soon, this time forever. Te amo, mi cariño. Michael.*

I turned the page over and examined the back. Blank. "Was there an envelope?" I asked.

"No. Just this, stuck to the refrigerator."

I held it up to the light, hoping to decipher a hidden message.

"What are you doing?" Shannon asked.

"Looking for the punch line."

"You think this is a joke? It doesn't seem very funny to me."

"I have no idea what it is, but it's not from Michael."

"I hate to second-guess you, Kate, but how do you know?"

"First off, who types a love letter?" She didn't reply. I handed her the paper. "Second, look at that signature. It's not Michael's hand-writing."

Shannon's voice matched her incredulous expression. "You think Gabby forged a love letter to herself and then hung it on the fridge?"

"Either that or someone was deliberately trying to deceive her."

Shannon handed the note back to me. "That doesn't make any sense."

I folded the page and stuck it next to the credit card statement in my pocket. "You're right, but none of this makes any sense. Let's keep looking. Maybe she has more letters somewhere."

We searched the rest of the kitchen. Nothing but the usual assort-ment of pots, pans, utensils, and a surprisingly well-organized junk drawer. The refrigerator and pantry were essentially bare, except for a couple of cartons of yogurt, a box of saltine crackers, and a bottle of desiccated-looking ketchup. "I guess Gabriella wasn't much of a cook."

Shannon shrugged. "I don't know. The few times I came over, Michael did the cooking." She waved her hand around the empty space. "There's nothing here. I'm going to search the bathroom."

While Shannon moved on to the bathroom, I headed to the bed-room, which was also decorated with Frida Kahlo posters. The dresser top displayed more candid photos of Michael and Gabriella next to a jewelry box filled with costume jewelry. No rings, wedding or otherwise. After twenty minutes of searching Gabriella's bed-room, all I'd concluded was that she had great taste in lingerie and a truly kick-butt shoe collection.

What was I missing? There was something important in this apartment. I could feel it, as clearly as Bella felt the mailman turning onto her block. But what was it and where?

I flopped across the bed and stared at the poster mounted above it, frustrated. *The Two Fridas* stared back at me. The heart of the

Frida on the left had been ripped open. The Frida on the right's heart was still whole. Which one represented Gabriella?

I spoke to the painting, pretending that I was speaking to Gabriella. "What are you trying to tell me?"

The poster didn't reply, at least not verbally.

Nonverbally, though...

I stood. My woo-woo yoga teacher senses were vibrating at high alert. The energy emanating from this portrait was strong. If I allowed myself to be vulnerable, what would it tell me? I glanced at the open doorway to make sure Shannon wasn't looking, then placed my palm against Left Frida's oozing heart. I closed my eyes, quieted my mind, and took a deep breath.

Come on, Gabriella, talk to me.

"Kate, what on earth are you doing?"

Shannon's voice startled me, and I jumped. I whipped around to face her, knocking the poster off-kilter. It crashed onto the bedspread with a muffled thud, toppled over, and landed facedown.

"Shannon, you startled me!" I chided.

She ignored me and pointed at the back of the frame. "What are those?"

She was pointing at envelopes. Five of them, each stuffed a quarter-inch thick. I pulled off the first and tore it open.

A stack of hundred-dollar bills stared back at me.

FIFTEEN

BY THE TIME SHANNON and I had finished taking down all of the artwork, we'd counted almost twelve thousand dollars.

"I don't get it," Shannon said. "Didn't you say Gabby's bills were all past due?" I nodded. "Why would she risk having her electricity and water turned off if she had all of this money?"

"I'm not positive, but I have a theory." I dialed Dale's cell phone. For the first time in twenty-four hours, my call didn't go to voice-mail. "Dale, thank goodness you answered. We need to talk. I found out some useful information today." By *we*, I meant everyone who'd helped with my sleuthing efforts thus far, including Shannon, Sam, and Rene.

Dale squashed that idea with a firm, absolute, no-arguing-allowed no. He did, however, reluctantly agree to bring Michael—who hadn't been arrested yet, thank goodness—to the beach house so I could meet with him in Dale's presence. Shannon was far from happy at being excluded, but she acquiesced.

Michael and Dale still had business to finish, so we agreed to meet in an hour and a half. I picked up my car at Shannon's and promised to fill her in on everything I was allowed to share when I saw her the next day at the fun run. In the meantime, she vowed to quiz Michael herself later that night.

Since Dale forbade anyone but the three of us from being present, Sam and Rene decided to go out for a late dinner in Seaside. Nine o'clock was well past the babies' bedtime, so I agreed to babysit.

"I just finished nursing them," Rene said, "so they should sleep for a few hours. But if they wake up and get fussy, I have some backup breast milk in the fridge."

"Are you sure you're okay being booted out of the house?" I asked.

Sam smiled. "Are you kidding? A night out on the town with my sexy wife while you're stuck here playing slave to our evil progeny? Consider yourself lucky if we come back." His eyes grew serious. "Tell Michael to keep the faith, okay?"

Bella minded the puppies while I checked on the girls, who were fast asleep dressed in animal print onesies—one giraffe, one elephant. I lightly brushed Alice's cheek with my fingertips, blew Amelia a good night kiss, carried the baby monitor downstairs, and poured myself a glass of oaky Chardonnay. I took a deep drink, sighed, and refilled the glass. Resolutions to cut back on drinking be damned. Tonight I needed liquid courage.

Dale's pickup coughed in the driveway. I threw open the door and for the first time in what felt like a decade, wrapped Michael in a huge, heartfelt hug. "I'm so glad to see you."

"I should get almost-arrested more often." Michael smiled, but the movement seemed forced. Purple-blue smudges bruised the skin under his eyes.

"You look exhausted," I said.

He reached up and brushed the ends of my hair, which were a good eight inches shorter than the last time he'd seen them. "You look fabulous." I would have chided him for being sarcastic, but the look in his eyes was sincere. I could only assume that exhaustion had struck him blind.

Dale strode purposefully through the door, all traces of Southern façade gone. "Where can we meet without being overheard?"

"The house is all ours." I smiled, trying to lighten the mood. "Except for the twins, and they're no problem. They can't talk yet, so they won't be able to testify." I pinched my chin between my thumb and my forefinger, pretending to think. "Bella, however, may be a problem. We taught her how to speak on command."

Dale's stern expression remained firmly in place.

I wiggled my eyebrows. "You know, *speak*. As in bark?"

Nothing.

"It was a joke." I shrugged. "I guess it wasn't that funny."

Dale's whiskers trembled. "Nothing about this is funny, Kate. I'm one hundred percent serious. You should be, too."

So much for my stand-up comedy routine.

"I am serious, Dale," I replied. "Nobody's here except the three of us, the babies, and the dogs. Let's go to the living room." I led them inside and sat on the couch. Michael kneeled next to Bella, who was resting on a throw rug, two exhausted puppies curled up next to her chest. She lifted her head, thumped her tail, and flopped back onto her side. An exhausted mother trying not to wake her rambunctious children.

Michael rubbed her ears, assured her that she was a good girl, and sat next to me. Dale, still all business, perched on the edge of a guest chair and pulled out a legal pad.

"Okay, Kate. Talk."

"That's not how this is going to work, Dale." I replied. "You two have been shutting me out, and I'm tired of it."

"We haven't—"

"Save it, Dale. I know you've both been screening my calls." I turned to Michael. "And Shannon told me about that text message the police found. You know. The one where you supposedly asked Gabriella to meet you at the beach?"

Michael peered at me earnestly. "I didn't send that text, Kate, I swear."

"Michael!" Dale scolded. "We talked about this. We are here to get information from Kate, not give it to her. Say nothing about your case—to anyone—unless I explicitly give you permission to do so."

Now I was getting cranky. "Come on, Dale. This is me, remember?" I gestured to Michael. "I'm on his side."

Dale opened his mouth to snark back, then closed his eyes and dropped his head. "God, I hate this." When he lifted his face again, his expression had softened. "Kate, you're my friend. Hell, you're practically family."

I waited for the "but." He didn't disappoint.

"But not tonight. Tonight, I'm Michael's attorney. You are a witness in the case against him. Lord knows what the DA will ask you if the case goes to trial. I'm sorry, but that means we'll have to keep some secrets from you. Got it?"

I didn't like it. Hell, let's be honest. I hated it. But I understood. I would have told Dale that I agreed, but I didn't get the chance. Michael interrupted.

"I don't care."

We both turned to him, confused.

"No more secrets. Not from Kate. That's what got me into this mess to begin with. I'm telling her everything." Dale started to argue, but Michael stopped him. "I'm serious, Dale. You're my attorney, and you're probably right. But this is my life. My decision. Kate hears everything."

Dale's lips grew so thin, they disappeared in his whiskers, but he remained silent.

Michael took my hand. "I didn't send any texts to Gabriella that night. I didn't have my cell phone, remember? I thought I'd left it at Shannon's, but maybe it got taken shortly after I went out."

"You think someone stole it?"

Michael shrugged. "It's the only theory that makes sense."

My spirit lightened. That might be good news. "If you're right, your phone might lead to the killer." I glanced at Dale, feeling suddenly hopeful. "Can we trace it?"

Dale shook his head. "The police already tried. No luck."

"Seriously?" I asked.

"Don't believe everything you see on TV," Dale said. "It's darned near impossible to track a cell phone that's been turned off. If the battery's been pulled, no one can do it. Not even the CIA."

Ugh.

I hated what I was about to say next, but I had to get it out in the open, for Michael as much as for me. "Michael, you blacked out. When you woke up, you were parked near that beach. What if you … what if you did something that you don't remember?"

Michael dropped my hand and jumped to his feet. "Kate, how can you ask that? How can you even think it? I'd never kill anyone. Especially not someone I cared about."

"Settle down, Michael," Dale interjected. "She's not saying anything that the prosecuting attorney won't say."

"Dale's right," I said, "but that's not what I mean. I know you didn't kill Gabriella, honey. You're not capable of that level of viciousness. It's not in your DNA." I paused. "But are you sure you didn't text her?"

For the first time all evening, Dale agreed with me. "It's the weakest part of our case, Michael. If you don't remember what you *did* do that night, how can anyone know for sure what you didn't?"

Michael's jaw clenched. "Actually, I do know. I got wasted, made an ass out of myself, and passed out in a pile of my own puke. I'm an idiot, but the only life I was hell bent on destroying that night was my own. Even if I'd had my phone, I wouldn't have asked Gabriella to meet me alone on a deserted beach after dark. It wouldn't have been safe for her."

I believed him. "Why didn't you shut off your cell service when you noticed that the phone was missing?"

"I assumed it would turn up at Shannon's. I didn't figure out that it had been stolen until the police cornered me about that text message."

Michael's story made sense. Not that a jury would believe it.

"I wish you'd told me about this last night." I thought for a moment. "Though I'm not sure it changes anything I learned today."

"Which was?" Dale asked.

"In a minute. You haven't told me everything yet. Shannon said the police have new evidence."

In spite of Michael's earlier resolve, he shot Dale a questioning look before answering. Dale gave him a single, curt nod yes.

"Two new pieces of evidence, actually. They found a hundred-thousand-dollar life insurance policy in Gabriella's files."

"Life insurance on Gabriella?"

"Yes."

I had a feeling I knew the answer, but I asked anyway. "Who's the beneficiary?"

"Me."

"Did you know about it?"

"Yes. I have a policy with her as the beneficiary, too. We took them out when we got married. It was all part of legitimizing the marriage. Both names on the apartment lease, joint credit cards, life insurance policies, photos. The feds put green card marriages under the microscope these days. We didn't want to take any chances."

"How could you afford such high life insurance policies?"

"We were young and healthy, so the premiums were cheap. We joked that it was our form of a lottery ticket. We planned to cancel them as soon as she got citizenship."

I leaned back and frowned. "If Gabriella needed money so badly, why all the drama over the divorce? It would have been more lucrative to kill you."

"Your joke's not nearly as funny as you think," Dale replied. "That insurance policy gives Michael a hundred thousand more reasons to want Gabriella dead."

The heart-wrenching cry of an unhappy infant screeched through the baby monitor. Bella lifted her head and stared toward the sound, ears pricked forward with concern. If I didn't act quickly, a second baby's scream would soon follow. "Hold that thought. I'll be right back."

I jogged up the stairs and picked up a giraffe-spotted Amelia. Alice slept in the crib next to her like an elephant-adorned angel. I carried Amelia back to the living room, bouncing her against my hip and cooing. "Who's one of the two cutest babies in the world?"

Amelia was obviously Rene's child; flattery worked every time. She stopped crying and reached for my locket, transfixed by the shiny gold.

I allowed her to play with it and continued the conversation where we'd left off. "Okay. So Michael had a life insurance policy on Gabriella. Lots of married couples have life insurance. He already had motive; he wanted a divorce. How is having life insurance that much worse?"

Michael's face turned from gray to a sickly, yellowish green. Neither he nor Dale would make eye contact with me. Dale finally spoke. "There's something else. The medical examiner released the results of Gabriella's autopsy."

I stopped bouncing Amelia. "Were the police wrong about her cause of death?"

Dale shook his head. "No. She was beaten to death, probably by a piece of driftwood. They found wood particles in her skull."

Grisly, but not new information. "Did they match it to the driftwood at the scene?"

"They're still testing, but not so far," Dale replied. "I suspect the murder weapon is floating somewhere out in the ocean, probably with Michael's cell phone."

"Then what did they find?" I asked.

Both men remained silent.

"Spit it out already!"

Michael swallowed hard, as if trying to clear a bone lodged in his throat. "Gabriella was three months pregnant."

I sagged against the arm of the couch, hugging Amelia close. *Of course.*

Part of me felt distraught. Horrified, even. Gabriella's murderer had ended two lives. But mainly I felt a sort of weird, melancholy resolution. "Of course she was pregnant. I should have known."

"The baby wasn't mine, Kate, I swear. I hadn't seen Gabriella in years."

"I know, Michael. That's not what I mean. Gabriella's pregnancy explains everything. Why she was demanding money from you, why she was running up bills while stockpiling cash, why she was running away."

Dale set down his legal pad. "Stockpiling cash? Running away? What are you talking about?"

I filled them in on everything I'd learned in the past twenty-four hours: that Gabriella had left a voicemail message quitting her job the night of the murder, that she was past due on her bills, and that we'd found almost twelve thousand dollars in cash hidden behind her artwork. Dale was so fascinated by the new information that he forgot to chastise me for searching Gabriella's apartment. I finished by handing him a brown paper bag containing the cash-filled envelopes we'd discovered.

Dale opened the bag, glanced inside, and closed it again. "That's a lot of cash to carry around in a grocery bag."

I shrugged. "I grabbed the bag at Gabriella's apartment. I was afraid to leave the money there, so I decided to bring it to you."

Michael's expression flickered between confusion and astonishment. "How did Gabriella stockpile that much money? She made decent tips, but the cost of living in Cannon Beach is almost as bad as Seattle. Worse, in some ways. Without me to help cover the rent, Gabriella must have been living paycheck to paycheck."

"At least part of it came from cash withdrawals on your joint credit card." I handed him the statement. "She stopped paying most of her other bills two months ago." Michael scanned the paper. His brow furrowed. "I think she was stockpiling cash so she could disappear without being traced. That's why she wanted money from you, too. She even asked Crystal for a loan, supposedly to help you pay off business debts."

Michael groaned. "She was planning to stick me with this whole mess, wasn't she?"

"Probably," I admitted. I glanced down at Amelia. Warmth surged from her tiny body to the core of my heart. "Don't judge her too harshly, Michael. I think she was protecting her child."

"What makes you say that?" Dale asked.

"The timing. She started racking up bills and scamming for money two months ago, which is right about the time she would have realized that she was pregnant." Amelia cooed, as if agreeing with me. "My only question is, why pull the trigger on Tuesday?"

"What do you mean?" Michael asked.

"Mona said Gabriella was a good employee. Was she?"

He nodded.

"Then she wouldn't have liked leaving Mona in a lurch. Besides, there was no reason for her to leave before Sandcastle Weekend. She would have raked in tons of tips. She was still in the first trimester, so she could easily have hidden the pregnancy for another week or two. She didn't have much food, but I didn't see any evidence that she'd started packing, did you?"

Michael shook his head no.

"The money she'd stockpiled was still hidden, too." I kissed the top of Amelia's head. "I'm telling you, Gabriella thought she had more time. Something happened on Tuesday. Something that made her speed up her plans."

"Maybe the father found out," Michael volunteered.

Dale frowned. "Which begs the question, who in the hell is he?"

"Can't they do a DNA test?" I asked.

"Only if they have something to compare it to. The police asked Michael for a sample today, but I wouldn't let them take it. I told them to get a court order."

"Why? A DNA test would prove Michael's innocence."

"No, it wouldn't. It would only prove that Michael wasn't the baby's father. That could hurt us. The DA may claim that Michael killed Gabriella because he found out that she was cheating on him. At this point, our best strategy is to slow the investigation down. The longer we keep Michael out of jail, the more time I'll have to dismantle the prosecution's case."

I walked with Amelia to the window and stared out at the darkness. Rhythmic white waves crashed in the moonlight, stark harbingers against a backdrop of black. Mesmerizing. Disconcerting. Haunting.

"Michael, how often did you speak with Gabriella?" I asked.

"I contacted her to ask for a divorce two months ago, right after you told me you were ready to start a family. Before that, I hadn't spoken to her since I left Cannon Beach. I was trying to start my life over."

"And since then?"

"A few times. Enough for me to realize that she was serious about wanting money for the divorce."

"Did she ever mention that she was seeing someone?"

"Not once."

I thought about the mysterious stranger I'd seen twice now. "I still wonder about that creepy-looking guy."

"What creepy-looking guy?" Dale asked.

"The one I saw lurking around both the spaghetti dinner and Gabriella's apartment. Remember? I thought he might be Gabriella's ex-boyfriend from Mexico."

"Gabriella was terrified of her ex. She would never have taken him back."

"Well, whoever that guy is, he's up to something. As soon as he saw me watching him yesterday, he took off. I chased him down an alley, but he disappeared before I could catch him."

"You what?" Michael leaped to his feet, startling Bella out of her cat nap. "Kate, what the hell? Do you have some sort of death wish?"

Michael's loud, cranky voice woke Amelia, who started wailing again. Alice's plaintive cry joined over the baby monitor. I glanced up at Dale. "Do you mind?" He jogged upstairs to retrieve her.

I rocked Amelia back and forth. "Don't be scared, little baby. He's just a big, grumpy caveman protecting the little cavewoman." I lowered my voice, pretending to whisper. "Your mama would kick his ass."

"Not funny, Kate."

I sighed. "I know it's not. But you're in real trouble, Michael. The last thing you should be worried about is me jogging down an alley."

Dale appeared behind me, cradling an unhappy infant. "I'm with Michael. Chasing a stranger—any stranger—was a boneheaded move."

I ignored them both and paced back and forth, trying to soothe Amelia back to sleep.

"Let's say you're right," Dale replied. "Let's say this guy—whoever he is—killed Gabriella. Why would he still be loitering around?"

My reply came out sharper than I'd intended, but I was frustrated. Submitting to male overprotectiveness had never been my strong suit. "How should I know? You're the defense attorney. You tell me. Why do criminals return to the scene of their crimes? Guilt? Fear? Keeping tabs on the investigation?" Dale didn't answer. "My point is, someone should question him."

"How do you propose we find him?" Dale asked.

"Cannon Beach is a small town. Someone is bound to know who he is. Rene and I could ask around and see if anybody recognizes his description."

Michael rolled his eyes. "Why stop there? Why not meet with a sketch artist and publish the drawing in the *Clatsop County Herald*? Be sure to tell everyone your address and offer a reward like you did when George was killed. That strategy worked out so well the first time."

"Michael, I told you before not to—"

Dale stepped between us, hugging Alice close to his chest. "Knock it off you two." He reached for Amelia with his free arm. "Give me that baby before you traumatize her." He gently took Amelia, made kissy noises at both babies, and then leveled a stern look at Michael and me. "Sit. Both of you."

Michael and I gave each other looks that clearly said *This isn't over*, then claimed opposite ends of the couch. Dale disappeared up the stairway. Bella abandoned the pups, jumped between us, and rested her chin on Michael's thigh, leaving me with a much less attractive end. Traitor.

Dale returned a few minutes later and spoke as if our conversation had never been interrupted. "Kate, if you see that guy again, don't chase him. Call me. If I don't answer, call 911 and report a prowler.

The police probably won't get there in time to catch him, but it will put him on their radar. That's the best we can do for now."

Which reminded me of Boyle. "Speaking of the police, I have another suspect." I told Dale and Michael everything I'd learned from Mona about Officer Boyle. "I hate to suspect a police officer, but in this case, I can't help it. He and Gabriella may or may not have had an affair, but he had some sort of interest in her. Mona saw them arguing. From the sounds of it, he got violent."

Michael frowned. "He certainly seemed protective of Gabriella the other night at the spaghetti dinner. He hasn't exactly been friendly to me since then, either. Then again, none of the cops have."

"They wouldn't be," Dale replied. "Unless they were trying to scam you into a confession, and I haven't let them get you alone long enough to do that." He picked up his legal pad. "How sure are you about this…" He looked down at his notes. "This Mona. Any chance she was lying or simply mistaken?"

Michael shook his head. "Mona's not perfect, but she's sharp and she's got a good heart. In spite of her bias against immigrants, she gave Gabby a job when no one else would. I don't think she'd lie."

"I agree," I said, then corrected myself. "Not about the good heart. She seemed like a garden-variety bigot to me."

Michael frowned. "People aren't simply good or evil, Kate. They're complex. Don't be so quick to judge. Gabriella learned how to get along with Mona, and she had a lot more reason to resent her than you do."

I felt my face redden, mainly because he was right. Example number 483 of how Michael forced me to be a better person. "Well, complex or not, I never got the sense that she was lying about the argument."

Dale's expression had darkened.

"This is bad, isn't it?" I asked.

"It's not good. To my knowledge, this Boyle character hasn't divulged any relationship with the victim, and he should have. At best, he's biased. At worst, he may be framing Michael."

Michael paled. I reached across Bella's back and took his hand.

"So what do we do now?" I asked.

"That's a good question," Dale replied. "I have to handle this carefully. If one of the investigating officers is the killer, I can't trust the evidence. Then again, I don't dare accuse Boyle without some proof of my own. It could come back to bite Michael." His shoulders squared. "It's time to up my game. I'm hiring a private investigator."

"I can't afford that," Michael replied. I opened my mouth to argue, but he stopped me. "Neither can you, Kate."

"I can if I sell the house."

"Not yet," Dale said.

"Not ever," Michael said louder.

I drowned out both of them. "It's my house."

Dale stood and raised his hand in the universal *stop* sign. "Settle down, both of you, and listen. I have a PI friend in Portland who owes me a favor. Let me talk to him before you do anything rash. Michael, if you get arrested, you'll need the house as collateral for bail. Provided I can get you bail, that is."

Michael buried his face in his hands. "How did everything get so messed up?"

It was an excellent question. I wanted to assure Michael that everything would turn out okay, but I would have been lying. I had a terrible feeling that things might not ever be okay again.

Dale broke the silence. "I'll go to Portland tomorrow."

"Why not just call?" I asked. "Shouldn't you stay here?"

Dale was adamant. "Trust me, I'm a helluva lot more persuasive in person."

"What should Michael and I do while you're gone?"

"For now, nothing. And in case I'm not being clear, that means no amateur sleuthing. No searching apartments, no interviewing suspects, no trying to corner wayward police officers."

He couldn't be serious. "Dale, I —"

"I said *for now*, Kate. I need time to think. Give me twenty-four hours. I'll talk to my investigator friend and formulate a plan."

"What if Michael gets arrested in the meantime?"

"He won't. At least I don't think he will. I raised a pretty big stink at the station today. I suspect that the police will wait for a court-ordered DNA test before they move forward with any arrests. Besides, tomorrow's that sandcastle contest. Small-town cops are much more efficient than television would lead you to believe, but a huge event like the one tomorrow will drain their resources. I suspect they'll wait until Sunday before they focus on Michael. Keep your heads low, spend the day at the festival, and try not to think about anything serious. Enjoy your time together." He paused. "While you still can."

SIXTEEN

In the end I agreed, albeit reluctantly, to part of Dale's advice. Michael and I would take the day off from investigating Gabriella's murder and attend the Sandcastle Festival together. Dale was right. The festival would give us a short reprieve, and lord knew we could use it.

As for not thinking about anything serious? Good luck with that. In spite of Dale's reassurances, I didn't hold any illusions. Michael could be arrested at any moment. We needed to have a conversation about our relationship, and if I didn't want to hold it through a sheet of bullet-proof Plexiglas, we needed to have it soon.

Shortly after ten, Dale headed back to Shannon's, vowing to tell her nothing and imploring Michael and me not to talk to anyone either, Rene and Sam included. I asked Michael to stay overnight at Rene's. "In one of the guest rooms," I added. "I'm ready to talk about our future, but no promises on anything else."

I took the pups outside for a potty break, then put them to bed in their playpen. Michael grabbed a Guinness and poured me another glass of wine. "For strength," he said.

He took a long pull from the bottle and followed me back to the living room. I ordered Bella off the couch and patted the seat next to me. Michael took it but sat ramrod straight, so far from relaxed I was afraid his spine might shatter.

I wasn't sure how to begin, so I started with the most obvious topic: Gabriella. "I know that your marriage with Gabriella was a sham, but that doesn't explain everything. Neither does Shannon's story, which is that you and Gabriella were 'friends with benefits.'"

Michael didn't reply, so I continued. "I need to know what she meant to you. Did you simply fall in lust?" It wasn't exactly what Shannon had said, but it was close. And all things considered, that would have been the easiest explanation—the one most easily forgiven. Boys will be boys and all that. I didn't buy it, though. Not with Michael. Michael simply wasn't that shallow.

Michael thought for a moment, as if unsure how to answer. Not because he was hiding something, but because he didn't know himself.

"No. At least I don't think so."

I'd been afraid he'd say that. "Michael, tell me the truth. Did you love her?"

"I love *you*, Kate." Michael's smile was more sad than romantic. "Like I told you before, Gabby's and my relationship was complicated. Looking back on it now, I think we were codependent. I was her white knight, destined to save her. She was my damsel in distress. Believe me, Kate, our relationship wasn't healthy, for either of us." He ran his fingers across the label of his beer bottle. "I wasn't completely honest with you earlier."

Big surprise there.

"Gabby and I dated for a couple of months. We started to get serious, fast. For a very short time, I thought she was the one." He sighed. "Then I woke up. I couldn't deal with all of the drama. Gabby was intelligent, beautiful, and sensitive, but she was also damaged. I'm pretty sure she had PTSD. She picked fights with me constantly. In some broken, subconscious way, I think she was trying to prove me worthy."

"You must have passed her test."

"What do you mean?"

"She trusted you."

"You could have fooled me. If she'd trusted me, she would have been honest. Instead, she stonewalled me and stuck me with a bill for a maxed-out credit card."

"That was to protect the baby." Deep in my gut, I knew it was true. "And she had enough faith in you to marry you, even if the marriage wasn't real. That has to mean something."

Michael sighed. "I suppose." He looked down at the sofa. "She told me that I was the first man in her life who didn't force her to sleep with him." His voice grew soft. "Including her father." When his eyes met mine, they were wet. "That's what killed me. It was like life set her up to be victimized. Her father abused her until she ran away at sixteen. She ended up on the streets, where she was 'discovered' by a modeling agent who got her addicted to cocaine. Every guy was worse than the one before. Then that last boyfriend..." Michael shuddered. "He almost killed her, Kate."

I thought back to my recent conversation with Shannon. She was firmly convinced that Gabriella had been using Michael. Could she have been right? "It's a horrible story." I softened my voice to take the sting out of my words. "But are you sure it's the truth?"

"I saw the scars, Kate, and not just the physical ones. Gabby wasn't mentally healthy. How could she be? The few times she and I were together physically, she had panic attacks. She lashed out at me like I was abusing her all over again."

His words surprised me. "Shannon told me that you and Gabriella had a more... satisfying love life than that."

"She told you that our relationship was one big sex party?"

"Not in those exact words."

Michael grimaced. "I can only imagine. That's what Shannon wanted to believe, and I let her. Gabby didn't want people to know about her past. It was important to her to seem..." His voice trailed off. "To seem normal, I guess." His eyes begged for understanding. "Kate, I'm a good man—at least I try to be—but I wasn't strong enough." He took a long swig of beer. I had a feeling he was gathering the courage to continue. "So I broke up with her. I felt terrible, but honestly, I think she was relieved. We ended up being much better as friends."

I paused for a moment, trying to reconcile the person in Michael's story with the man I'd come to love. Michael *was* a good man. He might not believe it, but he was also a strong man, with healthy boundaries. If I hadn't been able to change, our relationship would have ended a year ago. Yet another reminder of how Michael forced me to grow.

But Gabby wasn't me. My support systems—my roots—were solid. I was healthy enough to change. Gabriella's roots had been rotted—poisoned by men who should have protected her. The more I learned about her, the more I understood her attraction to Frida Kahlo. A beautiful woman. Physically damaged. Emotionally lost. A woman with tumultuous intimate relationships—with women as well as with men.

I paused for a moment, not sure how to phrase what I needed to ask next. "You keep mentioning the men in Gabriella's life. What about the women?"

Michael's eyes grew bitter. "Her mother was no better than anyone else. She knew about the father's abuse—she certainly knew about the beatings—and she did nothing."

"What about Gabriella's relationships with other women? Besides her mother, I mean."

Michael's expression softened from bitter to confused. "What are you getting at?"

"The artist tattooed on Gabriella's breast may have been more symbolic than you realized. She was bisexual. Von thinks that Gabriella and Crystal were closeted lovers. I didn't buy it for a while, but now I wonder ..."

Michael jolted in surprise. Then his eyes widened. "Von thinks they're gay? As in not interested in men?" His eyes moved up and toward the left. "I wouldn't have guessed that. Not of either of them."

I shrugged. "Not gay, necessarily. One or both of them could have been bisexual. Or experimenting, for that matter.

He took another long swig of beer, thinking. "Maybe. It would explain why Gabby and I worked so much better as friends. Also why Crystal and Gabby got so close after I left. They certainly weren't friends when I lived here."

We were both silent for several long seconds, serenaded only by the occasional contented snuffle through the twins' baby monitor.

"One thing about that theory doesn't make sense, though." I ran my hands through my hair. "When Crystal gave me this delightful haircut, she described you and Gabby as a devoted couple. She was downright cranky when she figured out that I was your 'mistress.'" I made finger quotes around the last word. "She never hinted that Gabriella was anything more than a friend."

"Would she, though? If they weren't going public, that is? Cannon Beach is pretty liberal, but it's still a small town. Besides, what would a closeted relationship have to do with Gabby's murder?"

"If they were lovers, Crystal had motive."

Michael looked at me quizzically.

"Gabriella was pregnant, which by definition means she'd had sex with someone other than Crystal. And she was planning to bolt.

From the looks of it, she was planning to leave town alone. Cheating and abandonment? People have killed for a lot less."

Michael set his beer bottle on the floor. "I don't know, Kate. Something seems off in that scenario. Crystal struck me as a little obsessive, so I could definitely see her lashing out if she was jilted. But every time I saw her flirting—and I saw her flirting a lot—she was trying to seduce a man. Usually me. And if Gabby truly was gay, how did she end up pregnant?"

"If her history with men is any indication, it may not have been her choice."

Michael closed his eyes and groaned. "I don't want to think about that right now, Kate. I just can't."

"Okay. I understand. But we need to bring it up with Dale tomorrow. We shouldn't dismiss any suspects—no matter how unlikely—until we find the real killer." I'd mull over how to handle Crystal's accusations about Shannon later. Michael had already gone through enough mental drama tonight.

Well, almost enough.

I reached into my pocket and pulled out the letter from Gabriella's refrigerator. "You were at the apartment during the police search, right?"

"For most of the time."

"Did you notice anything unusual?"

"Not really, but I wasn't exactly looking around. I basically stuck to the living room and tried to avoid Boyle. I didn't see any envelopes stuffed with money, if that's what you're asking."

"No, I mean the pictures of you and Gabriella." I swallowed. "There were a lot of them. In the living room and in the bedroom."

"We were creating a fictional life, Kate. We needed more than a single wedding snapshot."

"Shannon told me that they weren't on display when you lived in the apartment."

"A couple of them were, but no, not all of them. Not by a long shot. I assume Gabriella put them up after I left. Having us plastered all over the house probably made my moving raise fewer suspicions."

I handed him the paper. "What about this?"

Michael glanced at it, then did a double take. His eyes slowly scanned the letter from beginning to end. When he finished, he handed it back to me. "Where did this come from?"

"Gabriella had it on display in the kitchen."

"I didn't write it, Kate. I swear."

"I know. Any idea who did? Could it have been Gabriella?"

Michael examined the signature. "I'm not sure. Maybe."

"Shannon gave me the gist of it, but I don't speak Spanish. What does it say?"

"Not much. Just that I miss her and I'll be back for her soon. This letter makes no sense. Why would she write it to herself? Displaying the photos, sure. I get that. Anyone who stopped by would see them. But how many guests would feel they should read a personal letter?"

I didn't have an answer. It didn't make sense to me either.

Michael stood. "Look, I'm exhausted. Can we start this conversation again in the morning? Maybe it will all make sense after a good night's sleep."

Part of me wanted to let him go. The man was obviously dead on his feet. I couldn't. Dale might be confident, but I wasn't: Michael could be arrested at any moment. The time for avoidance was over, whether I liked it or not.

"Not yet. We need to talk about us."

Michael sagged back onto the couch, looking deflated. Like he knew where the conversation was headed and didn't want to go there.

I took a deep breath and forced myself to speak. "Michael, I get it now. I understand why you felt compelled to help Gabriella even though it meant breaking the law. The more I learn about her, the more I wish I could have helped her myself."

Michael replied with a single word. "But?"

"But what I don't understand—what I can't understand—is why in the eighteen months we've been together, you never told me."

Michael's jaw tensed, but he didn't speak. His silence was punctuated only by a ticking clock and the rumble of Bella's contented snoring. I continued. "Committing to our relationship was tough for me, Michael. You knew that. Why screw it up this way?"

He stood and walked to the fireplace. "I wasn't the only one who avoided talking about my past, Kate. You hid plenty from me, too."

He was right. I'd let him believe that my mother was dead, at least until she got arrested for murder. An indiscretion about which I'd been chastised severely.

"You're right, I did. And you hated it, which is what upsets me the most. How could you harass me about not being open with you when you were hiding something epic—a marriage, for God's sake—from me?"

Michael kneeled next to Bella and rubbed her neck, I assumed to avoid making eye contact. "Would you believe me if I said it seemed like a good idea at the time?"

I didn't reply. Then again, I don't think he expected me to.

He stood and faced me again. "I don't know, Kate. I liked you when we first met, but I never intended to get serious with anyone. Then we had that amazing first date and I fell for you."

"I fell for you, too."

"Really? Sure didn't feel like it at the time. You were like that Katy Perry song. You ran so hot and cold, I felt like I was dating two different people."

I nodded. "I was pretty crazy there for a while."

"With all of the fighting we did, I didn't think we'd be together long enough for my arrangement with Gabby to matter."

"How could it not matter?"

"I was only married on paper, so I wasn't cheating, and you acted like you'd never commit to a long-term relationship. You practically dog paddled across Puget Sound when you thought I was going to propose on Orcas."

His memory of that weekend wasn't exaggerated, unfortunately.

"After the deaths on Orcas, you changed. We got serious. By the time we moved in together. I thought it was too late."

"Too late to be honest with me?"

He didn't reply, at least not directly. "No matter how often we discussed our future, you never mentioned getting married. Not once. Given what had happened between Dharma and your father, I assumed you were against it."

"Even when I started talking about having kids?"

"That was only two months ago. Like I said, by then it felt way too late. So I decided to ask Gabby for a low-key divorce." He frowned. "I deluded myself that you'd never need to know."

"That's pretty lame, Michael."

"I was a coward. I know that now. Believe me, though, I never meant to hurt you."

"But you did. You hurt me a lot."

"I know, but no matter how much I want to, I can't go back and change it. The question is, what do we do now? If by some miracle I don't end up in prison, are we ever going to get past this?"

I gave him the only honest answer I could. "I hope so." I sighed. "You're right. It's late, we're both exhausted, and we need rest." I stood and patted my thigh. "Come on, Bella, let's go to bed." I desperately wanted to invite Michael to join us. I could tell Michael wanted it, too.

I almost did.

I lifted my hand to take his, then stopped and dropped it back to my side. If we went upstairs together, we'd make love. Before we took that step again, I needed to know that I could commit to Michael without reservation. We both deserved that much. "I'll see you tomorrow morning."

I trudged up the stairs, Bella reluctantly following behind me. She stopped on the landing and gazed at Michael, concern clouding her soulful brown eyes. I kneeled next to her and whispered, "It's okay, sweetie. He needs you tonight more than I do."

My confused canine trotted back downstairs, stood next to Michael, and leaned her weight into his thigh.

"Looks like you're on dog duty tonight," I said.

Michael smiled at me sadly and mouthed the words *thank you*. The bedroom door clicked hollowly behind me.

SEVENTEEN

THE NEXT MORNING CAME early. Earlier still for Rene and Sam, who had come home well after midnight, then spent the rest of the night placating unhappy twins and trying to calm overly stimulated puppies. If Sam was surprised to come downstairs and find Michael sipping coffee at the kitchen table, he didn't show it.

Rene was a different story entirely. She burst into my room, chanting in a voice so chipper it should have come from a purple dinosaur, "Wake up, sleepyhead! It's almost noon!"

I sat bolt upright and yelped. "Geez Rene! You scared the crap out of me." I glanced at the alarm clock. "Eight o'clock? You seriously barged in here and woke me up at eight o'clock? You're lucky I don't sleep with a gun."

"What, you shoot everybody who gives you a personal wake-up call?"

"I do if they sound as chipper as you do." I held the sheets to my chest with one hand and reached toward Rene with the opposite, doing my best impression of a bedbound zombie. "Caffeine. Must have caffeine."

"Funny, Kate. Consider yourself lucky that I didn't get you up earlier. I've been on pins and needles since Alice got me up at five. Michael's making breakfast, but Sam refuses to let me interrogate him, so I've been stuck waiting for you. Let's start with the most important item first. Are you two back together?"

I ignored her diatribe and, more importantly, her question. "You're letting Michael cook? I hope you enjoy scraping eggs off the ceiling."

"Stop changing the subject," Rene grumbled. "Besides, I just came from the kitchen and it's not bad. I think you've been exaggerating about his messiness. Now spill. Are. You. Two. Back. Together?" She grinned, exposing a mouth full of shiny, white, meddlesome teeth. A ferret who'd learned how to open the sock drawer. "Oooooh. Maybe that's why you're so sleepy. Did you two stay up all night playing conjugal visit?"

"Sorry to ruin your fantasy, but Michael spent the night in the downstairs bedroom with Bella."

Rene's grin wrinkled into a scowl. "Kate, what is wrong with you? Forgive the guy already! You belong with Michael and you know it!"

She was right, of course. After a full night's rest, I was on the cusp of admitting it too. I loved Michael. That had never been in doubt. I needed Michael. That was also a no-brainer. One question still haunted me: could I trust him?

I was beginning to realize that the answer was yes. Michael was a good man. He'd made a mistake—a big one—but he'd never intended to hurt me. Rebuilding our relationship might take a while, but for the first time in almost a week, I believed it could happen.

Provided the universe gave us a chance.

"I'm not giving up on Michael and me, but the first step to our happily ever after is keeping him off of death row, and that might not be easy."

Rene winced. "My conjugal visit joke wasn't funny, was it?"

"Don't worry about it. Honestly, we all could use a little humor right now."

Rene perched on the edge of the bed, all flippancy gone. "Seriously, Kate. What happened last night?"

I gave Rene an outline of what Dale, Michael and I had discussed, focusing primarily on the details the police already knew. Namely, Gabriella's life insurance policy and her pregnancy. I wanted to tell her my suspicions about Officer Boyle, but Dale's stern admonishment to not talk about it had scared me to silence.

Rene wrinkled her brow. "That's everything?"

I didn't reply.

"Why do I get the feeling that you're holding out on me?"

"Because I am. I'm sorry, Rene, but that's all I can tell you. I'll fill you in on everything else as soon as I can, but for now, Dale has sworn me to secrecy."

Rene was usually nosier than a small-town spinster, but she didn't press me. A Herculean effort that must have used every last drop of her willpower. "I'll hold you to that. In the meantime, what are your sleuthing plans for today?"

"I don't have any."

"There's no need to lie, Kate. A simple 'I can't tell you' would suffice."

"I'm not lying," I insisted. "Dale went to Portland to meet with a private investigator, and he asked Michael and me to keep our heads down until he gets back." I shrugged. "So I guess we play tourist at the festival for the day."

Michael's voice called from the kitchen. "Go get her, Bella!"

"Oh no! Rene, take cover!" I yelled.

A hundred-pound, fur-covered cannonball charged up the stairs. I covered my head and curled into a side-lying fetal position in a futile attempt to protect my stomach. Bella crashed through the door and flew onto the center of the bed—or rather onto my body, which was lying on top of it. She pranced back and forth across the mattress with pure German shepherd abandon, scratching the covers and licking at my face.

"I know, I know," I said. "It's good to see you too. It's only been eight hours, you know." I popped out from under the covers and scratched my fingernails up and down her ribs. "I'll bet you're hungry."

Bella tilted her head. *Hungry? Me? Always!*

I raised my voice loud enough for Michael to hear. "I'm up already. Remember, payback's a bitch."

A toothbrushing and a quick comb-through of my hair later, the three of us meandered downstairs to an aroma so heavenly, it was worth scraping bacon grease off the windows. Tomatoes, peppers, cheese, onions, and the tiniest hint of garlic. Obviously one of Michael's famous omelets. The scent of cinnamon-laced vanilla hinted that he'd baked cinnamon rolls for dessert.

Michael looked up from a spattering skillet. "It's about time you got down here. Rene had some soft tofu in the fridge, so I made you a tofu scramble. The rest of us are having omelets. Pour yourself a cup of coffee and pull up a chair. The cinnamon rolls are almost done."

I would have opened my mouth to thank him, but I was shocked silent. A single thought resonated through my brain. *Who are you and what have you done with my boyfriend?*

The kitchen was spotless. Sure, there were a few dirty dishes, but they were neatly stacked in the sink. The stovetop had been wiped clean. The dishtowel, folded in a perfectly aligned rectangle on the counter beside it. I surreptitiously glanced up at the ceiling and along the floor. Nothing. Even Bella looked confused. Where were all of the tasty food droppings?

"I see Sam got stuck with cleanup duty," I said.

Sam shook his head. "Not me. This is all Michael's doing."

Michael had cleaned while he cooked? Inconceivable. Cooking, for Michael, was an exercise of chaotic creativity, done with the joyful abandon of a child stomping through mud puddles. Neatness ruined the fun. At first I assumed that the out-of-character cleanliness was done in a valiant effort to placate me. But one look in Michael's clouded eyes and I realized pleasing me had nothing to do with it. He was overwhelmed. My normally laissez-faire boyfriend was struggling—trying to create order in a newly unpredictable life.

The realization made my whole body feel heavy.

He smiled, but the expression didn't seem genuine. "Go on, sit."

I sat.

We ate breakfast, then spent a surreal morning pretending to be friends on vacation, making small talk while focusing on the mundane details of life with three dogs and two infants. Feeding, walking, diapering, and entertaining. We completely ignored the fact that Michael could be whisked away in an instant.

It was our new normal. A weird but somehow comforting routine of denial. I convinced myself that my avoidance was enlightened, not simply a distraction. Yoga, after all, teaches us to live in the moment. To not angst about the past. To not worry about the future. And each wonderful moment I spent with my loved ones that morning was precious. So, like a child cowering under the covers, I pretended that if I couldn't see the bogeyman, he couldn't see me. It was a delusion, of course, but man did it feel good at the time.

We continued our pretense of normalcy until almost noon, when we loaded up the twins and headed off for the Sandcastle Festival. Michael and I drove in the Honda; Sam and Rene followed with the twins in the Volvo. Bella sat with her rear in our back seat and her head pressed through the bucket seats to the front, obviously ecstatic that her pack had reunited. I pulled out my cell phone and glanced at the screen. Dale hadn't called.

"Kate, can I ask you a favor?" Michael asked.

"What?"

"Can you leave your cell alone for a while? If Dale calls, we'll hear it. I'd like to act like everything's normal for a few hours."

"Michael, I—"

"I know it's not real. I know nothing has changed. But can we pretend?" His voice trembled. "If things go sideways, I want to remember one great day."

I smiled. "You didn't let me finish. I was going to say that it's a great idea." I paused, hoping I wasn't about to lie. "This is all going to work out, Michael. I promise."

Blissful denial.

Our two-car caravan pulled into Tolovana Beach's completely packed parking lot at twelve-fifteen. "Wow, the lot's full already," I said. "I thought the judging wasn't until two."

"It isn't," Michael said, "but the teams started working at eleven. People get here early to watch from the start. It's like one of those reality cake decorating shows. Truly, you're not going to believe it."

"I'm not going to *see* it," I countered. "We'll never find a parking space."

"No problem," Michael replied. "Sandcastle competition day is the one day each year that cars are allowed on the beach." He pointed to a sign in front of the iconic Mo's restaurant: *All vehicles must be off the beach no later than 3 p.m.*

"What happens if we're still parked there after three? The fun run doesn't start until three-thirty, and I have to teach yoga afterwards."

"We'll be long gone before three, unless you want to wave good-bye to the Honda as it floats out to sea. Don't worry. There's a huge exodus after the judging. We'll move the car then."

I chewed on my lower lip, doubtful.

"Seriously, Kate. Don't worry. After fifty-two years of running this event, the committee has it down to a science. Trust me."

I wasn't completely comfortable, but I agreed. A teenager wearing a kelly green 4-H T-shirt directed us to a makeshift parking area that was eight cars deep and stretched a quarter-mile down the beach. We parked next to Sam and Rene and began the complex series of tasks required for a day trip with four adults, three dogs, and two babies. I hooked on Bella's two-foot-long city lead. Sam inserted the twins into their tandem backpack. Rene held a flexi-lead in each hand—one attached to Ricky's collar, the other to Lucy's. An ill-advised setup that would inevitably result in her being split in half like a wishbone.

"Rene, didn't you bring shorter leashes?"

"The pups like to roam."

Novice.

Michael was stuck with pack mule duty. He slung a diaper bag over each shoulder and tucked three dogs' worth of waste bags into his pockets. He pointed north, toward Cannon Beach's majestic Haystack Rock. "The sandcastle contest is that way."

The organizers couldn't have hoped for a better day. The weather was a perfect blend of early fall crispness and late summer warmth. Haystack Rock stood like a green-black sentry watching over rainbow-colored kites that dotted a bright blue sky. The huge basalt formation was Cannon Beach's most famous attraction: a bell-curve-shaped monolith that was an ecosystem all to itself, providing a home for orange and purple starfish, green sea anemones, and orange-billed puffins.

An ecosystem that had been invaded.

I felt surprisingly melancholy as we walked along newly dug tire tracks toward the sound of the crowd. It was as if the tourists—Michael and myself included—were an infestation. A parasite of some kind. I missed the beach's quiet, natural beauty. The rhythmic whisper of waves against sand. Fearless seagulls searching for sand dollars. Scatterings of driftwood that Bella could chase to her heart's content.

Fortunately, the human invasion would be short-lived. The evidence of today's projects, washed away by tomorrow morning. That thought made me sad, too. So much in life was temporary. What took a lifetime to build could be whisked away in a heartbeat, no matter how much we wanted to hold on to it.

Good lord, Kate. Get a grip. Remember the teachings. Be. Here. Now.

Here now was pretty darned good. Here now was worth cherishing. I reached over and grabbed Michael's hand. He glanced at me as if surprised, then interlaced his fingers with mine. The connection felt warm. Comforting. Right. My sadness didn't disappear, but it lightened.

Michael pointed to a canopy topped by a lemon yellow sign with the word *Refreshments* painted on it in bold black letters. Bella lifted her nose and sniffed, clearly scenting fresh-grilled hamburgers. "If we get separated, go there," he said.

"Consider us separated," Rene replied. "I'm starving!" She tore off toward the food tent, dragging along two bewildered puppies.

"Rene, wait!" Sam yelled, jogging after her. The twins bounced like brunette and blonde bobbleheads over his shoulders.

"Want to eat?" Michael asked. "There aren't many vegetarian options, but they usually have grilled cheese sandwiches."

"Thanks, but I'm not hungry." I gestured toward Rene, who was angling her way to the front of the line. "I'd rather check out the sandcastles. Let's wait until she goes back for round two."

The contest area had been broken into at least fifty thirty-by-thirty-foot squares, each delineated by four metal stakes linked together with green gardening twine. Not far away, ten-foot-diameter water holes had been dug into the beach. Mini-mountains of sand were piled next to them. Artists hurried back and forth from the sand piles, carrying raw materials for their creations in five-gallon buckets. Back at the plots, their team members poured the sand into frames, wetted it with water, and stomped the mixture solid. T-shirts proudly advertised team names ranging from Team Oyster to Boogie Monster to True Grit.

As the time moved closer to one o'clock, the crowds began to converge. I'd been surprised at the number of people in Cannon Beach a few days ago, but that was nothing. Thousands upon thousands of people flooded the area around Haystack Rock. I saw many of the locals I'd spoken with earlier, but in the spirit of keeping my head low, I avoided them.

Von and a team called the Sand Doggers were creating a giant dog house complete with a ten-foot-long wiener dog. Jimmy's mother, Zoey, was there with an older version of herself that I assumed was her mother. Both tried valiantly—and futilely—to hold on to the toddler. I was pretty sure I even glimpsed Crystal's pink-tinted hair.

The only potential buzz killers were a half-dozen police officers gathered around their white and blue police SUV. I shaded my eyes and squinted into the light. Officer Alex, dressed in her familiar blue-black uniform, chatted with a blonde officer dressed in brown. Officer Boyle wasn't with them.

By one-thirty, the atmosphere was thick with swarms of people, the voices of happy beachgoers, and the energy of too many people crowded into too small a space. Rene—who reunited with us after inhaling two hot dogs—asked Michael to watch the puppies while she and I tried to elbow our way closer to the exhibits. No matter how close I got, I could still barely see. The contest area was surrounded by too many people, most of whom were significantly taller than my five-foot three-inch frame. All Jimmy would be able to see from his three-foot-tall perspective would be the back pockets of strangers. No wonder he tried to escape. Who wouldn't want to leave that sight behind?

At twenty minutes before two, the artists traded their shovels for water sprayers, screwdrivers, chisels, and putty knives. Their expressions were serious, their voices harried. Sandcastle Picassos at work.

By the time the ending whistle blew at two, I'd come to one firm conclusion: the term *sandcastle* was an obvious misnomer. Castles were the definite minority. The creations included Komodo dragons, gorgeous sea princesses, human-sized chess sets, and yes, even a ten-foot-tall castle, dragon and moat included. My favorite was a family of bullfrogs sunning themselves on a half-dozen lily pads. I had so much fun that I almost forgot about Gabriella's murder. Almost.

An announcer came over the loudspeaker. "Thank you for attending the fifty-third annual Cannon Beach Sandcastle Contest. The time is now two-thirty. Please remove your vehicles from the beach no later than three. The Family Fun Fest and 5K Fun Run begins at Whale Park at three. Join us back here for the bonfire and beach concert at eight."

"That was amazing," Rene said as we trekked back to the cars.

"Are you coming with us to the run?" I asked.

Rene and Sam exchanged the look of exhausted parents everywhere. "Sorry, the twins are wiped out and so are we." He reached down and ruffled Ricky's ears. "These two monsters even look sleepy. We're heading back to the house."

Michael helped them load the puppies into their crate. I didn't think it was possible, but the bruises under his eyes seemed darker than they had earlier.

"You look beat, too," I said. "Why don't you and Bella go back to the beach house with Rene and Sam? I'll move the Honda and park closer to the fun run. After all, I'm the only crazy person who agreed to work this afternoon."

Michael shook his head vehemently. "Not a chance. I'd love to watch you teach, and I know where to find the best parking spots. Besides, Shannon needs the moral support. The run is usually the least popular event of the weekend, and Shannon's really put her heart into it. She's convinced that if it goes well, she can get Cannon Beach to sponsor a half marathon next spring." He sighed. "I have a feeling she's going to be disappointed. We may be the only two people there."

"In that case, I'll teach yoga. You do the running." Jogging was not in my repertoire.

"Yeah, take Michael with you," Rene quipped. "The run will be good practice for him. He needs to get in shape so he can run from the cops."

I rolled my eyes. "Not funny, Rene."

But honestly, it was. Even Michael managed to crack a smile. I truly hoped her words wouldn't be prophetic.

EIGHTEEN

MICHAEL WAS WRONG. PLENTY of people attended the run. Hundreds, by my estimation. Dressed in a variety of shorts, jeans, T-shirts, and running gear, they all looked ready to have a good time. This part of the beach was much less crowded than the sandcastle competition's location had been, so I traded Bella's short leash for her normal six-foot variety. Bella immediately showed her teeth to a standard poodle.

"No mischief from you, missy, or there'll be no chew treats for you tonight," I said. Bella seemed affronted by the idea.

Michael and I found Shannon at the registration booth, which had been set up under the gazebo in nearby Whale Park. The small, grassy park provided easy beach access, picnic tables, and restrooms, but it was most famous for its namesake: a ten-foot long, cedar statue of a whale. A large handmade sign declared, *Join us at four-thirty for a post-run yoga class taught by Seattle Master Teacher, Kate Davidson!*

Shannon jogged up to us and gave Bella a hug—a move universally hated by most canines.

"Easy, Bella," I whispered.

Bella sneezed to show her frustration but otherwise didn't react. She might score a treat tonight after all.

Shannon released Bella and peered earnestly at Michael. "How are you? Dale told me he has everything under control, but he wouldn't give me any details. I've been so worried that it's been hard to concentrate on the festival!"

Michael's smile looked so genuine, it almost fooled me. "I'm good, Shannon. Really. Dale has a plan. A good one. You can stop worrying now."

Liar. But I didn't contradict him. We were, after all, under Dale's gag order. I pointed to the sign and changed the subject instead. "Master Teacher?"

"Well, I needed to say something. 'Post-run stretch substitute' didn't have the same ring. I have to impress the masses, don't I?"

"Masses is right," I replied. "What a huge turnout!"

"I know. I can't believe it," Shannon replied. "There are over four times as many people as last year. I guess all that advertising paid off."

"The ice cream social afterwards is brilliant," Michael said. "Who thought up that idea?"

Shannon pointed her thumb at her chest. "Yours truly. Nothing brings people together like free ice cream. With four ice cream parlors in town, we had plenty of portable coolers. All I had to do was convince them that donating a few gallons of inventory would be good advertising."

"So, what's the plan?" I asked. "The ice cream social is after the yoga class, right?" Yoga is traditionally practiced on an empty stomach, but that wasn't why I asked. I had a feeling that once the free sweets disappeared, my yoga students would, too.

Shannon handed me a printed schedule. "The event runs from three to six. We'll kick it off with the warm-up class and a few kid competitions at three. The 5K run begins at three-thirty, and your yoga class will start at four-thirty. We start dishing out ice cream an hour later."

"Is that enough time?" I asked.

"Aren't most yoga classes an hour long?"

"They're usually longer, but I can work with an hour, no problem. I'm concerned about the run. There's only an hour between when it starts and the yoga class. Are you sure people will be finished by then?"

"You're obviously no jogger, Kate. Five kilometers is a little over three miles. Most people finish in thirty minutes or so. My grandma can leisurely walk it in an hour."

Which meant that it would have taken Bella and me twice that long.

Shannon waved to someone across the crowd. "Sorry, I have to go. You two enjoy yourselves. Take Bella on the run if you want to. Just make sure that you're back by four-fifteen. She pointed to a roped-off area near the water. Your class will be over there." She gave Michael a hug. "Thanks for coming, Baby Brother. It means the world." They bumped knuckles and she jogged off to her friend.

When she was halfway down the beach, I turned to Michael. "I'm surprised Shannon didn't press you for details about Dale's so-called plan."

"I'm not. When she's working, she shuts out the rest of the world."

"What's going to happen when she finds out you were lying? About Dale having a plan, that is."

"It's not lying, it's wishful thinking. Besides, I don't want to think about that right now. Let's go back to pretending everything's normal, okay?"

Which was a fabulous idea for the ten minutes it lasted.

Everyone we'd successfully avoided at the sandcastle competition sought us out at the fun run. Von and his boyfriend Andreas found us first. Von strode up to Michael, looking paradoxically joyful, wary, and serious at the same time. He pointedly ignored me. Still angry about my earlier subterfuge, I assumed.

He placed his hand on Michael's shoulder, which earned him a foul look from Andreas. Bella nudged Von's leg, clearly hoping he'd brought her a cookie. He ignored her, too. Clearly anyone—even an adorable, cookie-loving canine—who hung out with me was on Von's do-not-befriend list.

He spoke to Michael in an almost tender voice. "I'm sorry about Gabriella."

Michael's face grew pink, but his expression remained somber. "Thanks." He placed his hand on my forearm. "This is my—" He stumbled at the end of the sentence. "This is Kate."

Von stiffened. "I know. We've met."

Goose bumps covered my forearms. His tone was that cold. I tried to diffuse the tension between us by offering pretend sympathy. I pointed at the bandage still covering his forearm. "How's that bite healing? Puppy teeth are the worst."

Wrong move.

Andreas's eyes opened wide. He grabbed Von's arm and twisted it back and forth, as if examining the wound through the bandage. "Bite? You told me you cut yourself."

Von groaned.

Andreas machine-gunned questions at him in rapid-fire succession. "Did you go to the hospital? What did the doctor say? Do you need stitches? Are you on antibiotics?" His eyes widened. "Oh good lord, what if it had rabies!"

"Thanks a lot," Von grumbled at me under his breath. He yanked his arm away from Andreas. "I didn't go to the doctor," he snapped. "It was a puppy, for God's sake. Puppies bite."

Andreas jolted. "Don't grump at me like I'm the one being unreasonable. You lied to me."

"I was afraid that you'd go all crazy-hypochondriac, as usual." Von's expression grew cruel. "Looks like I was right."

The two men continued arguing, but I tuned out their words, suddenly overwhelmed by an uncomfortable suspicion. How had Von *really* injured that arm? Did the bandage cover a cut, a dog bite, or something significantly more incriminating? Like a wound obtained in a late-night struggle with an unarmed woman?

The hair on my arms quivered. Von was obviously fond of Michael—maybe even romantically. He'd resented Gabriclla. I'd heard him disparage her under his breath. Was that enough of a motive to kill her?

I would have continued puzzling out Von's motives but a high-pitched squeal interrupted my thoughts. "Michael!" Crystal threw her arms around Michael's neck. He stiffened at first, then returned her hug.

"I'm so glad you haven't been arrested," she said. "What happened to Gabby was horrible, but I don't believe you hurt her. Not for a second. None of us do."

A low, seething voice came from behind us. "Speak for yourself." *Boyle.*

He glared at Michael, his upper lip trembling. "You have a hell of a lot of nerve coming here."

We all reacted to Boyle's unwelcome arrival. I gasped and tightened Bella's leash. Michael tensed; Von frowned; Andreas flinched; Bella growled. Crystal's expression hovered somewhere between wariness and confusion.

"Easy, girl," I said to Bella automatically. "This is our friend."

Bella usually reacted to those words by sitting and offering the stranger her paw. Not this time. She remained standing at high alert, teeth bared, leaning toward Boyle. *Go ahead*, she seemed to say. *Make my day.*

Officer Boyle flexed and unflexed his fists, laser-focused on Michael the same way Bella was focused on him. "If it weren't for your fancy lawyer, you'd be in a jail cell in Astoria right now. Hell, if I had my way, you'd be swinging from the end of a noose. You certainly wouldn't be sauntering around town living it up with your mistress." He brought his beet-red face to within an inch of Michael's. "Make no mistake, mister. You. Will. Fry."

A low, threatening growl vibrated from deep in Bella's throat. Boyle leveled a hard stare back at her, right hand hovering dangerously close to his gun. "Oh, please. Give me an excuse. I'd love to put a bullet between your eyes, too."

I grabbed Bella's collar and backed her away. "Bella, be quiet." I leaned down to her ear and whispered, "He has a gun!"

Michael's growl sounded more threatening than Bella's. "Leave them alone. Kate and Bella had nothing to do with Gabby's death, and you know it. Neither did I. If you had enough evidence to arrest me, you'd have done it already. Back off or I'll sue you for harassment."

As threats went, it was pretty darned empty, but it was the only leverage Michael had.

Boyle sneered. "Try it. I guarantee you won't like the results. Soon you'll be mine, trapped inside a cell. Jail's a dangerous place, you know..."

The radio on Officer Boyle's shoulder crackled. He kept his eyes locked on Michael but spoke into the microphone. "Boyle here. Go ahead." Garbled static obscured the reply. "I'm on a code eight." More static. "Be there in five. Over and out." He turned back to Michael. "This isn't over." He marched toward the beach and disappeared behind the carved whale.

Crystal stared after Officer Boyle, slowly shaking her head. "What a jerk," she mumbled.

"Do you know him?" I asked.

"No, not really. I mean, a little. I've seen him around." Her guarded expression belied her words. I would have pressed her further, but I didn't get the chance. She kissed Michael's cheek and said, "I need to sign in for the run. Everything is going to be okay, I promise." She joined the growing line at the registration table. Andreas and Von followed behind her, still grumbling at each other.

I waited until they were all out of hearing range before I spoke. "So much for pretending things are normal."

Michael didn't reply.

I squeezed his arm. "Maybe Boyle's right, in a way. Dale told us to keep a low profile. You probably shouldn't be here." I handed him my car keys. "There are more than enough people to support Shannon. Take Bella and go back to Rene's."

"How will you get home?"

"I'll call a cab or hitch a ride back with your sister."

Michael considered my offer for a couple of seconds, then squared his shoulders. "No. I'm innocent. I'm not going to act guilty." He gave me a forced smile, handed back the keys, and pointed at the schedule. "Come on. Let's go watch the Toddler Trot."

The Toddler Trot—a hundred-foot dash for kids three and under—was one of Shannon's new events. Eight deadly cute almost-babies lined up on one end of the beach, held back by their captors (aka parents). A hundred feet south, other family members prepared to coax the toddlers to run in their direction. The first child to go from one end to the other would win a fifty-dollar gift certificate to a local toy store.

The athletes consisted of five adorable girls and three precocious boys, Jimmy among them. His mother held him on her hip at the starting line. The woman I assumed was his grandmother stood at the finish.

I put Bella in a sit next to me. "This should be interesting."

And it was.

The chaos began with the bang of the starter gun. Three baby-girl athletes plastered their palms to their ears and burst into tears. The rest of the runners ran full speed—in every direction except toward the finish line. Two careened toward the ice cream area; one headed for the beach. Jimmy beelined it straight toward Bella.

"Puppy!" he screamed. He tore off to the left, run-wobbling his way toward my toddler-loving canine.

His mother's eyes widened. "Jimmy, come back!"

His grandmother yelled, "Come this way, baby!"

"Bella, down!" I yelled.

We all might as well have been swearing in Sanskrit. Jimmy and Bella were Romeo and Juliet, separated by parental buzz killers. Jimmy reached out his hands; Bella reached out her tongue. The two collided in a puddle of fur, giggles, and German shepherd saliva. Jimmy wrapped his tiny arms around Bella's neck and pulled. She flopped to the sand and nibbled his chin. Neither boy nor beast had ever looked happier.

Jimmy's mother slid next to him and tried—unsuccessfully—to pull his arms off his canine best friend. "I'm so sorry. I swear, I don't know what's gotten into him. He's obsessed with your dog."

I should have been horrified, and part of me was. But mainly I was enchanted. "The feeling's obviously mutual. I think Bella is happier than he is."

Meanwhile, back at the finish line, a curly haired toddler staggered into the happy embrace of a man I assumed was her father. The crowd cheered; two children cried. Every child got a medal, whether they finished the race or not. Michael and I laughed so hard that tears streamed down our faces. For that brief moment, Gabriella and Officer Boyle—and even Dale and his PI friend in Portland—were long forgotten.

It felt wonderful.

Next up was the 5K run, which had about three hundred participants of all ages. They jogged. They walked. They dragged along erstwhile canine companions. Some carried water bottles, others dog waste bags. Most wore huge smiles and not nearly enough sunscreen. No doubt about it: Shannon's event was a rousing success.

Shortly after the first group of runners crossed the finish line, Michael and I made our way to the roped-off space designated for the yoga class. Participants—about sixty, by my estimation—started filing into the area a few minutes later. Andreas pulled a reluctant-looking Von to the front. Jimmy's mother, Zoey, took a space in the middle. Jimmy must have been with his grandmother. Either that, or Zoey had buried him up to his chin in the sand.

I ducked under the rope and handed Bella's leash to Michael. "Looks like I'm on deck. Bella seems pretty calm, but keep her away from other dogs, just in case."

"No problem." Michael pointed to a spot about ten feet behind me. "We'll hang out here."

"Watching people practice yoga is as exciting as watching paint dry. Wouldn't you rather go for a walk?"

"Are you kidding?" The right side of Michael's mouth lifted into a rakish grin. "Watching your backside could never be boring."

My throat—and a few places significantly lower—tingled. Michael and I were getting back to normal. Normal was good. Normal was easy. Normal was heaven.

Normal was short-lived.

I raised my voice to be heard over the crowd. "Welcome to yoga class. My name is Kate. How many of you have done yoga before?" To my surprise, about eighty percent of the participants raised their hands. "Wonderful. How many of you have done Viniyoga?"

No one. Except Michael, and he wasn't practicing.

"The beauty of Viniyoga is that there's no 'right' way to do a pose. All that matters is that you feel better at the end of practice than at the beginning. If anything doesn't feel safe, don't do it." My students smiled back at me. An easy crowd. So far so good.

After making sure there were no injuries, I asked everyone to stand and touch their palms together at their hearts in the Anjali Mudra, often called Prayer Position.

"Close your eyes and deepen your breath."

I closed my eyes, too, so I could visualize our upcoming practice. I'd teach most of it standing, since the participants didn't have yoga mats. We'd begin with poses that stretched the muscles involved in running. A variation of Warrior One would stretch the calves. Dancer's Pose would open the front of the thighs. A Staggered Legged Forward Bend would release hamstrings. We'd finish with some symmetrical forward bends to ease the low back and include plenty of arm sweeps to erase shoulder tension and relax participants' necks.

Plan in place, I opened my eyes.

And came face-to-face with Officer Boyle.

He stood straight across from me on the edge of the yoga space, arms crossed, face scowling.

I glanced back at Michael. He nodded to let me know he'd seen him, gave me a double thumbs-up sign, and mouthed the words *knock 'em dead*. Probably not the most appropriate statement, given how Gabriella had died, but at least he didn't tell me to break a leg.

I tried to focus on teaching, but Boyle's scowl evaporated my attention. Instead of conjuring up visions of peace, I pictured Gabriella's body. Where was her wedding ring? The tan line on her fourth finger indicated that she wore the ring regularly. If she'd taken it off at home, why hadn't Shannon and I found it in her apartment? If the killer stole it, why?

"Take a deep inhale and raise your arms up to the sky. As you exhale, fold forward and bring your face toward your front knee."

Gabriella's face. I shuddered. Her beautiful face had been destroyed by her killer. Bludgeoned over and over and over again. Her killing wasn't a random act of violence. She was beaten to death by someone she knew. Someone she might have hurt back. I glanced at Von, who was wrapping his hands around the backs of his ankles. The bandage on his forearm haunted me. What was it hiding?.

Officer Boyle stopped glaring and strode toward Michael. I kept teaching. "Let's do some modified Sun Salutations. I'll do the first repetition with you, then allow you to move at your own pace."

I moved slowly, timing my instruction so students could easily follow along. My body relaxed into the flow of breath-centered movement, but my mind refused to obey, jumping from thought to disconnected thought. Starfish ankle bracelets. Bulging white envelopes. Happy wedding photos. Tragically unborn children.

I performed the first repetition with the class, then asked them to move on their own. My eyes found Boyle a few feet away, still staring at Michael, who was now chatting with Crystal. For the moment at least, Michael seemed safe.

"A few more repetitions, and then we'll move on."

The students were finishing the last Downward Facing Dog when Jimmy's grandmother ducked under the rope. She whispered something to her daughter, who stopped moving.

"You *what*?" Zoey shrieked. "You *lost* him?" The rest of the class stopped moving and started mumbling. Zoey shielded her eyes and peered up and down the beach. "Jimmy!" she cried. "Where are you?" Her eyes grew wild. "Jimmy!"

A tiny voice wailed in the distance. "Mommy!"

Everything next happened in an impossible fast-forward slow-motion. Zoey pointed toward the toddler's voice and screamed. "Stop him! He's kidnapping my son!"

I followed her finger—straight to the man with the camouflage hat. He held the struggling toddler in a vice grip under his elbow. He glanced at Zoey and started running. Fast.

Bella ran faster.

She whipped toward the child's cry and lunged, ripping the leash out of Michael's hand. Before he could stop her, she tore after Jimmy's abductor. The rest of us humans—including Michael, Zoey, Officer Boyle, and me—sprinted excruciatingly slowly behind her.

Bella reached the camo-hatted man a good ten seconds before the first human. She flew through the air, planted her front feet on the would-be kidnapper's back, and knocked him flat to the ground. He dropped Jimmy, scrambled to his feet, and kept running. A male bystander tackled him near the sidewalk. Bella stayed with Jimmy, circling around him, snarling and snapping. Anyone who didn't know her would have thought she was rabid.

My heart dropped to my toes. Bella was guarding Jimmy. Protecting him. I knew it. Michael knew it. I had a feeling Jimmy's mother knew it, too. But we might be the only three.

"Somebody stop that dog before it kills him!" a stranger's voice yelled.

"Bella, it's okay!" I yelled louder. "Leave it!"

Officer Boyle pulled his gun.

"No!" I screamed. "Don't shoot her!"

Boyle didn't pause. Then again, I couldn't blame him. Police officers are trained to act on split-second impulses, and Boyle believed a child was in imminent danger. To a cop—any cop—human life trumped animal. Every time.

He raised the gun and pointed it at Bella.

A feral "Nooooooo!" echoed behind me.

Michael flew through the air, tackling Officer Boyle from behind and knocking his gun to the ground.

I dove next to Bella and grabbed her collar, praying that in her near-crazed state of arousal, she wouldn't accidentally attack me.

Michael and Boyle scuffled in the sand, yelling at each other. Neither one paused long enough to listen to the other.

"Don't move! Get on the ground! Now!"

"She wasn't going to hurt that kid, you idiot. She was protecting him!"

Jimmy's mother skidded next to me and wrapped her arms around her sobbing toddler. "Thank you. Oh my God, thank you." She pushed Jimmy to arm's length and scolded, "I told you not to run away from Grandma," then immediately wrapped him back in a deep embrace. Bella whined and licked every square inch of his face with her long, black-spotted tongue.

When I stopped shaking long enough to look up again, Officer Boyle was securing Michael in handcuffs. Blood dripped off Michael's chin and splattered in crimson droplets across the front of his shirt. An unfortunate side effect, I assumed, of an untimely collision with Officer Boyle's fist. The camo-capped man—whose fallen hat revealed a sweaty, balding head—was being led away by one of the officers I'd seen earlier.

Shannon, who'd come from lord only knew where, screamed at Officer Boyle. "He wasn't resisting arrest, you moron. You didn't have to coldcock him!" Crystal stood beside her, crying and reaching toward Michael.

Von grudgingly grabbed Bella's leash. "I'll hold her. You should go talk to the cop."

By the time I arrived next to Michael, I was shaking so hard again that my teeth chattered. His nose was still bleeding; his right eye was blackened and swollen. I ignored the cuffs on his wrists and the injuries to his face and wrapped my arms around him. "I'm so glad you're okay. You could have been shot!"

Then reality hit.

I shoved him away. Relieved anger spewed from my mouth. "What were you thinking! You could have been shot!"

"I *didn't* think, Kate. I just reacted. Bella was a hero. I couldn't let her get hurt."

Officer Boyle grabbed Michael by the elbow and jerked him roughly away. "You just made a huge mistake, buddy. You're under arrest for assaulting a police officer. You're mine now. You and I are gonna have ourselves a little talk."

Boyle recited the Miranda warning as he led Michael away.

NINETEEN

THE NEXT TWENTY MINUTES passed in a dark, ominous fog that provided paradoxical clarity. A tear-filled thank you from Jimmy's mother later, I'd learned more than I'd ever wanted to know about bitter divorces and contentious custody battles. Evidently, moving across the country didn't protect you from a crazy man hell-bent on destroying you.

My theories about the camo-hatted man had been simultaneously correct and dreadfully mistaken. As I'd surmised, he'd been up to no good, but his actions had nothing to do with Gabriella. He'd been scoping out his ex-wife Zoey's home town, waiting for an opportunity to abduct their son.

I'd eliminated a suspect, but that gave me absolutely no comfort. Michael was in Officer Boyle's custody now. At best, Boyle was a rogue police officer who had no problem using his fists on a prisoner who wasn't resisting. At worst, he was a killer. What if a few punches to the face were only the beginning of his plans for Michael? What if Michael was in imminent danger?"

In that moment, any suspects other than Boyle seemed ridiculously unimportant. All that I cared about was keeping Michael safe. I jogged over to Shannon, who had officially closed up the remaining fun run activities early. She huddled near the yoga area with Crystal and Von, looking distraught. Andreas was nowhere in the vicinity.

I grabbed Bella's leash from Von and pointed in the direction of Boyle's disappearing patrol car. "Shannon, he might be the killer."

Shannon's face wrinkled in horrified disbelief. "Michael? Jeez, Kate. What's wrong with you? My baby brother risked his life to save your dog! Now you accuse him of murder?"

"Not Michael, the cop," I replied.

Disbelief turned to dismay. "Michael drove off alone with a killer?"

Von rolled his eyes. "That's ludicrous. Why would a police officer kill Gabriella?"

"Guys, that's not imp—"

Shannon interrupted me. "Well, Michael certainly didn't kill her. He'd never hurt anyone. And that cop is obviously violent. He beat the crap out of Michael."

"Listen. I need you to—"

"Oh, get over it, Shannon," Von snapped. "Michael deserved a good clock cleaning. He tackled an armed police officer. Someone could have been killed. He's lucky he got off with the jab to the nose."

Shannon pressed her purple-red face up to Von's. "You can't say that about my baby bro—"

I interrupted them both with a loud finger whistle. "Both of you! Shut up!"

The look they passed my direction could have fried ice cream.

"Sorry, but I need you to listen to me. Michael could be in danger." I blurted out the whole story—including everything Dale had ordered me to keep secret—not omitting a single detail. Gabriella's pregnancy, the money Shannon and I had found taped behind the posters, the argument Mona had witnessed between Gabriella and Boyle, and my new fear that Boyle might be planning to harm Michael. I ended with, "We have to do something."

One thing was certain: Shannon wasn't angry with Von anymore. She was *livid* at me. "Michael lied to me. And you let him! 'Dale has a plan,' indeed." She yanked out her cell phone. "You and that damned lawyer keep too many secrets. You should have told me all of this. What's his phone number?"

"I'll call him." I pulled out my phone and pressed Dale's number on speed dial.

I started talking the instant he said hello. "Dale, I'm so glad you answered. We have a problem." I told him about Jimmy's attempted kidnapping. When I got to the point where Michael tackled Boyle, Dale interrupted with a string of swear words so foul I didn't even know what all of them meant. "I think Michael might be in danger, Dale," I finished. "Boyle arrested him for assaulting a police officer."

"You two couldn't stay out of trouble for one single afternoon?"

"It wasn't our fault. We—"

"Can it, Kate," Dale snapped. "I don't have time for your excuses right now."

I jerked the phone away from my face. *What the hell? First Shannon, now Dale?*

In the year I'd known Dale, he'd never lost his temper with me. Not once. Not even when I'd deserved it. I lifted the phone to my ear, fully intending to snark back, but a terrifying realization froze the retort before it emerged from my throat. Dale wasn't angry with me. Not really. His frustration was an escape valve. A release that covered up a more primal emotion.

Fear.

For Michael.

"Dale, please," I choked. "Don't be mad. I'm scared."

Silence. I imagined Dale counting to three. "I know, Kate-girl, I know. I'm sorry. I shouldn't have snapped at you like that. It doesn't matter, anyway. What's done is done. Where did Boyle take him?"

"I don't know. The police station, I assume."

Shannon interrupted. Her face had faded from purple-red to a flushed pink. "If he's asking where Michael is, he's probably on his way to Astoria. That's the closest police station with a jail."

"Did you hear that?" I asked.

"Yes. Hang on for a minute." Another few seconds of silence. "Damn. It will take me two hours to get there. I'll call my lawyer friend to see if he can get to Astoria sooner, then I'll head to my car. I'll be there as soon as I can." More whispered swear words whisked through the phone line.

"Dale?"

"Yes?"

"Drive fast."

I clicked off the phone and shoved it in my pocket. "Dale says he'll get to Astoria as soon as he can."

Crystal wore an odd expression, simultaneously thoughtful and distressed. "How long will that be?"

"Two hours."

She glanced at her watch. "Do you really think Michael's in danger?"

I paused, willing myself to not overreact. "I don't know. Maybe." Officer Boyle's face flashed through my memory, followed closely by Michael's swollen nose and purpling eye. "Yes."

Crystal's shoulders squared. "Then that's two hours too long. We can't stand here twiddling our thumbs while Michael gets hurt."

"We're not going to," Shannon said. "Come on, Kate, I have an idea." She grabbed my elbow and pulled me down the beach. Bella trotted behind me.

"Wait a minute! I'm coming with you!" Crystal yelled.

Shannon whipped around and gave her a hard stare. "No, you're not." She turned back to me. "Kate, I said *now*. Get moving."

Bella and I scrambled through the deep sand behind her. "Shannon, slow down!" I stopped, lungs heaving, and tried to catch my breath. "Where are we going?"

"Away from Crystal and Von."

"Why?" The word came out in a scratchy, asthmatic half gasp. If Shannon didn't slow down soon, she'd either lose me or I'd drop dead of heart failure.

We finally caught up to her under the gazebo at Whale Park. She was scrolling through the contacts on her cell phone.

"Why did we ditch Crystal and Von?"

"What good are they? Von's on Boyle's side, and Crystal is useless. We need help. Inside help. I think we can get it, but not if we have those two numbskulls tagging along. I'm mad enough to leave you behind too, but I can't. If my plan's going to work, you need to be part of it." She touched her index finger to the screen, pressed the phone to her ear, and mumbled, "Come on! Pick up, pick up, pick up."

"Who are you calling?"

She turned her back to me and frowned, plugging her free ear with her index finger. "Hi, it's Shannon. We need to meet." Silence. "I know, but it's important." She walked to the edge of the gazebo and back again. "My brother's girlfriend and I have a confession to make."

———————

Which was how, four days after Gabriella's death, Bella and I found ourselves race-walking behind Shannon to Arcadia Beach. At almost seven in the evening, the horizon glowed indigo-pink, a hue so gorgeous I wanted to bottle it for Rene's fall onesie collection.

247

Shannon didn't slow down until we'd skirted around the final rock outcropping toward the stairway that led up to the parking lot. Officer Alex stood, or rather paced back and forth, near the bottom step. Static crackled from the microphone on her shoulder. She ignored Bella and me and spoke directly to Shannon. "I can't believe I let you talk me into meeting you here. Alone, no less. I only agreed because…" She scowled and shook her head. "Oh hell. I don't even know why I agreed."

"I do," Shannon replied. "You don't think my brother's guilty."

"Not true," she replied. "And it doesn't matter what I think, anyway. Deciding his guilt isn't up to me."

"It's not up to Boyle, either," Shannon argued.

Officer Alex didn't reply.

Shannon stepped close to her and placed a hand on her forearm. "Come on, Alex. We're friends. I know you don't trust Boyle."

She jerked her arm away. "Make no mistake. Tonight, I am *not* your friend. I am an officer of the law. My loyalties do not lie with you. Or with that damned brother of yours, for that matter." She glanced at me, then frowned back at Shannon. "You said you had a confession to make. Now what is it?"

I was curious about that myself. I would have quizzed Shannon on the way but we were moving too fast. Anything but the shallowest of breathing was an unaffordable luxury. In-depth conversation? Out of the question.

"Kate and I searched Gabriella's apartment," Shannon said. "We found evidence that you missed."

Oh good lord. Shannon was going to tell Officer Alex about the money we'd found in Gabriella's apartment. Dale had been cranky with me before. Now he'd be apoplectic.

Officer Alex wasn't far off herself. "You two have been concealing evidence? Since when?"

248

Shannon and I replied at the same time.

"Since never," I said.

"What difference does it make?" Shannon said louder.

Officer Alex pointed to me. "You. Talk. Now."

I chose my words carefully, hoping I wasn't about to end up in a cell next to Michael. "You'd already searched the apartment when we *legally* entered and looked around ourselves. We found something that may be relevant to Michael's defense and gave it to his attorney, Dale Evans." I crossed my arms. "I'm not saying anything more until I get Dale's permission."

Shannon whirled at me and snapped, "You and that damned lawyer. If you two had told me what you were thinking about Boyle last night, I'd have called Alex then and Michael wouldn't be in this predicament. What good will some Podunk attorney do if Michael is dead?"

Officer Alex's expression flipped from frustrated to confused. "Dead? Why would your brother be dead? And what does Boyle have to do with any of this?"

"He killed Gabriella," Shannon replied. "He's going to kill Michael next."

Officer Alex threw up her hands and started marching back to the staircase. "You're insane. I never should have come here."

Shannon grabbed her arm. "Hear me out, please."

Officer Alex stopped walking, but she didn't look happy.

"You and I both got a little tipsy the night we closed on your house, remember?"

The officer's eyes grew wary. "Yes..."

"You told me that the only bad thing about living in Cannon Beach was dealing with Boyle and his harassment. When I asked you to explain, you claimed it was just the alcohol talking."

Silence.

"It wasn't the alcohol, was it?"

Officer Alex glanced uneasily at me, then glued her eyes on Shannon. "What does that have to do with your brother?"

"Nothing. Not directly, anyway. It's about Gabriella. Boyle was harassing her, too."

Officer Alex jolted. "Harassing her? Did he even know her?"

"Kate, tell Alex what you learned from Mona yesterday." Shannon glared at me, lips thinned, jaw set. Clearly unwilling to take no for an answer. "We need her help. If you don't tell her about Boyle, I will."

I flashed on Michael's bloodied face. I didn't want to admit it, but Shannon might be right. We'd kept too many secrets, and Dale was too far away to help. We needed someone on the inside. Someone who could set bias aside. Maybe that someone was currently staring at me, wearing a blue-black police uniform.

Please forgive me, Dale.

I told her everything.

"First off, I don't know for sure that Officer Boyle killed Gabriella, but at the very least, he shouldn't be a lead investigator in the case. He has a conflict of interest." I told Officer Alex about Boyle's frequent visits to Tuscany, Gabriella's place of employment. "According to Gabriella's boss, Boyle spent a lot of time there."

She shrugged. "Maybe he likes Italian food. Big deal."

"Have you ever eaten there?"

"Once."

"Then you know it's pricey. A special-occasion place. Not some diner you eat at multiple times a week. Not on a cop's salary, anyway. Besides, Boyle never ordered a meal. He just sucked down coffee and monopolized one of the tables in Gabriella's section."

"Again, big deal. Maybe he was interested in her. That's not a crime, either."

Shannon interrupted. "If he was interested in her romantically, shouldn't he have divulged that when he was assigned to her case?"

No reply.

"From what I learned, he was more than simply interested in her," I continued. "I think they had an affair. Gabriella ended it right around the time she realized she was pregnant." The last part was pure conjecture, but it made sense. "Mona—the boss—saw them fighting. Boyle got so mad he kicked the headlight out of his police car."

For the first time, Officer Alex's voice didn't sound confident. "That's how his car got trashed? He told the captain that some kids vandalized it while he was using the gas station's restroom."

"He lied." Shannon's voice was deadpan.

"I don't think Boyle took Gabriella's no for an answer," I said. "I think he kept hounding her, asking—maybe even demanding—that she take him back." I spoke faster, warming to my new theory. "When we saw Gabriella at the spaghetti dinner, she seemed frightened of something—or of someone. I'm almost positive that someone was Boyle. He certainly didn't seem happy to see Michael."

Officer Alex stared at me without blinking. "If your theory is true, your brother's arriving in town would have been a good thing. He came to Cannon Beach to demand a divorce. He admitted that much before he lawyered up."

"Michael and Gabriella knew that," Shannon said, "but what if Boyle didn't? What if he thought they were getting back together?"

I leaned toward Officer Alex, as if physical proximity would make me more credible. "You saw Gabriella's apartment. She had photos of Michael and her everywhere. It practically looked like a shrine. She even faked a love note from Michael and taped it to her refrigerator."

Officer Alex's face showed no expression.

"Don't you see?" I said. "Gabriella was trying to get rid of Boyle— or at least buy time—by telling him that she was reconciling with her husband. She was pretending that she and Michael were getting back together, even though their marriage was clearly over."

Officer Alex crossed her arms. "You're overlooking one very obvious explanation. Her relationship with her husband may not have been as 'over,' as you've been led to believe."

Shannon and I spoke simultaneously, for once in agreement.

"No way," Shannon said.

"Not a chance." My head shook so hard, I was surprised it didn't fly off my shoulders.

Officer Alex frowned. "Fine. Let's say you're right. What was she buying time for?"

"To gather enough money to disappear. Shannon and I found cash hidden all over the apartment. Almost twelve thousand dollars. Gabriella quit her job the night of the murder, too. She was definitely running. The question is, from who?"

Officer Alex rubbed her forehead and sighed. I hoped that meant I was getting through to her. "She wouldn't have been running from Michael. Like you said, he wanted a divorce. She could have gotten rid of him with the swipe of a pen."

"Alex," Shannon whispered. "I know you don't trust Boyle. What I don't know is why. Has he physically threatened you?"

Officer Alex avoided eye contact by reaching down to rub Bella's ears. Her voice was barely a whisper. "No. He's never touched me. He didn't physically assault the officer in Portland, either, at least not as far as I know."

"Portland?" I asked.

She lifted her eyes and met mine. "Boyle was suspended in Portland for sexual harassment. He wallpapered a gay officer's locker with porn photos."

"Suspended? Not fired?"

Her voice grew bitter. "Yes, and barely that. He got a couple of days without pay, a note in his file, and a week's worth of sensitivity training. When he applied for the job here, he convinced the asshole who hired him that he'd learned his lesson." She huffed. "What a joke."

"He's harassing you now." My words were a statement, not a question.

Alex replied with a single, almost imperceptible nod. "Turns out he's an equal opportunity homophobe."

"Why don't you file a complaint?"

"I did, but nothing came of it. It's my word against his. Evidently he learned one lesson during those classes in Portland: don't leave any evidence. He limits his ugliness to whispered slurs when no one else is around."

Her story both saddened and surprised me. "I thought everyone in the Pacific Northwest under the age of seventy-five had outgrown those ancient biases. Especially now that same-sex marriage has been legalized."

Alex laughed, but without humor. "In some ways, the hostility has gotten worse since gay marriage became legal." She picked up a rock and threw it toward the ocean. "Look, you've raised some legitimate concerns about Boyle, but I'm still not convinced he's a killer. He's a jackass for sure, but I deal with jackasses every day. Most of them never commit murder."

"Maybe not," I said. "But listen to your gut. Is it *possible*?"

She didn't reply, which was an answer all by itself.

"Alex," Shannon whispered. "Someone else might get hurt."

"What do you expect me to do? I can't accuse a fellow officer of murder. Not without more than a few unfounded suspicions."

"Maybe not," Shannon replied. "But you can help keep my brother safe."

"How?"

"Go to the jail. Make sure Boyle doesn't spend any time alone with Michael. If we're wrong, what harm will it do? If we're right, you might save my brother's life."

Officer Alex slowly closed her eyes. When she opened them again, all hesitation was gone. "I'll head to Astoria now."

She jogged up the stairwell and disappeared. A few seconds later, her patrol car's lights strobed in the gathering darkness.

TWENTY

SHANNON AND I HUSTLED back along the beach, heading toward our separate vehicles. We agreed to meet at the police station in Astoria. Hopefully between Dale, Officer Alex, Shannon, and me, we could keep Michael safe until Dale arranged bail.

Hopefully.

When we hit the entrance to Tolovana Beach, Shannon jogged right and headed up the ramp toward her car in the parking lot. Bella and I continued race-walking toward mine, which I'd moved to a side street near Whale Park. A male voice spoke over a loudspeaker, introducing the night's band. Eight o'clock. Three hours since Michael's run-in with Officer Boyle.

I skirted around the crowd, trying not to drown in a complex emotional stew: hope, worry, frustration, longing. Dale and Officer Alex were on the case. That gave me hope. We'd done everything we could to help Michael, but it might not be enough. That caused the worry. I had an uneasy feeling that I'd missed something, but I couldn't put my finger on what. Hence the frustration.

The most surprising emotion, however, was longing. Longing to be here with Michael, enjoying this place under happier circumstances.

Bella slowed and began sniffing, a sure sign that she needed a bio break. I stopped walking and loosened her leash. "Okay, sweetheart, go ahead."

In that blissful moment of stillness, I could almost imagine Michael standing next to me. I could almost feel the warmth of his fingers intertwined with mine, enjoying the night.

The sky was a sparkling ebony, lit by brilliant white stars and yellow-orange campfires. The scent of burnt marshmallows wafted on the cool evening breeze. A retro band belted out '80s tunes from a makeshift bandstand: "Girls Just Want to Have Fun."

The song jolted me back to reality.

This girl just wanted to break her boyfriend out of jail.

"Come on, Bella, we have to go." I upped our pace from race-walking to jogging.

We were steps away from my car when my cell phone rang. I glanced at the area code: 503. Northwest Oregon. I considered letting the call go to voicemail, but I couldn't. What if it was someone calling with news about Michael?

It wasn't. At least not directly.

The hysteria in Crystal's voice sounded real. "Kate, thank goodness you picked up. I didn't know who else to call."

The question that popped from my mouth was largely irrelevant. "How did you get my cell number?"

"You put it on your client intake form. That's not important, though." Her voice dropped to a whisper. "Kate, I think I screwed up. I think Officer Boyle is after me."

Her words were so ludicrous, at first I thought I'd misheard them. "What?"

"I was freaked out about Michael, so I decided to leave the bonfire and head to Astoria. When I got to my car a few minutes ago, the tires were slashed. At first I figured it was some stupid teenagers. The local kids get pretty wild during the festival. I came back to the hair salon to call the police, and it's been trashed, too." I could hear her swallow through the phone line. "Kids might do one or the other, but not both. I'm being targeted."

"I don't blame you for being upset, but what makes you think Boyle did any of this?"

"He's trying to intimidate me." Her voice shook. "It's working."

Crystal kept talking, but I didn't listen. Instead, I leaned against my Honda, feeling frustrated and struggling to hold back an insensitive retort. Arguing with a crime victim wouldn't be yogic, but Crystal's theory about Boyle didn't make any sense. Boyle already had what he wanted: Michael. He had no reason to waste time intimidating Crystal. She simply wasn't important enough. Her initial assumption was right. The vandals were probably some misguided kids blowing off steam.

Unless…

What if we were wrong about Boyle being the killer? What if he was simply a rogue cop locked on the wrong suspect? What if the real killer was still out there? Could that killer be Crystal's vandal?

My mind whirled through suspects, but none of them felt right. The camo-capped man was out. He might be a nut job, but his nut was firmly fixated on his ex-wife. Shannon? She'd hated how Gabriella was using Michael, and she'd have done anything to protect him. But we'd been together until a few minutes ago. When would she have had time to trash Crystal's shop? Von. Von was hiding something under that bandage, and he resented Gabriella. But Crystal? Why would he go after Crystal?

I turned and thudded my forehead against my car's roof.

Argh.

Maybe I had it all wrong. Maybe the killer was some psychopath that I hadn't even met yet. If so, Gabriella's life wouldn't be the only one in jeopardy. Dad told me once that when a psychopath commits their first murder, something inside of them breaks. Life loses all value. Their first kill, he claimed, isn't their last. A psychopath's first kill is simply a prelude to their second.

My entire body flashed cold. "Crystal, you need to get out of there and call the police. Now."

"He is the police. And I can't leave without a car. Where would I go?" She started sobbing. "Oh lord, why did I threaten him?"

"Threatening a psychopath is never—" My mind snapped back to Crystal. "Wait a minute. Who did you threaten?"

"Boyle!" Crystal shouted. "Haven't you been listening? I threatened *Boyle!*" Her voice squeaked, hovering on the edge of hysteria. "You and Shannon dropped that bombshell about Boyle and then took off without me. I couldn't stand there like an idiot while Michael was in danger. Von refused to get involved, so I called the station and asked for Officer Boyle. He didn't answer, but I left a message on his voicemail. I told him that I had proof that he'd killed Gabriella."

"Proof? We don't have any proof."

"I know that, Kate, but Boyle doesn't. I told him that if he ever hurt Michael, I'd make sure he rotted in prison." She started crying again. "How could I have been so stupid? Boyle's a cop. He can easily find out where I live. He's probably at my house now."

She was right. A police officer—any police officer—could easily obtain her address. If Boyle was the killer, Crystal's phone call put her in grave danger.

I stared at my car keys, conflicted. Shannon should be halfway to Astoria by now. Hopefully Dale was already there. Michael had three people riding to his rescue; Crystal had no one. Threatening Boyle had been stupid, but she'd been trying to help. I couldn't leave her stranded at the salon.

"I'll come and get you. You can stay with Rene and me until we figure this out."

"Thanks, Kate. Please hurry."

"I'll be there in five minutes."

I made it in four. Or I would have, if I could have found parking. I finally left my car in a not-quite-legal spot four blocks away, pulled Rene's pepper stray out of my purse, promised Bella I'd be back in a few minutes, and jogged toward CB Cuts.

I didn't slow down until I reached the salon's dark second-floor landing. Prickly unease tickled the back of my neck. The *No Dogs Allowed* sign had been torn from the door; the window it used to cover was shattered.

I moved the pepper spray off its safety setting and squeaked the door open.

"Crystal?"

The formerly immaculate space smelled strongly of rubbing alcohol (courtesy of a broken jar of comb disinfectant) and resembled my kitchen after Michael had baked one of his infamous seven-layer lasagnas. Glass littered the floor. The retail shelves were empty. Bottles of shampoo, conditioner, makeup, and hair spray were scattered everywhere.

The shampoo bowl was filled, not with water and suds, but with a muddy concoction of water, planting soil, chopped ivy, and shredded photos that had once framed the cutting station's mirror.

Crystal huddled on the floor, sobbing. "My beautiful shop. Ruined. What am I going to do?"

I reached for her hand and pulled her to standing. "Don't worry about that now. Let's get you out of here."

She pointed to her kitten, who was huddled underneath the shampoo bowl, ears flattened against her skull. "Not until I catch Mouse. She's freaked out and she won't let me near her. She'll jump through the broken window and escape as soon as we leave the room."

Mouse's eyes flitted back and forth between Crystal and the shattered window. Frightened, feral energy electrified the air around her.

"See? She's going to bolt the first chance she gets."

"We can't stay here, Crystal."

"I know. Now that you're here to help, I can trap her in the cat carrier. I need to assemble it in my office. Otherwise she'll go berserk. Stay here and don't let her escape, okay?"

A vision of Rene—swollen-eyed, red-nosed, and violently sneezing—flashed through my mind. The question was idiotic, but it popped out of my mouth anyway. "Can't you leave the kitten behind? My friend is allergic."

Tears flooded Crystal's eyes. "If she gets loose, I'll never catch her again."

I didn't have time to argue, and I wouldn't have won anyway. I'd never have left Bella behind in similar circumstances. Hopefully the cat could stay at Shannon's, at least temporarily. Provided Shannon wasn't the killer, that is.

This day sucked.

Crystal disappeared into the back room to assemble the cat carrier. I put the pepper spray back on safety, kneeled, and tentatively reached my fingers toward Mouse. The kitten seemed calmer now that her stressed-out owner was out of the room. "Hey there, little kitty. Want to go for a ride?"

The unmistakable screech of a cat carrier's metal-on-plastic jolted the air, startling us both. Mouse screamed and flew at my face; I yelped and dropped the pepper spray. That damned cat careened out from under the shampoo bowl and skidded across the floor, racing for the base cabinet where Shannon kept the linens. The wooden door thumped solidly closed behind the white tip of her tail.

Dammit! At the rate we were going, Michael would serve twenty-to-life before I got out of this hair salon. I marched to the cabinet, pulled out the towels, and stacked them on the floor.

Fervently wishing I'd worn leather gloves, I kneeled on the floor and reached my arm inside the cabinet. "You don't want to bite me now, do you, little kitty?"

Mouse replied with a snake-like hiss-spit, but I couldn't feel her. She must have hunkered down out of my reach. "Nice try, little kitty. But you won't get away from me that easily." I lay on my belly and serpent-crawled inside the built-in cabinet, reaching my fingers all the way to the back.

Wooden walls, empty corners.

No warm fur. No sharp claws. No finger-chomping teeth, either. Nothing but a small, hollowed-out space on the left that was filled with loosened insulation and a plastic, cylindrical pipe.

The water line to the shampoo bowl.

So this is where Mouse goes when she disappears inside that wall. She skirts along the plumbing line between shampoo bowl and the cabinet.

I crawled deeper into the cabinet and swept my hand around the hole, hoping to grab her. My fingers wrapped around something decidedly unkitten-like.

What the heck?

The object I grasped was three inches square by a couple of inches deep. A box of some kind. The sides had a rough texture, but something smooth—paper, perhaps?—was affixed to the top. I worked it free from its hiding place and slithered out of the cabinet to examine it more carefully.

I glanced down at the intricately carved jewelry box and suppressed a gasp.

Michael stared back at me.

I recognized the photo from Gabriella's apartment. Michael on his wedding day. Heartbreakingly handsome. Only in this copy, he was alone. Gabriella had been carefully cut from the photo.

Every fiber of my being knew what Crystal kept hidden inside that tiny hope chest, but I needed to be certain. I glanced around the empty room. No one with me but Mouse, who had scampered through her favorite escape route and emerged from the hole underneath the shampoo bowl again. She glared at me as if to say, *Touch me again and I'll amputate your pointy finger*. Crystal was still fiddling with the cat carrier in the other room.

"What do you think, little kitty?" I whispered. "Should I do it?"

Mouse didn't answer, but her golden eyes clearly said yes.

I gripped the jewelry box in both hands and quietly eased open the top.

Gabriella's wedding band.

Her murderer—who I now knew was Crystal—had indeed stolen it. Turned it into a keepsake. A grisly souvenir. Crystal had killed Gabriella, likely in a demented attempt to win Michael. I suspected she'd trashed the salon, too. But why?

Dad's voice whispered inside my head. *A psychopath's first kill is simply a prelude to their second.*

My mouth filled with cotton. *Of course.* Crystal wanted Michael. In her disturbed worldview, I was the only person still standing in her way.

I needed to get the hell out of Dodge. Now.

I stood up, tucked the box inside my jacket pocket, turned toward the door—

And came face-to-face with Crystal.

She held six-inch haircutting shears in her right hand. Her left hand was clasped in a white-knuckled fist. "I didn't say you could snoop around, Kate." Her voice sounded calm. Too calm.

I pretended ignorance, which wasn't much of a stretch. "I wasn't snooping. I was trying to catch Mouse. She ran inside the cabinet." I hoped against hope that Crystal wouldn't check underneath the shampoo bowl.

Crystal's eyes darted to the shampoo bowl, then fixed steadily on me. "Nice try, Kate. Mouse is right where I left her. I really am afraid she'll try to escape, though. I scared her half to death when I broke the window."

My voice squeaked. "You broke the window?"

"Playing dumb doesn't suit you, Kate. My damsel-in-distress story was pure genius, don't you think? I couldn't figure out how to get you alone. Your asinine theory about Boyle gave me the perfect idea." She raised the shears toward my chest. "I hated to vandalize the shop, but I needed you to believe that I was in danger. Otherwise, why would you meet me, much less go off alone with me? You certainly won't be coming back for any more haircuts." She grinned at her own joke.

Then she frowned at the kitten. "I'd planned to take care of you outside, but Mouse wouldn't let me catch her, and she'll escape if I leave her here alone with the broken window. And now you know that I killed Gabriella. You'll probably scream if we go outside." She paused for a moment, as if thinking. "I guess I'll have to do it here."

My stomach did back flips. If what she'd done to Gabriella was any indication, Crystal's version of "taking care of me" involved a dozen or more blows to the head. I had to get away from her, but how?

Mouse's tail flicked up and down as if she was trying to get my attention. My eyes flitted to the rhinestone-covered vial on the floor next to her. *Rene's pepper spray.* If I could somehow manage to get to it...

Crystal spoke in a monotone, clearly reciting a story she'd told herself hundreds of times before. "Michael was mine until that sorceress Gabriella put a spell on him."

"A spell?"

"Once he met her, he couldn't see me."

Ah, yes. I knew that syndrome well. I called it *The Rene Effect*. Part of me felt sorry for Crystal; I knew how demoralizing it was to be lost in another woman's shadow. I had news for her, though. There was no magic involved. Just the inescapable magnetism of unflawed beauty.

Crystal touched the point of the shears to my throat and pulled the box out of my jacket pocket. "Gabriella never deserved that ring. It should have been mine. No matter. It's my turn now."

I edged toward the shampoo bowl, millimeter by millimeter. "Your turn?"

"My turn to have Michael. I knew Gabby's spell would force him to come back, so I stayed close to her, waiting. Hoping that when he did, he'd see me again." She twirled a lock of pink-blonde hair around her index finger and pulled. Blush-colored strands floated to the linoleum. "But he didn't, so I had to get rid of her." Her eyes were flat, her expression absent. "It worked. You were there this afternoon. He saw me. He talked to me." Her lips trembled upward. "He hugged me."

I opted not to point out that I'd seen him flinch first. "Did you know that Michael had asked Gabriella for a divorce?"

"Not until the night of the spaghetti dinner. Like I said, Gabby told me on the drive home that Michael had been seeing someone else—you. She said she still loved him but it was time to let him go." Crystal's eyes deadened. "I told her to text him and tell him that as soon as she got home."

Poor Gabriella. Even in her final hours, she was forced to live a lie. To pretend that her scam marriage was real. But I didn't say that. Instead, I said, "You knew Michael would never see that text."

"Michael dropped his phone during the scuffle with Gabriella in the parking lot."

"And you stole it?"

"Not exactly. I was planning to give it back later. I thought 'finding' his phone would give me the perfect excuse to see him. I answered Gabby's text pretending to be Michael and asked her to meet at the beach." The right side of Crystal's mouth lifted into a creepy half smile. "Man, was she ever surprised to see me instead of Michael."

"You didn't have to kill her. Once she divorced Michael, she would have been out of your way."

"She never would have gone through with it. She would have hypnotized him again."

I risked a glance at the pepper spray, still lying on the floor eight feet away, next to the shampoo bowl. Mouse arched her back and fluffed out her tail, ready to make a run for it. *Please, kitty. Please don't bolt now. Please don't draw attention to the pepper spray. If you're a good kitty, I'll make sure you get a great new home. One without a crazy lady.*

"Gabriella was pregnant." I couldn't keep the accusation out of my voice. "You murdered an innocent child."

"She told me," Crystal huffed. "All of this time she claimed to be madly in love with Michael, and then when she realized I'd never let her have him again, she changed her story. Like being an incubator for Boyle's parasite spawn would save her. She stole Michael from me and then *cheated* on him? She claimed Boyle was violent—that she was planning to run away." Crystal snorted. "I'll bet. Straight to Seattle. Back to Michael." She frowned. "Now the only person left in my way is you. You're just like her. Michael is blinded by you, too." Crystal reached up and ran her fingers across my locket. "I saw you touch this when I mentioned him the other day at your haircut. He gave it to you, didn't he?" I didn't answer, which was evidently the reply she expected. "It's mine now." She ripped the chain from my neck.

A shuffling sound came from the stairwell. Crystal turned toward it, accidentally lowering the shears.

That was my chance, and I took it.

I raised both palms to her chest and shoved, knocking her off balance. I dove for the pepper spray.

Mouse assumed I was coming for her. She flew at me, yowling, and sank fourteen of her twenty-four claws into my flesh. I ignored the searing pain in my hand and wrapped my fingers around the pepper spray's canister.

"Don't hurt her, you monster!" Crystal screamed. "She's just a kitten!" She raised the scissors overhead, ready to strike. Mouse careened through her feet toward the linen cabinet. Crystal tripped and stumbled toward me.

Looking back, I'm still not sure which one of us would have prevailed. I kid myself that I was about to subdue Crystal, but truthfully, I'd probably still have been trying to get the pepper spray off safety when Crystal plunged the scissors into my jugular.

Looking forward, it doesn't matter.

The door slammed open and a deep voice boomed, "Police! Drop your weapons!"

I threw the pepper spray on the floor. Crystal's scissors clattered next to it. Officer Boyle kicked both weapons out of reach but kept his gun trained on Crystal.

"It was you. This whole time I blamed Gabby's husband, and it was you! How could you kill Gabby? You were her only friend."

Crystal backed away, hands in the air, golden heart dangling between her fingers. Boyle crept menacingly toward her. "Gabby was my—" His voice broke. "She was pregnant, with my child." His grip on the gun tightened. "You. Killed. My. Child."

All of my emotions, all of my fears, flipped in an instant. I wasn't afraid for Michael anymore. I wasn't frightened for myself, either. I was terrified for Crystal. I used my most steady, soothing yoga voice. "Officer Boyle, she doesn't have a weapon anymore. Her hands are up, just like you asked."

He didn't respond.

"Crystal isn't a threat," I reiterated. "Please, lower your weapon."

For a long, painful moment, I didn't think he heard me. In fact, I'm still not sure that he did. I honestly don't know what kept him from shooting. Maybe his police training kicked in. Maybe he realized that I was a witness. Maybe Gabriella's spirit yelled from the afterlife, ordering him to stand down.

Whatever the reason, his shoulders finally relaxed. His grip on the gun did, too. He ordered Crystal to turn around. When she complied, he kicked her feet apart and cuffed her.

———

Boyle called for backup. Officer Alex arrived fifteen minutes later and took Crystal into custody. Other than a discrete nod as we passed, she didn't acknowledge me or our recent conversation.

When Boyle returned to the hair salon, I was on my knees, talking to Mouse through the metal grid of her cat carrier. "Okay, kitty. Thanks for finally letting me catch you. We got off to a bad start, but since you foiled Crystal's plan to kill me, I figure I owe you one. You're stuck with me, at least for now. Someday you might even like me."

Boyle handed me the locket. "I pried this from Crystal's hands, but it's obviously yours. It has pictures of your boyfriend and dog in it."

"It doesn't have to go into evidence?"

"Not if I never found it." He shrugged. "I figured it might be important to you."

"It is. Thanks."

Boyle gazed uncomfortably at his shoes. "I owe you and Michael an apology."

I placed my hands on my thighs and stood. "Michael, definitely. But not me. You saved my life tonight. That's apology enough."

"I was so sure that he did it. Killed Gabby, that is." Boyle's shoulders slumped. "Maybe my captain was right."

"About what?"

"That I was too close to the case. He ordered me off the investigation a couple of hours ago. Evidently some 'anonymous source' called and told him that I'd been romantically involved with Gabby. I couldn't lie to him, at least not and get away with it. He's furious that I didn't ID her body when I saw her tattoo. I'll probably lose my job."

"Why didn't you? Identify her, I mean."

"How could I explain seeing Gabby's breasts without admitting that we'd had an affair? I was convinced that her husband had killed her. I wanted to be the one who arrested him. I *needed* to be the one who arrested him. I didn't count on Crystal calling the station and ratting me out."

I didn't say anything, but I was positive that Crystal hadn't made that phone call. Officer Alex had come through for us, just like Shannon knew she would.

"Don't get me wrong," I said. "I'm grateful. But what were you doing here tonight?"

"Like I said, the captain tossed me off Gabriella's case. I was on my way home when some tourist called in, saying they heard someone break a window near the coffee shop. I was checking it out when I overheard you and Crystal." His voice cracked. "Do you think she was telling the truth? That Gabriella was skipping town because she thought I was violent?"

I didn't answer. Then again, I didn't need to.

Boyle stared over my shoulder as if looking for comfort somewhere outside the picture window. "That's why she didn't tell me about the baby." When he looked back at me, his face was stricken. "I would never have hurt Gabby. *Never*. I loved her."

His face cycled through a kaleidoscope of emotions. Confusion. Grief. Pain. Betrayal. Remorse. But not anger. Not even a trace. Certainly nothing close to violence.

Boyle was, in many ways, a jerk. Homophobic. Likely obsessive. Trashing a cop car wasn't exactly pacifistic, and I'd never choose him as my lover. But in that moment, I knew: I'd been wrong about him, and so had Gabriella. I doubted he'd ever laid a hand on her. As for harming her child? Not a chance. But Gabriella would never have risked it.

I picked up the cat carrier. "If you don't have any more questions for me, I'd like to go home now."

"You're taking the cat?"

I shrugged. "I doubt Crystal will be free to care for Mouse anytime soon. I suppose she might have a family member who wants her, but I suspect she's mine now. Unless you're looking for a kitten, that is…"

Boyle leaned his face toward the carrier. Mouse spit and swiped at his beard with all seven claws on her right paw.

"Nope. It's all yours."

I suppressed a smile. Another pet that didn't like beards. Mouse and Bella might be a match made in heaven.

TWENTY-ONE

FOUR AFTERNOONS LATER, I meandered along the beach near Haystack Rock, allowing the ocean's waves to lap against my bare feet. The huge monolith centered me. Gave the moment more meaning somehow. A reminder of how I'd chosen to live my life. Strong. Dark. Alone. I reached down and stroked Bella's fur. Well, maybe not so alone.

Rene spoke softly behind me. "Kate, hon, it's time. Are you ready?"

Was I?

Deep down inside, I'd always believed that Michael's and my story would have a fairy-tale ending. An ending set in a crowded church bursting with dusky pink roses and burgundy calla lilies. An ending sweetened by a three-tiered, dark chocolate wedding cake. I never dreamt it would end here. Not now. Not like this.

Had I made the right choice?

For a moment, I allowed my mind to get lost in all that had happened since Saturday.

Michael was released from jail shortly after my confrontation with Crystal. Dale got the charges against him dropped. In exchange, Michael promised not to sue the police department for excessive use of force. Boyle voluntarily resigned. Part of me felt bad for that. Somewhere deep inside Boyle lived a good man. I hoped he'd find him someday.

After everything we'd been through since Gabriella's death, we all needed a few days to decompress before heading back to Seattle. It took some negotiating, but eventually Shannon (who, like Rene, was allergic to cats) agreed to temporarily move in with Rene, Sam, and the twins at the beach house. Michael, Bella, Mouse, and I stayed in separate bedrooms at Shannon's cabin. Dharma joined Dale soon after.

Crystal was denied bail. She had very few friends, and no one in her family wanted her kitten. So for now at least, Mouse was mine. The kitten still didn't trust me, not that I blamed her. From her perspective, I'd kidnapped her from the hair salon and now held her captive at Shannon's cottage. She wasn't all that fond of Michael, either, but she'd grown to adore Bella, and Bella was ecstatic about her new job as cat slave. Rene was less than pleased about my new cat-dander generator, but she scheduled an appointment to meet with an allergist as soon as she got back to Seattle.

Michael and I spent two long days in serious, tear-filled discussions. Not only about us, but also about Gabriella. Since he'd still been married to her at the time of her death, he'd inherited all of her possessions. He kept the photos but donated everything else—including the money I'd found in her apartment—to a local domestic violence shelter. Part of the life insurance money would pay for Gabriella's burial and settle her overdue bills. Michael offered to give the rest of it to Dale for his legal services, but Dale refused. Michael decided to donate it to a nonprofit that served illegal immigrants. I thought it was a fabulous plan. We all wanted Gabriella's death to have meaning.

Two nights after Crystal's arrest, the four of us—Bella, Mouse, Michael, and I—bonded in the living room. Bella and Mouse cuddled in front of the fireplace. Bella groomed the top of Mouse's head while Mouse kneaded Bella's chest with her claws. The kitten's loud purr competed with the crackling fire.

I cemented a final photo of Michael's pretend life in a faux leather photo album. Gabriella, smiling, on their fake wedding day. Pink Gerbera daisies brought out the color in her cheeks. Young. Happy. Vibrant. Alive.

I traced Gabriella's outline with my fingertips. "Her death seems so meaningless. And the baby ..." My voice trailed off. "I was furious with you, Michael. In some ways, I still am. But if I'd known that her life was in jeopardy, I would have helped her. I would have helped both of them. You know that, right?"

"Of course." He kissed my forehead. "That's who you are. That's why I love you."

"I understand why she didn't tell Boyle about the baby; she was frightened of him. But why not tell you? If she'd been honest with you, none of this would have happened."

Michael sighed. "For the same reason our relationship was such a disaster. Gabby could never trust any man. She was too broken."

Michael closed the album and pushed it to the edge of the coffee table. When he turned to face me, he wore a resigned expression. We both knew: it was time for *the talk*.

I stared at the fire, pretending to be mesmerized by its dancing flames.

"You need to decide, Kate."

I lifted my eyes to meet his. I desperately wanted to continue postponing the discussion, but I couldn't. It wouldn't be fair. To either of us.

"I screwed up," Michael continued. "But how I felt for you never changed. I think we belong together, but I'm smart enough to know that most stories don't end happily ever after. If you still want to get married, let's do it, as soon as possible. If you need more time, you've got that, too." He stared at his hands. "And if you want to end things—at least for now—I'll respect that decision, too. But I need to know where you stand. Now."

I closed my eyes and tried to tap into my inner wisdom. Like Bella—like Gabriella, for that matter—trust didn't come easily for me. And when that trust was betrayed...

Rene's voice startled me out of my revelry. "It's not too late to change your mind."

I turned toward her and grinned. "What? You think I'm going to swim for it?"

She smiled back. The smile of my best friend. The best friend who knew me—flaws and all—and loved me anyway. "I can never tell with you."

I interlaced my fingers through hers and squeezed. "Come on, let's go."

Rene and I ambled toward the tiny gathering of everyone Michael and I held dear. Once I'd said yes to Michael's proposal, neither of us wanted to wait. So we'd planned a tiny ceremony for two days later and limited our guests to those we truly thought of as family.

Rene and Bella moved to the maid-of-honor position. A few seconds later, my father's ex-police partner, John O'Connell, took my elbow as we prepared to walk down the makeshift aisle. My cornflower blue dress hovered below my knees in perfect complement to the bright blue sky.

I looked left and right, memorizing the faces of our extended family. Sam sat in a folding chair, holding a frilly-frocked twin on each knee. The puppies and Dale's Jack Russell terrier, Bandit, wrestled in the sand next to him, play-growling and tangling their leashes. Tiffany and Alicia, who'd driven down together from Seattle that morning, sat on their right. Tiffany bounced up and down and waved, wearing a tight, bright red miniskirt that clashed perfectly with Alicia's conservative blue dress. Alicia gestured with her eyes toward Tiffany and shrugged.

Michael's parents and Shannon occupied the groom's side, whispering, snapping photos, and laughing at the puppies' antics. Even Mouse was present, at least in spirit. I held a snapshot of her in my left hand. My "something new."

The person I most wanted to see waited at the front. Michael stood between Dharma, who was acting as our officiator, and Dale, who was his best man. Michael was grinning like a fool, which was appropriate given that he was crazy enough to marry me. The right side of his face still glowed a brilliant purple-blue from Boyle's pounding. I sported a deep red scratch across the bridge of my nose, courtesy of this morning's attempt to befriend Mouse. My wedding pictures would never be as gorgeous as Gabriella's, but then again, who cared? I'd never need to create a shrine to a fake life with Michael. I had the real thing.

Rene reached down and turned on a portable CD player. Pachelbel's *Canon in D* floated along with the soothing, breathlike rumble of the ocean. Dharma fingered a notepad containing Michael's and my wedding vows. The wildflowers laced through her long braid matched the bouquet in my hands. She looked beautiful. Happy. When I smiled into her eyes, I saw my own future. Also beautiful. Also happy. How could it be anything else?

I'd planned to march down the aisle in time with the music, but my trickster mind refused to keep tempo. Instead, it chanted my favorite mantra with each step: *Arriving home.*

When Michael's hand replaced John's, I understood why my subconscious was chanting. No matter how messy. No matter how much we bickered. No matter the challenges we faced or how hard we had to work to overcome them: this relationship—this man—would always be home.

I didn't listen to the words Dharma uttered, though I knew they were beautiful. Instead, I focused on the sensations: Michael's warm hand, Bella's soft fur. The sweet scent of honeysuckle. The cool afternoon breeze. The imagined smile of my father, telling me how much he approved.

When the words "I do" left my lips, I knew one thing for certain. Today wasn't Michael's and my happily-ever-after. Happily-ever-afters take place at the *end* of the story.

Today was ...

THE BEGINNING

© Jason Meert

ABOUT THE AUTHOR

Tracy Weber is the author of the award-winning Downward Dog Mystery series. The first book, *Murder Strikes a Pose*, won the Maxwell Award for Fiction and was nominated for the Agatha Award for Best First Novel. *Pre-Meditated Murder* is her fifth novel.

A certified yoga therapist, Tracy is the owner of Whole Life Yoga, a Seattle yoga studio, as well as the creator and director of Whole Life Yoga's teacher training program. She loves sharing her passion for yoga and animals in any way possible. Tracy and her husband, Marc, live in Seattle with their mischievous German shepherd puppy, Ana. When she's not writing, Tracy spends her time teaching yoga, trying to corral Ana, and sipping Blackthorn cider at her favorite ale house.

For more information on Tracy and the Downward Dog Mysteries, visit her author website at TracyWeberAuthor.com.